WELCOME TO SUGARTOWN

WELCOME TO SUGARTOWN

USA TODAY BESTSELLING AUTHOR
CARMEN JENNER

WELCOME TO SUGARTOWN
Copyright © 2013 Carmen Jenner
Published by Carmen Jenner

This is a work of fiction.

Names, characters, businesses, organisations, places, events, and incidents are either of the author's imagination or used in a fictitious manner. Any resemblance to actual persons, living dead, or actual events is purely coincidental.

Thank you for respecting the author's work and not making me set various motorcycle gangs and a very pissed off Elijah Cade on you.

Published: Carmen Jenner 3 November 2016
carmenjennerauthor@gmail.com

Editing: Lauren K McKellar
www.laurenkmckellarauthor.blogspot.com.au

Cover Design and Formatting: Be Designs
www.be-designs.com.au

Photo Credit: Perrywinkle Photography
www.perrywinklephotography.com

For Ava & Ari
May you find a love of your own
as big as this someday.

For book bloggers everywhere
Thank you!

ANA

*T*here's a mind-numbing restlessness that comes with living in small towns. The gossip, the people, and the unending monotony that makes you want to poke your eyes out with a fork. I've lived my whole life in Sugartown, so I should probably expect nothing to ever change, and each new day to be just as dull as the last. And yet, every day I wish for the unexpected. I wish for big cities, for open-mindedness, for the ability to jump on my bike and ride the hell out of town and never look back.

Every day I dream of leaving Sugartown. And every day I open this crummy pie shop, I make pies and serve customers, and stay several hours after closing to make pies for the following day. I'm nineteen. The world should be full of endless possibilities, right? Wrong. Oh, so very wrong because I've just finished high school and my family happen to own this joint. So instead of making the world my oyster and all that, I'm stuck wearing this retro waitress uniform for the rest of my days—my mum and dad had some kind of rockabilly diner fetish, it's sad really, don't ask.

Sugartown sits smack bang on the highway in the middle of nowhere. It's a quaint little town and a pleasant enough place to stop on your journey from there to anywhere but here, but no one ever stays. And why would they? It's surrounded on both sides by nothing but cane fields and the ancient sugar mill, that spreads its sweet acrid stench in a smoggy cloud over the whole town, making everything smell like burnt toffee. There's nothing to do, nowhere to go, and the nearest town is 25 kilometres away.

I sigh and lean over the counter, staring out the window. Across the road, my dad has shut the doors to his other business, a garage specialising in custom Harley-Davidson fittings: Big Bob's Bikes and Auto. He leans against his bike and smokes a cigarette as he waits.

My mum's dream was to open a diner and make pies all day. My dad's? To run a garage and customise Harleys. That way he could combine his early midlife crisis with his love of mechanics. They were both lucky enough to have had their dreams realised, and both unlucky enough to have them shattered when she found out she had cancer. Amid the chemo and the hospital visits, mum taught me how to bake from her recipes. Now I make pies in her kitchen, dad runs his garage across the street, and in a way it's like my mum's dream is still alive and kicking. Though I doubt she expected the dragon stepmother to be a part of that dream.

"Ana, are you even listening to me?" My friend and long-term tormentor Holly screeches in my ear. Holly works every shift with me. She's all kinds of crazy gorgeous with wild red curls, green eyes and more 'personality' than a whole ward of mental patients.

"It's kinda hard not to listen to you, Hols." I say, and then laugh as I add, "On account of you never shutting the fuck up."

"Shut up, biatch, I know you haven't been listening to a word I've said. Lucky for you, I've got no problems repeating myself."

"Yippee," I deadpan.

She waves that away as if I'm the one with all the crazy and begins wiping down the counter with a dirty rag, smearing grease all over the Formica. I love her, but I think Holly may have been dropped on her head when she was a baby. "Anyway, as I was saying, are you going to Nicole's party next week?"

A scruffy looking kid with strawberry blonde curls and bright blue eyes comes strutting through the shop, saving me from a tiresome conversation in which I continue to argue all the reasons why going to that party would be disastrous for someone like me and where Holly manages to twist the entire conversation back around to the fact that not going would be social suicide. The little brat acts like he owns the place, pokes his tongue out at me and jumps up on the counter that Holly just finished wiping down.

I ruffle his hair and he smiles up at me. "What's up, Sammy?"

"Nothing. Whereth mum?"

"The dragon's out the back, primping her dragon lady curls for my dad."

I was an only child, until I wasn't any more. Until former Belle's Pies employee Kerry sunk her talons into my dad after Mum died. Eventually they got married and she fell pregnant. Kerry sat around on her big-fat-pregnant bum while I worked double shifts on the weekends in the shop.

I was thirteen.

I can't fathom what Dad sees in her. It must be the sex, because I can't find a single redeeming quality. The only good thing to come out of that woman was Sammy. He's six now, every second word comes out with a lisp and, despite his unfortunate parentage, he just may be my favourite person in the entire world. It appears I'm his favourite, too, a fact that irritates the dragon beyond belief, that I may or may not play in my favour just to piss her off.

"But thee thaid thee was going to take me for ice cream tith afternoon."

"It's Friday night. Sorry, kiddo, but you're stuck with me."

"Ith OK. I liketh being thuck wif you, Ana Cabana." He beams, and it's so hard not to pick him up and squeeze him until his adorable little guts squish out.

"Aw, thanks, brat. I liketh being thuck wif you, too." I mock and ruffle his hair once more for good measure. "Now, go do your homework and I'll bring you a milkshake once the dragon lady is gone."

"Thweet." He jumps off the counter, poking his tongue out at Holly who pokes out her own in return and then proceeds to make monkey faces at him. I swear, sometimes it's like Holly and Sam are the same age. She makes out like she can't stand him when the opposite is true—she adores him just as much as I do.

Sammy bounds over to a booth in the back, pulls out his supplies and gets to work, his tongue poking out in concentration.

A few minutes later the dragon stalks through the back door and into the kitchen, huffing when she sees Sammy through the giant serving window. She struts over to him, leaving a cloud of cheap perfume in her wake.

"Sammy baby, you didn't come and say hi to mummy." Dragon ruffles his hair the way I do, but he pulls away when she touches him and glares at her.

"My nameth noth Thammy, ith's Tham. And I'm not a baby." He says indignantly and goes back to his studies.

Dragon shoots me a look. "Daddy and I have a party to go to tonight, so don't wait up."

God, it's so gross when she calls him Daddy. The mental images those words conjure when they come from her mouth are enough to make me vomit for days on end. The sad thing is he's almost old enough to be her dad. And now for the second time in as many minutes I'm thinking of my dad having sex, which is wrong on so many, many levels.

Without even a kiss goodbye for Sammy, Dragon sashays through the shop in her short skirt and too-tight singlet top with the cut outs and her high heeled boots.

"Do you ever want to crash one of their parties?" Holly pipes up, as we watch Kerry cross the street. She kisses my dad full on the lips and then straddles the seat behind him. He revs the throttle and they ride away into the sunset.

"And watch a bunch of drunk, greying old bikers boast about how big their engines are while their trampy women drape themselves across their laps? Not my idea of fun, Holly."

"Yeah, bunch of hussies. Though I wouldn't mind draping myself across Red Hot Rob's lap again."

"Whath a huthy?" Sam's little lisp pipes up from beside me.

"Yo' momma." Holly shoots back with a cheeky grin.

"Seriously Holly? You don't think he's going to repeat that?" She shrugs. "It's true."

"Hussy is a bad word," I tell him sternly, giving Holly a pointed look. "If I ever catch you saying it there'll be no more Banana Chocolate Cream Ana Cabana Surprise Pies, okay?"

They're Sam's favourite. It's a concoction I made up one night when Dad and the dragon were at one of their booze fests, and Holly and I had raided their stash. Sam had been sound asleep, until we began marauding the kitchen with a serious case of the munchies. I'd pulled it together enough to bake a pie with the only edible things left in the house: chocolate, bananas, beer and mini-marshmallows. The beer was downed before it had a chance to meet chocolate and banana—probably for the best—and after passing out before we had a chance to taste the creation, we woke to Sam covered head to toe in chocolate. He'd devoured the whole thing. The name stuck, and oddly so did the recipe—minus the beer, of course—and now it's one of our best sellers.

Sammy's eyes go wide as saucers and he vigorously nods his head. "Okay."

"And I thought I asked you to do your homework?"

"You thaid you wath gonna get me a milkthake when the dragon left, and the dragonth been gone for a hundred yearth, already."

"If I get you a milkshake will you please go and do some schoolwork?" He nods enthusiastically and scurries back to his booth.

The sound of a bike tearing up the street draws the attention of all three of us. Growing up around a motorbike enthusiast I've come to learn the sounds that the engines make. Dirt bikes sound all high and whiny, like something got caught in the garbage disposal unit. Well-oiled machines, like the Harley-Davidsons my dad rides and customises, have almost a growling purr to them. It's musical and primal all at once. It sends chills up your spine and sets your teeth and nerve endings to vibrate.

And then there's the hard and fast variety, the Japanese models made for speed and not endurance, or so my dad says. He calls them pushbikes because that's exactly what they sound like, a motorized pushbike.

This bike, though, this bike sounds like it's on its last legs. It's low and gravelly, and kind of sounds like a lawnmower on steroids. Which tells me one thing—the rider is more than likely not from around here, or my dad would have had that baby on a hoist the first time he'd laid eyes on it.

A black beat-up bike pulls up to the curb in front of Dad's garage. The rider's decked out head to toe in black: leather, jeans, boots and helmet. Of course, from across the street I can't make out how good looking, or even how old he is, but the cut of his shoulders in his leather jacket kinda makes me melty.

He removes his helmet, runs a hand through his faux-hawk and my heart practically stops. I look at Holly, who turns, then looks back at me, "Oh my—"

"HOT!" I finish. We glide over to the window to get a better look at the newcomer. He can't see us, of course. Well, he probably could, if he bothered to look over here, but he's not. He has his face pressed to the glass of Big Bob's Bikes and Auto. He walks to the roller door of the workshop and knocks hard, three times.

Holly runs her finger up and down the glass before her, as if she's stroking his body through the window. "He's way hotter than your cousin."

"He *is* way hotter than my cousin."

"And it wouldn't be incestuous for you to sleep with him." She presses her palm flat against the glass, and then smiles appreciatively at me.

Oh no. I know that look. Nothing good ever comes from that look.

"You should go over there," Holly states, as we watch him remove his jacket and get the full effect of his profile. The t-shirt he wears is fitting and black, and there are tattoos almost everywhere. *Oh, sweet mother of god.* I've never wanted to lick anyone's bicep before, but even from across the street I can see how edible this guy is.

"What, are you crazy?" Heat claws at my cheeks because that's exactly what I want to do; go over there and ride this guy's bike. *Sweet baby Jesus, even my thoughts need to be censored.*

"Ana, you should totally go and talk to him."

"I'm not going to talk to him."

"He's at your dad's shop. What if it's a life or death situation?" she screeches, and I swear it's so loud that it causes hot decrepit-bike guy to stop looking at his watch and glance up at us. He shields his eyes and squints into the sun. His head cants to the side just a little when he finds us watching him. Holly, the traitor that she is, pulls the cloth from her apron and pretends as though she's innocently cleaning the window. I, on the other hand, simply stare as he crosses the street towards us.

"Crap. Now he's coming over." I turn and head back to the counter. Holly just keeps wiping at the window with her cloth, but all she's doing is smudging sticky caramel over the clean glass.

"You're welcome." She giggles like a hyena on crack.

"You're cleaning that window properly before you leave."

She lifts her fingers to her forehead in some kind of wacked out girl-scout salute. "Yes ma'am."

The bell above the door jingles and I feel my spine stiffen. The smell of leather, motor oil and boy sweat fills our tiny shop and I start inhaling hard and fast. I'm kind of surprised I don't hyperventilate.

"Hi, I'm Holly. Holly Harris, what can I get you?"

"Uh, hi." I turn and see him withdrawing his hand from Holly's too tight grasp. "The shop across the street, do you know the guy that owns it? I was supposed to meet him there earlier today, but I got held up in traffic."

"Ana, would you like to field this one?" Holly asks, drawing me into their conversation and forcing hot decrepit-bike guy's eyes to look me over. Is it my imagination that his hungry gaze glides over me from head to hip? Twice?

"He's gone for the day. Friday night's bonfire and booze night down by the river."

"Shit. I knew I shouldn't have stopped earlier."

"Shop opens again at ten am."

"Nah, that'll be too late. Any idea where I could find this river?"

"Eight blocks down, second turn on your right, then you wanna follow the cane fields for another five kilometres, you'll run right into it."

Holly's standing behind Hot Guy making lewd hand gestures and snapping her teeth at his bum like she wants to take a bite. I shoot her a warning glare and jerk my head in the direction of the kitchen several times, but it's Holly, so of course she doesn't take the hint, which leaves me looking like a stroke victim.

Hot Guy's brows furrow. They're killer brows, all tapered in the right places but rugged enough so you can tell they haven't been trimmed or plucked. Dipping my eyes a little lower, I notice how long his lashes are, thick black lashes that any women would kill for, but the observations don't stop there. His eyes are such a deep, dark chocolate that they're almost black and I think I see the first hint of a dimple when he gives me a bemused smile.

Dimples, for crying out loud!

Like he wasn't already perfect enough with his lashes and his leather and his freaking melty dark chocolate eyes!

He dares a look over his shoulder and Holly smiles innocently. I'm pointing back and forth between her and the kitchen like a crazy person and threatening murder with my eyes when he turns back around, and I have to pretend like I'm adjusting my ponytail in order to appear even halfway normal.

"You okay?" The smile is faint, but definitely there, and that brings me right back to the dimples again.

"Uh-huh," I mutter. Holly shoots me a warning look, a look that says if I don't get on with it she'll make this a million times worse for me. Resisting the urge to jump on Holly and body slam her into the pastry display case, I hear myself saying, "I could show you if you like? The river. I mean. Not show you something else. That didn't come out right. I meant—"

"What Ana's trying to say here, is that her shift ends in exactly one hour and since I'll be sticking around to watch the brat—" Holly inclines her head in Sam's direction, who's following our interaction as if it's his favourite episode of *SpongeBob SquarePants,* "—she'd be delighted to take you down to the river and show you her bonfire."

"Holly!" I chastise.

"You sure … uh, Ana, was it? I wouldn't wanna put you out."

"Ana loves putting out," Holly chirrups.

She is having way too much fun with this.

"Holly!" I say again, much louder this time.

"What? He knows I'm kidding." She turns to Ole' Melty Eyes. "Right?"

He runs his hand through his hair. I can practically feel the freak out going on inside his head. Any more from Holly and this guy's going to Kawasaki out of town, as fast as his wheels can take him. "Yeah, of course."

I sigh and give both him and my self-esteem an out, "I could just draw you a map, if you like?"

"No. I want you to take me." His brows knit together and the dimples pop out when he laughs at what he just said, but he doesn't make any attempt to rectify it. In fact, the smile he gives me is downright cheeky and full of challenge. I smile back, thinking he has no idea what he just walked into.

He thrusts a hand out in front of me and says, "Elijah Cade."

"Ana." I take his proffered hand. It's warm but not sweaty, calloused, and it engulfs mine completely.

"You got a last name, Ana?"

"Nope, just Ana."

His eyebrow quirks and the smile he pairs with it is as smug as smiles come. "Well, just Ana, you and I will be seeing a lot of each other from now on."

"Is that so?"

"I'm gonna be working across the street, and I'm gonna need a place to eat." I know he's provoking me, any idiot could see that, and yet the way his voice lowers and his dark eyes seem to hood over when he says the word "eat" makes me want to offer up myself as an all-night buffet.

I hear Holly gasp and I know I'm in trouble. Holly's very rarely shocked by anything. I don't know if it's what Elijah said, or the way I'm so obviously drooling over him, but the fact that she's gasping is so *not* good. I look away from Melty Eyes, but I'm afraid I'll need a cold shower before I can calm down enough to keep my inner hussy at bay.

"Really? I wasn't even aware that Big Bob was looking for another mechanic."

He looks surprised. Surprised and suddenly wary. "You know him?"

"You could say that."

"Tell me then, what have I gotta do to impress him? I really need to hold down this job."

"Okay, here's the thing. Big Bob's really big on pretty boys, so make sure you smile. Don't wear a shirt while you're working, and he's partially deaf so you'll need to talk REALLY LOUD!"

"You're shitting me, right?"

"Afraid not. Mr Boss Man is a partially deaf, raving homosexual. Still want the job?"

Holly stares at me in horror from across the room and mouths, "What are you doing?"

"Yeah, of course," he says, rubbing the back of his neck. He is clearly uncomfortable. "I mean, it's not like I'm going to be stripping or anything."

"Just your shirt. But something tells me you're used to people staring at your bare chest anyway."

His lips quirk into a slow smile and there's a moment when I can tell we're both thinking the same thing: Elijah without a shirt. Okay, well, *I'm* thinking of Elijah without a shirt and from the way he's smirking at me, I'm pretty certain his mind is on missing articles of clothing too.

"Tell you what, Elijah Cade, why don't you have a seat and I'll bring you some pie on the house."

"That'd be great."

"Sweet or savoury?"

"Sweet," he deadpans. "Definitely sweet."

"Sweet it is."

Shortly after Elijah sits down, Sammy sidles up beside him and they jump head first into a lengthy discussion about the bike Elijah rides. Sam's quick to point out that his older model bike has nothing on a Fat Boy. He even folds his arms over his chest and frowns the way our dad would.

Holly pinches my arm while I'm preparing Elijah's pie. I've really got to get a new best friend, one who's against physical violence.

"Wanna tell me what that was about?" she whispers.

"Just having a little fun, is all."

"A little fun? Ana, there's fun and then there's suicidal. You just told him your dad was gay and enjoyed seeing his employees prance around half-naked. That might work here; he did knock up the evil bitch stepmum, after all, but at the garage? Bob's going to annihilate this kid."

"I know, but think how fun it will be to watch him walking around shirtless and yelling at my dad all summer."

"You are a bad, bad girl, Ana Belle," she whispers conspiratorially.

"So they keep telling me." I grin like the cat that got the cream, but even I don't believe the smile that's plastered on my face.

I set the pie down before Elijah and Sam's eyes go saucer wide. "No way. You gave him a thlice of Ana Cabana thuprithe pie?"

"Yep. If you pack up your things I'll get you a slice *and* a milkshake."

"Can Elijah have a milkthake too?"

"If Elijah wants a milkshake?"

"Oh, Elijah wants a milkshake." He smiles and the dimples come out swinging. I just wanna sit down and admire the holy mother of hotness that is decrepit-bike-riding, tattoo-sleeved, dimple-popping, Elijah Cade.

He's staring at me expectantly. It's obvious he's spoken and, in all my fan-girling, I've completely missed it.

"I'm sorry, what?"

"Vanilla. The milkshake. Can you make it vanilla? It's my favourite." He winks and shovels more pie into his mouth.

Without another word I stalk back to the kitchen. My heart is in my throat, trying as best it can to abandon this sinking ship. What the hell was I thinking, flirting with a guy like that? He's going to be working for my dad, which means I'll see him every day. And probably sooner rather than later he'll figure out that I tricked him. He'll more than likely hear the rumours about me. Maybe he already has, and that's why he's coming on so strong. Elijah Cade is the last thing I need.

I can hear him and Sam talking out in the diner. The milkshake machine stops whirring and the noise of Holly slamming down the metal cups on the table in front of the boys reaches my ears.

"There's your vanilla milkshake," she snaps. Her footsteps pound toward me.

"Uh, thanks," Elijah calls after her.

"My mumth a huthy," Sammy pipes up and I cringe and curse Holly under my breath.

ELIJAH

I'm no stranger to women. Tall, short, thin, thick, I've been … friendly … with an awful lot. In fact, I like to think I know women pretty well, but I sure as shit don't know what the hell happened back there. One minute Ana was giving as good as I gave and the next, she was flying out the back door. *Maybe I came on too strong?* Nah, fuck it. Life's short. She's hot and she might be just the thing I need to keep my nose clean while I'm in this crap-hole of a town. Not that I'll be staying long. I never stay long.

After her psycho friend almost showered me with vanilla malted-milk Ana comes stalking out of the kitchen, grabs the kid by the arm and tells me to meet her round back in ten minutes.

I watch her usher the kid ahead of her through the kitchen door. She's untying her apron as she goes, causing the blue dress to pull against her ass and ruck up a little higher. Holy shit, I'm headed into boner territory. I tilt my head to the side and admire the view before the swinging doors make it disappear completely. Next thing I know I'm staring at 5'3 of pissed off waitress.

Aaaaaand there goes my boner.

The friend, Hannah, or Hailey, or something, gives me the double finger point between her eyes and mine, universal code for "I'm watching you."

Crap, did every girl within a 10 kilometre radius suddenly start PMSing the minute I rode into town?

I'm trying real hard not to laugh, so when she vocalises what her hand gestures apparently didn't convey I bite down on my cheek hard enough to taste blood. Chick's like a shark, though. I swear her eyes narrow when she scents my blood in the air.

"Okay." I say, 'cause I know she's waiting for me to say something and, to be honest, that's all I got.

"I'm glad we had this little talk."

"Yeah, me too."

Wait.

What the fuck?

Did we even have a conversation? This chick's messing with my head. She's also kinda creeping me out, so rather than sit here and risk her boiling my bunny while I wait for Ana I grab my helmet and my jacket, throw a twenty on the table and head out to get my bike.

"See ya round." I call as I'm exiting the pie shop.

"Not if I see you first, Elijah Cade," she singsongs, and I repress the urge to run for my life.

A minute later I'm parked in front of her garage as Ana comes down the stairs wearing jeans that cling so tight to her legs and arse that I can clearly see all the places I want to put my mouth and hands. She's also rockin' a barely there singlet top that I have no doubt I could see right through if it got wet.

God, I hope it rains.

Holy mother of whoring nuns she's hot. Fuck! I haven't just crossed the border into boner territory, Mr Happy's erected a tent from my jeans and is setting up camp there.

I clear my throat, shift in my seat and hope like hell she doesn't notice the raging hard-on before she gets on the bike. Once she's positioned behind me she won't see a thing. Her hot little body will be pressed into my back, her legs wrapped around mine ... shit. *Wrong thing to think with a hot girl in front of me, and a boner the size of Everest.* And no, that's not an over exaggeration, my man meat is huge.

"You okay?" Ana asks. Shit. I hate it when I get so lost in my head I forget what's going on around me.

"Yeah," I say, glancing down at the gravel beneath my bike to keep from gawking at her. "Just tired. Been a really long day."

"Right, well, let's get you sorted so you can hit the hay." She smiles, but it's nothing like the look she was giving me inside. *Did I offend her?* Crap. Why the hell are chicks so hard to read? In an effort to make things right I add, "Your pie is awesome, by the way."

Fuck. That sounded completely suggestive.

"That didn't come out right."

"It's okay. My pie *is* awesome," she says playfully as she backs away from me. Something in her expression makes me want to chase her.

"I have no doubt," I whisper, and then loud enough so she can hear, "Are you getting on, or are we gonna play chasies all night, Ana no last name?"

"Oh, I have my own ride." She lifts the roller door to the double garage where a beat up Holden, a Fat Boy on pits and a shiny yellow geriatric-looking Vespa sits. Ana dons a matching yellow helmet and buckles it beneath her chin.

"That's your ride?" I'm having a hard time keeping the smugness from my smile.

"Uh-huh."

"Alright, then," I say, trying not to laugh. A massive grin breaks out on my face.

Ana's scowling. "What?"

I hold up my hands to ward her off. "Nothing. Just, you do know I have to meet this guy tonight and not next week, right? Are you sure your little grandma bike is gonna cut it out there on the open road?"

"Hey! This 'grandma' bike could run rings around your decrepit little tricycle."

"Tricycle?" I laugh at the righteous indignation on her face, the sheer determination in her gaze that says she'd like to hand me my arse on a plate. I kinda want to let her. I stroke my bike lovingly. "This is a precision instrument of speed and t—"

"Toy parts?" she asks as she hops on her scooter, kicks out the centre stand and revs the engine.

"Baby girl, nothing about me or my bike is childish." I smile, but there's an edge to it.

"We'll see." She edges the Vespa forward so she's directly in front of me.

I rev my engine, pull on my helmet and slam my aviators into place.

"And I'm not your baby girl."

Ana fishtails in front of me, kicking up a cloud of grey dust and gravel in my face. I shake my head and jet after her. *I'm gonna have that girl naked beneath me before the week's end.*

ANA

I look at the clock once more. You know? Just in case someone miraculously invented a time machine and I find myself somewhere back in time before three am. The ceiling fan whirs overhead and the summer heat has sweat sticking my PJs to my body. I kick the covers to the end of my bed and resolve not to think about what it is I'm thinking about: Elijah Cade.

Although, if I have to think about Elijah, it's kind of nice to remember the look on his face when he finally caught up to me last night.

"I take it back," he'd shouted over the roar of our engines. "That's sure as shit no grandma bike."

The look on Elijah's face when I left him in the dust was priceless. I mean, yeah, I drive a Vespa, but my dad custom builds and restores Harleys. If he couldn't get me on a "real" bike he at least had to modify it so that I wouldn't be a laughing stock. He souped-up the engine one night while I was asleep, a fact I was not too happy about as it voided my warranty, but I guess when your dad's the best mechanic in the state little things like null and voided warranties never really come into play.

I'd given Elijah a smug smile and he'd shoved his sunnies back into place and sped off in front of me, copying my fishtail manoeuvre to a tee. I was so not having that, and I'd let him know by overtaking him at every possible turn. Of course, we'd been speeding and we'd overshot the turn-off by about ten kilometres, but it had been so nice just to drive and play that I couldn't have cared less.

An almighty crack of thunder had made me glance up at the storm clouds overhead, at which point I'd decided I didn't want to get caught in the rain and I'd let Elijah zoom past me, only to turn around and head in the other direction when he thought he had me beat. It had been a good five minutes before I'd seen him slip in behind me again and maintain a steady speed. When we'd reached the river, or as close to the river as the road would take us, I'd walked him through the rocky, overgrown trail and down the steep sloping bank. From the obscurity of the trees, I pointed out "Big Gay Bob" and hightailed it out of there, before my dad or the dragon could see me.

"You're not gonna stay?" Elijah had said.

"Nope." I'd called over my shoulder.

"What if I get lost?"

I'd turned and walked backwards without any fear of falling or making a complete dork out of myself. I knew that terrain like the back of my hand. When I was younger the bikers would drag their kids along to those bonfires. I knew every twist, turn and protruding rock of that path. "Then you'll have a really long trek back to your bike."

My reply had been rewarded with a flash of dimple. For a moment I'd forgotten just how dangerous Ole' Melty Eyed Dimples was. "Thanks for the ride, Ana No Last Name."

"Welcome to Sugartown, Elijah Cade."

Now, as I lie in bed, I can't stop thinking about him. I wanted to stop thinking about him, needed desperately to stop thinking about him if I was going to be any use at work tomorrow, but instead I found myself tiptoeing through the house, grabbing the keys to the shop and scurrying out into the rain in my singlet top and boy shorts to make pies in the industrial-sized kitchen until the sun came up.

And that's exactly where Holly found me at 9 am, with my head resting on the flour-covered bench and twenty Triple Chocolate Melted Fudge pies surrounding me.

Holly casts suspicious eyes around the room and arches her waxed-to-perfection brows. "Rough night?"

"The roughest."

"Well, considering there's not some tattooed motorcycle god half naked in this kitchen, I'll take it as a sign your date didn't go well."

"Pfff, he's hardly a motorcycle god. Bespa" —yes, I named my bike, don't judge me— "ran rings around that little tricycle of his. And it wasn't a date."

"You sound like your dad." Holly rolls her heavily made-up eyes and dips her equally manicured finger into the pie that I'd taste tested early this morning, "Mmmm, delicious. Wait, did you change the recipe for your surprise pie?"

"No. This is something different." I rise and stretch out all the aches and pains of spending the night in the kitchen, but not before I see her brow arch and a knowing smile slip across her lips. I busy myself wiping flour from the bench with a nearby rag.

"Whatcha doin'?"

"Cleaning."

"No I mean whatcha *doing*?"

"I don't know what you mean." I feign innocence, but she sees right through it. I am so busted.

"What's it called, Ana?"

"I haven't named it yet." I work real hard at scrubbing an imaginary stain on the bench.

Holly lets out a gasp. It's so loud, it has me jumping up on the chair, thinking she's seen a bluetongue lizard in the kitchen, "You sneaky little slutsky! You totally made him a pie!"

"I did not make him a pie!"

"You dirty whore!" she shrieks as she picks up a nearby broom and starts prodding my butt with the handle.

I swat at her with my floury dishrag. "Would you cut it out?"

"Oh Elijah, won't you try my pie? I made it just for you," she taunts in a high-pitched, girly tone that sounds absolutely nothing like me. "What's that, you wanna stick your fingers in my deliciously silky, warm pie?"

I'm so focused on Holly's taunting and the wickedly jabby broom handle currently tenderising my rump that I don't hear the bell signal a customer. And this is how Elijah finds us as he stares through the serving window: me in my underwear, covered head to toe in chocolate and flour, standing on the chair I'd slept on and having my arse poked by a very dead best friend—or at least, she will be, once I get him to leave. For a minute we are frozen, all three of us just gawking at one another.

"Mornin'." Elijah grins. And there they are, both dimples popping out to say hello. And it's not even ten am yet. The snide bastard makes no attempt to hide the fact he's ogling me from head to toe.

With a squeak, I drop the rag and attempt to cover myself, but in my haste the movement throws me off balance, which then causes my chair to tilt at an angle that's not conducive to keeping me on my feet. I fall flat on my face and, to my absolute horror, while I'm down there acquainting myself with the checked lino and the dust bunnies, Elijah sidles right up to the window and starts up a conversation about our brand new pies. Like he didn't just witness the single most humiliating moment of my life, and neither he nor Holly can see my half-naked arse sticking out from behind the island bench.

I. Am. Beyond. *Mortified.*

And, just when I'm thinking this day couldn't possibly get any worse, I hear the shop door open and my dad's gravelly greeting. Big Bob enjoys mornings about as much as I do.

I quit trying to dig myself a shallow grave through the linoleum floor, shoot up from behind the safety of my counter with a very calm head and nod to each of them.

"Elijah. Bob."

Dad's eyes narrow and his ever-present scowl threatens to divide his forehead in half. "Ana?"

Oh crap. I know that voice. I haven't heard that voice since I was ten-years-old and he caught Holly and I with a stolen packet of cigarettes. We hadn't even had a chance to light up before he was pulling us out from behind the supermarket and humiliating us in front of the whole town. The look on my dad's face now says he's about two seconds away from picking me up by the scruff of the neck and crucifying me where I stand.

And yeah, okay, maybe from his standpoint this looks bad, but despite me being a nineteen-year-old woman, Dad's still struggling with the fact that I've moved from training bras to push up bras, and thinking boys were stinky to maybe wanting to sleep with one. And since Elijah seems to be the only male within a 5 kilometre radius and he just caught his daughter half naked in the kitchen, things aren't looking good for any of us.

He turns the full weight of his scowl on Elijah, who is still smiling like he just won the freaking lottery *and* a Christmas ham. "Son?"

"Uh-huh."

"Haven't you got a bike to fix?"

Elijah still hasn't taken his eyes off me, but my dad's tone brokers absolutely no argument, and what's more, when he gets an eyeful of Bob Belle's infamous scowl, he clears his throat.

"YES, SIR! I'LL GET RIGHT ON IT …" he yells. And why wouldn't he yell? After all, it is what I told him.

Dad winces at the volume. Holly is laughing again, like a whacked out chimpanzee and I'm just too mortified for words. Elijah scurries back through the shop with a nod in our direction and an exclamation of, "I freaking love this town!"

"I'm. Just. Gonna. Go … now," I mutter and exit through the back door with my tail between my legs.

ELIJAH

*T*wo weeks on and I still can't forget seeing hot waitress Ana standing in her underwear. Not that I'd want to forget. In fact, that image has been on replay in my spank bank twice a day for a fortnight now. I'd give my left nut to get beneath those lacy little boy shorts. The fact that she's still playing hard to get is pissing me off and turning me into a fucking horn dog. I don't usually walk away from a challenge, but sometimes life throws you so much shit you've just gotta quit while you're ahead.

And other times life throws you a bone, or in my case, a raging boner for the hot waitress in the pie shop across the road. If I were a smart man I'd walk away, I'd cut my losses and move on to the next hot piece of arse, and I'd be better off—hell, that waitress would be better off. But no one ever accused me of being smart. Like all men, I think with the little head more than is good for me and I can't walk away without a taste of that girl.

And speaking of the "little head", I've got a date with a slice of pie and a hot waitress who's about to fill my spank bank fantasies for another fortnight.

I slide out from under the hood of a 1971 GTX Plymouth Road Runner. It's the kind of car you want to drape a warm body over the hood and fuck till you're both senseless. And, with all the bikes I've been workin' on lately, it's been nice to slide beneath a machine as beautiful as this. I'm pretty confident that I'll have this thing purring like a kitten before the afternoon is out.

I wash up in the sink in back, scrubbing the pungent smell of grease and brake fluid from my hands. My stomach growls.

My cock twitches when I think of the way Ana smells as she leans across the table to set my pie in front of me. I always sit in the very last booth, closest to the counter. I face away from the windows so I'm looking directly into the kitchen and sit as far back in the booth as possible so she has to lean in to slide my plate in front of me. It's kind of a dickhead move, I know, and I'm sure she knows exactly what I'm up to, but I don't care.

Fuck, I'm getting hard just thinking about her in that cute little uniform, those gorgeous tits spilling out the top. I squeeze my eyes shut and think about old ladies and nuns and sweaty old man balls, anything to take my mind off Ana's big, beautiful tits that are making me so hard I can't see straight. I'm playing these things on a loop and whispering, "Old ladies, nuns, sweaty old man balls" over and over, and just praying that the meat muscle will chill the fuck out and let me get through one friggin' day without getting a boner in public for the hot waitress, when I glance into the mirror above the sink and see Bob standing behind me. His arms are crossed in front of his chest and he's scowling. Nothing new there; he's always scowling.

"You heading to lunch?"

"YEAH, YOU WANT SOMETHING?"

"A word before you go."

"ALRIGHT." I tear off a chunk of paper towel and take the opportunity to readjust things below as he walks toward the back seat of a sawed in half Ford Falcon that Bob uses as a couch. I follow him and sit on an old milk crate that someone strapped a piece of foam to in order to make a stool. The tape is worn around the edges, it sticks to my jeans and the foam has worn down to nothing, picked away by tiny fingers.

"You got a problem with your ears, kid?"

"NO, SIR."

"Then quit friggin' yellin' at me."

"But I thought—"

"Son, do you own a shirt?"

I glance down at my tattooed torso, taking a minute to appreciate the fact that, although I haven't seen the inside of a gym for six months, my work, the mini workouts I do in my room every morning and my daily runs are enough to keep me pretty built. I look back up at Bob and he's not at all happy with the way I look. Maybe he's into hairy guys?

"Yeah, of course," I say, feeling a little uncomfortable at the way he's glaring at me.

"Well, why the bloody hell don't you ever wear it, instead of parading around here like it's the fucking Mardi Gras?"

I grab the shirt tucked into my back pocket and pull it over my head, utterly confused. "I thought … I thought you were into that?"

Bob turns three shades of pale. No shit, it's like I'm staring at a fucking ghost. "Look mate, you're a real good worker. You keep your head down, you don't carry on like a pork chop when I ask you to close up late Fridays. Now, I gotta be honest, I wasn't too sure about this whole … arrangement in the beginning, and despite riding some import pushbike, you know your way around an engine. I know you've had some trouble in your past and I can see you're trying to make amends for that. You're a good kid and what you do in your free time is none of my business. I like you, Son. As an employee. If you like blokes then … we'll find a way to co-exist, but you've got to start wearing a shirt. It'd be a shit fight if OH&S came in and saw you—"

"Wait. You think *I'm* gay?" I start laughing at how fucking ridiculous that notion is, considering I've been jacking off to the image of the same girl for the last two weeks. The same girl that told me my boss was partially deaf and that he'd require me to work half naked. *That sneaky bitch.* She is so going down for this. "Dude, I'm not gay. I thought you were."

"Son, I am not gay. I've been married twice. I have kids."

"I didn't know you had kids."

"Well, you should, you spend enough time with them at the pie shop."

"Hot waitress Ana is *your* daughter?"

"*Hot waitress*?" Bob's eyebrows shoot all the way back into his hairline. "Whaddya mean, hot waitress?"

Fuck! I just said that out loud, didn't I?

I shoot up from my stool. Bob's standing now, too. His arms are folded in front of his large body and I'm not afraid to say I'm shitting myself at the scowl I'm seeing on his face. This scowl is different from all his other scowls: it's a don't fuck with my daughter kind of scowl, and yeah, I may have seen plenty of those in my twenty-three years, but none have ever been this scary. It's the disapproving dad scowl to end all dad scowls and what makes it worse is that it's also coming from the dude who pays my wage.

Fuck! I am so screwed.

"I'm just gonna head out now," I mutter, as I take a step back, and then another, and soon I'm half way across the shop.

"Take one more step and I'll bust your nuts with my favourite wrench." He smiles but it's not a friendly smile. It's a we're-going-to-have-us-a-little-chat-and-then-I'm-gonna-cut-off-your-balls-for-even-thinking-about-what's-between-my-daughter's-legs smile. In other words, this is the moment where I'd normally run. "We're gonna have a talk you and me."

"It's not what you think."

"Really? 'Cause right now, son, my thoughts aren't fuckin' pretty."

I put my hands up in surrender. "I haven't touched her, I swear."

"You're not gonna touch her, are you, son." That really wasn't a question. He meant: do not fucking touch my daughter!

"No, Sir."

"You keep your mind on the job and your dick in your pants, are we clear?"

"Yes, Sir." I gulp. "Crystal."

Satisfied, Bob nods and stalks across the shop floor. He picks up a wrench and begins beating the shit out of a rusted old engine. I decide to skip lunch today, and tomorrow.

By closing time on Friday I was itching for a way to get back at Ana and, yeah, I'm not gonna lie, the thought of her tits spilling out of that uniform may have been responsible for my feet carrying me across the road to Belle's Pies instead of releasing the throttle on my bike and travelling as far away from hot waitress Ana as I could in order to keep the family jewels intact.

I smile at the girls behind the counter and slide into my usual booth.

"Hey, Ana Belle. How you doin' today?"

"What's up Cade? We haven't seen you here for a couple of days—" Her eyes widen, and she tugs her bottom lip in tight with her teeth. "You just called me Ana Belle, didn't you?"

"Jigs up, baby girl."

From the counter, Holly chortles, bending double at the waist as she holds her stomach. Ana chuckles too, like having me on is the funniest damn thing in the world. "You know I spent the last two weeks screaming at your dad and parading myself around half-naked in front of him because I was worried he'd fire me if I didn't. Now I think he might fire me because I was dumb enough to listen to you two little girls."

"We're hardly little girls." Ana frowns as if she's honestly offended. She's right, of course, Ana's the furthest thing from a little girl, but from the way her friend guffaws and throws herself over the counter, I'm convinced Holly's off her rocker. She may need to be sedated before she starts throwing pies at the customers.

"No?" I lean toward her, an obnoxious smirk playing on my lips. "What would you call yourselves then? Grown women?"

"Yes," she says indignantly.

I can't resist. "Prove it."

Shut the fuck up, dickhead. Bob is going to have your arse for this. Despite the warnings from my brain, my Johnson dances a fucking jig inside my pants and my mouth opens anyway, "Go out with me tonight."

"What?"

"You heard me."

"I'm not going out with you."

"Why not?"

"Because you'd more than likely leave me by the side of the road to get back at me."

"You could always drive."

"You'd ride with me on my scooter?" She sounds doubtful.

"Sure." I'm sure the look I give her says it's not my favourite idea, but the smile that breaks out across her lips is so fucking spectacular I'd consider riding on the back of her scooter every day of my life just to see that flash of pretty white teeth.

"I don't know if you've noticed, but this is Sugartown. There's not exactly an abundance of places to go."

"There's a pub isn't there?"

"Well, yeah, but—"

"There a pool table?" She nods, and I feel myself smile so wide I know my dimples are coming out. "You play?"

Her cheeks turn the prettiest shade of pink. I have to fight the urge to grab her face with my hands and force my lips down on hers.

"Not for a long time." She holds my stare for what feels like forever, and there's something calculating behind her eyes, but then she looks away. "Listen, I can't go out with you tonight, I have to babysit Sammy."

"I thought he was staying at what's-his-name's house tonight?" Holly pipes up from behind the counter. Clearly, pretending she's not listening to our conversation is something she's not fazed with.

"Holly!" Ana shoots her a look, it's one I wouldn't want to be on the receiving end of, but Holly just shrugs her shoulders and stares defiantly. Her friend may be as freaking crazy as a monkey on meth, but I think I'm beginning to like her.

"What? It's true."

"Well, it may be true, but you know what he's like at a sleepover. He's there ten minutes before he's begging an adult to drive him home."

"Couldn't you just go until you get a call to come pick him up?"

"Come on, Ana Belle, it's the least you could do after humiliating me in front of your dad for the past two weeks."

"Hey, you brought that on yourself."

"How so?"

"You came strutting in here all cocky, with your dimples and your tattoos and your big brown eyes and expected us to swoon."

"Baby girl, if that's all it takes to make you swoon then you just wait 'til you see what I do with my hands."

Ana's gaze grows misty eyed. She swallows hard, but her face shuts down into the scowl she often wears around me. "I don't think so."

She turns to walk away and I lurch forward and grab her wrist. "Come on, Ana. I'll be on my best behaviour."

"That's not saying much, Elijah."

"Do you judge every guy this unfairly, or just me?"

She turns with a cocky grin, but when she sees I'm deadly serious, the smile fades. I don't mean to be a dick, but I've spent most of my life living up to other people's bad expectations and I won't have that with her. I can't have her thinking of me that way, even if it's all I deserve.

"I'm sorry. You must think I'm a complete bitch?"

"Well, not a *complete* bitch, maybe 99.9 per cent of one—"

"Hey." She swats at my arm and, like a complete tool, I flex my bicep beneath her fingers. That shit wasn't even deliberate, just instinct. *Stupid.* She doesn't seem to mind though because her smile is back, wider than ever. For a half second I imagine what it'd be like to give into the urge to bend her over the table and fuck her senseless, but then I feel like a complete arsehole for objectifying her so blatantly. This should tell me I'm in over my head with this girl.

I'm not the guy who stays in one place long enough to have a second date. When they're seeing proposals and picket fences I'm checking out of shitty motels and watching road signs turn to dust in my rear-view mirrors. I'm practically married to that white line.

So why the hell can't I walk away?

"You can make it up to me by letting me pick you up at eight o'clock," I say.

She shakes her head, but the way her lips curl up in the corners and the twinkle in those pretty blue eyes tells me I've won. "I thought you said I could drive?"

"You can," I say and tuck into my pie. "You can drive my bike. As long as you can handle the pace, that is. I have to warn you, though; the steering's a little different from a Vespa."

"I can drive anything."

"Somehow I don't doubt that, Ana Belle. I don't doubt that at all."

ANA

*H*olly bounces up and down on my bed and I have to count backwards from one-hundred so I don't choke her. I can't believe she screwed me over so thoroughly. I tell her as much, and she pokes her tongue out at me in her typical response to being reprimanded.

"Come on, Ana, would it really kill you to go out with Mr I'm So Freaking Hot Even My Mother Would Sell Her Soul to Get a Piece Of This? Would it kill you to have a little fun for once?"

I wrinkle my nose. "You have some serious issues. That's gross."

"Gross, but true. Ana, he's gorgeous and you *need* this."

"I do not *need* a date with Elijah Cade."

"Okay fine, you know what? I need a date with Elijah. Take off that outfit, I'm gonna trade places with you." She grabs at my top and tries to lift it over my head but I bat her away.

"Elijah's my date, and I'm not having you steal him away like you did with Matt Roberts at Vanessa Carter's party in year nine."

Holly rolls her eyes. "Are you ever going to get over that? I told you, I was standing in the hall and he just happened to fall onto my lips. It wasn't my fault that the place was so crowded you could barely breathe without making out with someone. And I thought you said this wasn't a date."

"It's not. I mean, it is, but it's not." I sigh impatiently. "I don't know. He makes me all … twitchy."

Her gaze grows all soft and squishy and she grins as her fingernails sink into my arm in her excitement. "Aww, you really like him."

It's my turn to roll my eyes. "He's all kinds of wrong for me, Holly."

"Who cares? No one's asking you to marry him."

"He's trouble. Exactly the kind of guy I should avoid," I say. She's looking at me like I just strung up her kitten as a Christmas ornament. "You know what this town is like. Within five minutes of walking into that pub tongues will be wagging and Sugartown will be rife with gossip. You know how antsy my dad gets with talk like that? The next time Constable Davis sees him throwing down, he'll be locked up for weeks."

"Ana, this is exactly why you need a distraction like Elijah. Between Sam, your dad, the dragon and the shop you have too much stress in your life. If you don't blow off a little tension, you're gonna explode! And I am not cleaning up chunks of Ana from the shop floor."

"And you don't think a date with Elijah's just going to add to the stress?"

"Not with those hands, he's not. I wonder what kind of orgasm face he makes?" she asks and performs some kind of facial gymnastics. Either that, or she's having a stroke. I'm kicking myself that my phone is in the other room, because moments like this should be documented for all time. "Ooh, oh, take a picture of it for me, will you?"

"You are sick. You know that, right?"

"Yep." She leaps off the bed and scoops up a black top that I'd been considering. "Now, if you'll excuse me, I've got a hot date with Zac Effron. He is so freaking hot post *High School Musical*. I wonder what kind of face Zac makes? Wear the white top, not the yellow, it makes your boobs look bigger and don't forget to take pictures. I wanna see how far down those tattoos go."

After she leaves, I apply a little make-up and consider pinning up my hair, but then I think about dealing with the helmet hair that's bound to have me fussing all night and I decide to tie it in a loose knot at the back of my head until we pull up at the pub.

When I'm done, I hear Elijah's bike on the gravel drive outside. I tear through the house, scooping up my cross body purse and my helmet from the kitchen table.

I open the door and Elijah's standing before me with his hand raised to knock. He gives me a startled smile. "Hi."

"Hi," I reply.

I start to pull the door shut behind me and he looks over my shoulder, "Your dad home?"

"No. He already left with the dragon." Elijah's shoulders relax a little and I fight the urge the give him hell about it because it's obvious he's afraid of my father. I settle on torture instead, ensuring my hand grazes his hard oblique as I breeze past. "Let's go."

The resounding growl behind me makes me grin wider than I have in years.

I knew my entrance with Elijah would cause a stir. Walking into the only pub in town with the newest resident sexy biker after you've been labelled the town whore is bound to make waves. The stares and silence that ensued were deafening. And thank god my dad was down at the river or Constable Davis would be making good on his threat.

"We shouldn't have come here," I whisper to Elijah as he takes my hand in his and leads me to the privacy of the pool room—and, by privacy, I mean not-at-all-private, as there are at least two walls that open out to the main bar.

"No one's looking at you, Ana, they're looking at me, and I'm used to it. If I'm not worried, then you shouldn't be either." He takes his wallet from his back pocket and lines up four coins along one end of the pool table, securing it as ours for the next long while. "You know how to rack 'em?"

I nod and bite down on my lip to avoid the smile that wants to spring forth. If there's one thing my dad taught me to do, it's play pool. I've been hustling money off of his friends, men three times my age, since I was ten-years-old.

"Yeah, I think I've got it," I say, as I take the cues down from the wall and set about racking up the balls.

"What's your poison, Ana?" Elijah asks in a husky voice. My gaze locks with his. Heat spreads over my cheeks and between my thighs and as he stands there, challenging me with those melty eyes, I'm quite sure he already knows the answer to that question.

Instead of making a complete fool out of myself I smile sweetly and say, "Vodka, lime and soda."

"Lightweight," he whispers and the challenge is unmistakable. It's true. I am a lightweight, but that's not why I chose it. The truth is, I already feel so out of control around him that I don't really need the buzz of alcohol to impair my judgement anymore. "Vodka, lime and soda it is, but next time, I'm buying you a real drink."

"You planning on getting me drunk so you can take advantage of me, Cade?"

"Ana." He leans in close, sending a bolt of desire through me as his warm breath skates across my neck. "When I do finally get you naked beneath me—and trust me, it's not a question of if, but when—I'm going to make sure you haven't so much as looked at a drink. I want you to remember everything I do with my hands and my lips and my tongue."

My breath leaves me in a rush. I clutch the edge of the pool table behind me so tightly I can feel I'm losing circulation in my fingers. I'm having a hard time believing he's just whispered something so intimate in the middle of a packed bar and an even harder time believing I could be so turned on by it.

Elijah pulls away slowly, removing his hand that had somehow found its way onto my hip. *How did I not know his hand was resting on my hip?* His gaze is locked onto mine, clearly reading my every thought, because somewhere between him picking me up earlier this evening and him saying those words to me just now, the filter between us has vanished.

He smiles this playful lopsided grin that makes only one of his dimples pop out, and just when I think I'm about to melt into a puddle and let his hands fulfil all the promises he just made, he hands me a pool cue with a taunt of, "Your break, baby girl" before sauntering off toward the bar.

I take aim at the white, imagining that cocky self-assured smile he gave me, and the table explodes with the thundering crack of ricocheting plastic. Three balls find a home in the corner pocket. Elijah turns and cants his head to the side with a questioning look. I fold my arms in front of my chest, pushing my boobs up a little, marvelling at how easy it is to gain his undivided attention. I give my best attempt at a lopsided grin, like the one he shot me seconds ago. "You're gonna regret playing me, Cade. I'm gonna eat you for breakfast."

"Keep looking like that, baby girl, and I'll let you eat me for dessert, too."

My mouth drops open into a surprised little "O" and he chuckles and wanders off to get our drinks.

Once Elijah returns, we begin the first of many games, all of which I win—and I'm almost one-hundred per cent certain he's not holding back on me. In fact, he's seems to be trying his best to unnerve me with every shot I make, but two can play at that game and it isn't long before he's losing the battle of wills and wits.

"So, where's Mummy and Daddy tonight, Ana Belle?" Elijah asks as he breaks on our eighth game.

"Out at another club meet, and please tell me you didn't just call the dragon lady my mother?"

His lips tip up into a crooked smile that forces just one of his dimples to pop out. "I don't know, I can see a little bit of a family resemblance there."

"I will hurt you, Cade." I lean over the table and take my next shot. My boobs are spilling out of my top and I take a moment to readjust before I have a complete wardrobe malfunction—à la Tara

Reid. When I glance up, I find Elijah eyeing me like prey. His gaze clouds over with lust, but there's something darker hiding there, too. I haven't a clue what it is, but it makes me want to run away and throw myself at his mercy, all at once.

"I don't doubt that for a second, baby girl."

I sink another ball into the side pocket and try to pretend he doesn't unnerve me. "What about you? Did you leave a string of heartbroken girlfriends back in … where did you say you were from again?"

"Sydney."

Sydney. Wow. That only narrows it down to around 12,000 km². Give or take.

Elijah takes aim at a ball that's perfectly aligned to slide into the pocket, but he slams the cue against it with a loud crack. It rebounds off the cushion and sinks two of my balls as it slips into the pocket. "Nope. Don't do girlfriends."

"Oh," I mutter, feeling disappointment surge through me.

He's not exactly forthcoming.

A commotion from the pub's entrance makes me miss my next shot. Elijah glances between me and the group of guys that just walked in. I don't have to look to know that Scott and his posse of terrible tools just arrived, and that they're headed straight for us.

One of the reasons I was so anxious about coming here is because I know that this is where he and his collection of dickhead friends usually hang out on a Friday night. Between our awkward arrival and having so much fun whooping Elijah's bum, I guess I forgot to be concerned.

Elijah watches me closely, and I know he understands that the closer Scott's group drifts, the more anxious I get because he moves closer, too. He leans in and his warm breath skates the shell of my ear, sending a shiver down my spine. "Take the shot again, Ana, and this time forget about the room around you."

I nod, lean over and sink my last ball before the eight. Just as I'm raising myself up off the table I see a hand place a coin against the top rail. By now, our previous coins have vanished, eaten by the table in our pursuit of beating one another.

I look up into pale blue eyes. Scott winks at me, already guessing correctly that I'm the one winning this game, meaning his coin ensures he gets to play me next. It wouldn't matter, I've beaten him every time the two of us have ever played, but he's doing it to mess with my head—and, unfortunately, it's working.

"Hey, Blondie." Scott uses his stupid pet name for me, the one I always hated. His eyes slide over me from head to toe and I have to supress the urge to shudder. "Haven't seen you in a while."

"No, you haven't," I reply harshly. I don't add the part I'm really thinking, though. *Not since the night I turned you down and you called me a cock-blocker and dumped me for a girl who would "put out", then spent the last few weeks of our final year of school telling everyone I was a slut who banged you and three of your friends.*

Elijah slips his arm around my waist and playfully whispers in my ear, just loud enough for the room to hear, "You're making me crazy in this outfit, baby." Then he stops nuzzling my neck and nods his head in Scott's direction. "Who's this?"

I don't know who's more stunned, Scott or me?

Still, I'm not stupid enough to not take the boon Elijah is offering. The fact that he's deliberately marking his territory by wrapping me in his arms and calling me baby in front of a boy I trusted who broke my heart, even if it is mostly for show, sends a thrill through me, and I can't help but snuggle into him when I say, "Oh, no one. Just some guys I knew in school."

Scott's eyes narrow and he thrusts his hand out in front of Elijah, who has no choice but to step away from me if he wants to shake it. "Scott Turner."

Elijah shakes but doesn't offer his name.

"Nice ink, man," Scott says. The condescending tone he uses tells me he thinks it's anything but. He raises his brow and adds, "Did you get those in Juvie?"

Elijah smiles, "A few of them, yeah."

Scott smiles too, only it's smug, as if he was just trying to prove a point and is delighted to be right. Elijah cocks his head to the side and looks thoughtful for a moment before pointing to the tattoo that is playing peekaboo with his shirt collar. "Though this one was done in a maximum security joint just outside of Sydney."

Scott baulks a little. His friends, who'd been whispering and muttering oooohs and ahhhhs like the childish morons they are all fall silent. I glance at Elijah, wondering if that's true. *It can't be. Though I guess it wouldn't be the first time my dad gave an ex-con a job.* True or not, I decide that right now, I don't care. I'm just so thankful for Elijah's presence and the fact that he's not fazed by an idiot like Scott.

"'Scuse us a sec, boys." Elijah takes my hand and leads me into the hall, which is kind of pointless, considering there's a direct line of sight from the poolroom to where we're standing. Dissatisfied with the scene he's making by dragging me away he pens me in against the wall. His face is oddly serious when he asks, "Goldilocks in there, did he screw you over?"

I nod, afraid he's going to lose interest once I give him that clarification, and I'm thanking my lucky stars that Scott and his friends didn't mention anything else about me being the town bike.

"You want me to beat him up?"

I laugh. "No Elijah, I don't want you to get arrested for beating up some moron from my past."

"You wanna make him so fucking jealous he can't see straight?" he asks in all seriousness. It's absurd. I shouldn't give a crap about what Scott and his brainless goons think of me, and yet the idea of shoving someone as hot—and yeah, okay, pretty damn scary looking—as Elijah under his nose sends a thrill through me. I find myself nodding, though the way Elijah's smiling at me makes me realise that I've no idea what I just agreed to.

"Then kiss me."

"What? How do you even know he's looking?"

"You, in this outfit? Trust me, he's looking."

"What's wrong with this outfit?" I say, but the words peter off with the way his gaze slides over me. I know that look. That's the way he looks at my pies when he comes in for lunch, like he hasn't had a meal in days. I want to be the meal.

He leans in, so close I can feel his warm breath brush my lips. "You gotta kiss me back."

"Huh?"

"I'm going to kiss you now and, despite the fact that you don't like me, if you wanna make this dickhead jealous, you gotta kiss me with all you got."

The whiskey on his breath washes over me. I haven't touched whiskey since I was seventeen and got so sick I only narrowly escaped having my stomach pumped. I swore I would never touch the stuff again, and even the smell usually has me dry reaching but right now I'm finding it a very welcome scent, and the fact that I'm hyperventilating has nothing to do with alcohol of any kind.

"I never said I didn't like you. In fact, I don't know anything about you."

"Ana?"

"Yeah?"

"Shut up," he says, and mashes his lips to mine. His mouth is hot, his taste bittersweet from the whiskey, and at first, it's awkward. I have no idea if I'm kissing Elijah because I want to make Scott mad with jealousy or if I'm kissing him simply because I want to. He pulls back to study my face. I try to rein in my bemused expression, but frankly, I don't think I'm fooling anyone. I probably look like a stunned mullet. Elijah's expression is kind of intense. Intense and a little angry.

"That's all you got? Seriously? Are you even trying to make him jealous? 'Cause I gotta say, I think your method sucks." I pull his face back to mine and take him with my mouth. I force my tongue inside while his eyes are still on me. He's surprised, but when I clasp my hands behind his neck and push myself against him, his arm snakes around my back, his fingers tangle in my hair and he kisses me so hard and deep we're practically consuming each other.

Elijah walks us back a step, until I'm pushed up against the wall once more. He's found his way between my thighs and the pressure of his erection against my pubic bone elicits a moan from me. "You wanna get outta here?"

"Okay."

He takes my hand and leads me past the gawking patrons, past Scott and his idiotic friends, past the frowning publican, Dave, who's sure to give my dad a full report tomorrow, and out into the balmy summer air.

He holds out a hand for the keys, that I confiscated earlier in the night. "I'm driving."

"Where are we going?"

"For a ride." He watches as I fumble with the buckle on my chinstrap, hooks his finger in it and pulls me closer, kissing me as greedily as he did inside.

"I don't think they're watching out here," I say when we come up for air.

"That wasn't for their benefit. It was for mine."

I bite down on my lip to keep the smile from busting out and making me feel like a complete mental case. Elijah runs his thumb over my lip, snagging it out from under my teeth and slipping his calloused thumb inside my mouth. My tongue darts out on its own, grazes the rough edges, tasting whiskey and leather. He releases a groan and smiles down at me, but it's predatory and not at all sweet enough for his dimples to pop out.

He takes a few steps back toward his bike and then straddles it, his gaze never once leaving mine. "You have a curfew?"

"I'm nineteen, Elijah. Of course I don't have a curfew."

"Your dad's kind of a badarse. I wanna make sure he's not going to turn my balls into pumpkins if I don't have you home before midnight."

I slip onto the bike behind him, wrap my arms around his waist and hold on—and yeah, I may have trailed my fingers around a little slower and softer than was necessary. He flinches a little, his shoulders tensing, and the hard muscles of his stomach bunching beneath my fingers before he settles into the seat and my arms.

"Besides, he scares the shit out of me," Elijah adds.

"Aw, he'll be so proud when I tell him."

"You wouldn't dare." He puts on his helmet and slides on a pair of black wayfarers with clear lenses and yells, "Hang on" before careening out of the parking lot at breakneck speed. I wrap my arms tighter around him, squeeze my thighs tighter against his. I see his head shift down to glance at my thighs and he swerves a little. I tuck my head in away from the wind, lay my cheek against his back and breathe in the scent of leather and Elijah.

ELIJAH

Dropping Ana back at her house that night felt like one of the hardest things I've ever done. I know, I know, that's a gross pussy-arsed exaggeration, especially for someone like me, but it was damn hard returning her to her dad's house when all I wanted was to take her back to my motel, throw her on the bed and fuck her brains out.

You don't do that with girls like Ana, though. You take girls like Ana out to fancy restaurants, or to your kid sister's birthday party or home to meet your mum, but since I don't do fancy and have no family left to speak of, I drove around the outskirts of town for a little while before taking her home, because Ana is one girl I didn't want to screw over. Maybe the *first* girl.

Either way, the press of her thighs against mine made me crazy. All I could think about was how they'd feel wrapped around my hips as I shoved myself inside her. So instead, I drove her home before the temptation proved too much for me. As much as I wanted her, I knew this was a girl I'd have to go easy with before I choked and fucked everything up.

"Do you want to come in?" she'd asked with a coy smile.

Fuck. So not the question to ask a man who's fantasising about being balls deep inside you.

"You have no idea," I'd whispered beneath the revving throttle. "Some other time, maybe."

"Oh." *Did she look disappointed?* "Well, thanks for the drink, and for that thing you did with Scott."

"Ana, that really wasn't for his benefit." I lean forward. "I've been wanting to lay you out before me and kiss every inch of that fucking beautiful body since I first laid eyes on you in your parents' pie shop."

"Well, I guess it's a good thing the pub doesn't have beds, or I'd be in trouble."

"Why limit yourself to a bed, when any flat surface is fair game?" I'd winked and then gunned it down the gravel alleyway before she could lure me inside.

Now, a whole day later, as I scour the local supermarket for a decently priced microwave meal, I think of a hundred other ways that I should have said goodnight to Ana. My mind also constructs a hundred other scenarios where I've taken her back to my motel room and made good on that promise. I'm deciding between two different microwave meals, wondering which will be less likely to taste like dog food, when someone rams me with their trolley from behind.

"Ah! Fu—" I spin around to face a very chagrined Sam. "—uuuuudge 'n' ice cream!"

I squeeze my eyes tightly shut and take a few sharp shallow breaths to keep from Hulking out at hot waitress's little brother. "Hey Buddy, how's it goin'?"

I bump my knuckles against his tiny fist and he tilts his chin up at me before breaking out into a goofy smile.

"Aww, thorry dude, I didnth thee you there."

"Oh my god, Sammy you didn't hit someone else, did you?" asked a panicked disembodied voice from an aisle over.

"Ana Cabana, Elijath's here! And my trolley cut off his leg and totally made him bleed everywhere."

I glance down. Sammy's right, my ankle is bleeding, though not enough to warrant a hospital visit. Still, the impact had been enough to make me drop the items in my hands, and the carton of milk I'd been holding has busted open and spilled all over the floor.

Ana comes bolting around the corner, skidding to a halt in front of me, though not fast enough to avoid slipping through the spilled milk. Her legs go out from beneath her and we collide and go down in a tangle of limbs. The breath rushes out of my lungs as I take the brunt of our fall.

She leans back to see my face and there's the most beautiful pink blush in her cheeks. "I'm so sorry, are you okay?"

"You Belles pack a punch, you know that?" I feel my lips tug up at the corners.

Ana laughs. "Just be thankful it wasn't my dad that ran into you."

"Well, I can tell you right now, you wouldn't have your hands on my arse like you do my daughter's." Bob appears before us as if he's been summoned. As if the mere mention of his name calls him up out of the darkness like that dude from *Harry Potter*. I follow the line of his gaze and, whaddya you know, my hands are on Ana's arse, holding her in position as she's splayed on top of me.

"What the fuck, Ana?"

Sam laughs and starts jumping up and down in the milk puddle singing, "Daddy thswore! Daddy thswore!"

Ana jumps to her feet and reaches out a hand to help me up. I take it, but only because I like the feel of her tiny hand engulfed in mine.

"Son?" Bob looks like he's going to have a stroke right there in the middle of the grocery store.

"Dad …" Ana warns.

"I thought I made myself clear?"

"Yes, Sir."

"Wait, what do you mean you made yourself clear?" Ana glances between the two of us. At least I think she does. My mind is too focused on the 170-plus kilograms of pissed off dad in front of me to lay eyes on her and know for sure. "Dad?"

"Dad? Dad? Dad? Dad?" Sam parrots over and over again.

"That's enough, Sammy!" Bob and Ana yell above him.

"Oh my god. You totally warned him off of me, didn't you?" I do risk a glance at her this time. Her gaze is cutting and her jaw is set. She's incredibly hot and also kinda scary, not gonna lie. Bob at least has the decency to look sheepish.

"Maybe I should just let you guys—"

She whirls on me and scary takes on a whole new meaning. "Elijah, do not move a muscle."

I hold my hands up in surrender and thank Christ she turns her fury back onto her old man. "I can't believe you are still trying to pull this crap."

"Elijah and I had an understanding—"

"No. Just no! I am nineteen-years-old, Dad. You do not get to tell me who I can and can't date. And you especially don't get to ward off the only guy in town who might be interested." She accentuates each word with a jab to his chest and his big biker face winces with every poke of her bony little finger.

"In fact …" She pivots toward me and I flinch, thinking she's about to start laying into me too, but the next thing I know she's smashing her lips against mine and shoving her tongue down my throat as her soft body moulds into my hard one. I'm so startled that at first I don't respond, then she moans, all faint and breathy and shit, and my hands are on her arse again like it's a reflex.

"Hands, Kid," Bob growls.

I raise my hands in a "look, no touching" kind of gesture and pull away, but it's clear that Ana's not done with me yet. She pushes her glorious rack even closer, her lips teasing my own, and I can't help but fist my hands in her hair and kiss her harder than before.

"Daddy, why ith Ana thucking on Elijath's face?"

"I'm asking myself the same thing, Kid," Bob mumbles. "Alright, break it up you two. You've proved your point."

Ana pulls away and that blush I'd witnessed earlier is now an all-out glow. She smiles, a little sheepish, but it's tinged with only a hint of embarrassment and it seems like she's pretty proud of herself. "Sorry, that's twice now I've used you to prove a point."

"I'm not complaining."

"Hey, we're having a BBQ at the house tonight, you should come."

I dare a Glance at Bob. "Ah, I don't know if that's such a good idea."

"Gah!" Ana throws her hands up in exasperation. "This is because of him isn't it? Dad tell Elijah he's welcome to come to the BBQ tonight."

"Yes, Elijah, why not come and eat my food, drink my beer and manhandle my daughter some more?"

"Dad!" She shoots him a stern look before smiling up at me. "You should come. Holly will be there."

I cringe and scratch the back of my neck. "That's not really a selling point."

"Yeah, she does get kind of intense."

"Elijah, ith you come to the BBQ tonight, I'll totally thow you my collection of mathbox carths." The kid's eyes are so round with excitement; I couldn't bear to let him down. Even though it may mean Bob and his buddies have a chance to kick my arse for manhandling his daughter, I still can't say no to the little guy. Kids always hit me where it hurts. And before you start sprouting some sensitive new age guy bullshit, being a sucker for kids doesn't make me a pussy.

Does it?

"Well when you put it like that, heck yeah, I'm gonna be there. That'd be awesome, little man."

"Cool."

"So you'll really come?" Ana asks as she snags her bottom lip between her teeth and, just like I did the night before, I have this crazy urge to run my thumb over it and then kiss her till she's dizzy. Probably not the wisest move with her old man staring daggers in my direction.

"Ana, can you wrap this up? I'm gonna head over to Dave's to get the beer," he mutters, as he walks away. "Maybe I'll borrow his shotgun while I'm there."

"Dad!" she admonished. "Sorry, he's kind of a jackass when he wants to be."

I smile down at her and whisper, "You should try working with him."

He's still staring like he wants to tear me a new one. "Bob, if it makes you uncomfortable I can take Ana with me for the night." His answering scowl tells me I've just said the wrong thing. *Again.* "On a date, not … you know … for the night."

"Ith Ana Cabana having a thleepover at Elijath's? Can I go too, Daddy?"

"No!" everyone, including me, yells.

"Ana's not going anywhere, Son," he says this to Sammy, but his gaze never leaves mine the entire time. Then he starts laughing, until he's red in the face.

"What's so funny, Dad?"

"You know what, Kid? Why don't you come to our BBQ? Ana can introduce you to all her surrogate uncles." Ana's eyes go wide and Bob chuckles some more. "And then there's the old ladies, who're almost as protective of her as her mum was."

I swallow hard. Ana's eyes are still wide, and I could have sworn I just heard her make an "eep" sound.

"Can't wait," I reply, as Bob heads toward the exit, chuckling the entire way.

I am so screwed.

I park my bike in the alley beside Ana's house and follow the sound of Cold Chisel's "Khe Sanh". I hate Cold Chisel. They remind me of him and I do my best to avoid thinking of him. Ever.

It's not just the music that has me on edge, though. I debated coming here against staying in with another TV dinner for a good two hours before I told myself to stop being such a pussy and finally threw myself in the shower before I could chicken out again.

Truth is, I don't know what I'm doing here.

Ana's the first girl I've seen something more with. And that's a dangerous way of thinking. Not just because her dad has the ability to send me on my way—one call to my case worker and I'm back in the clink, maybe for good this time—but because, for once in my life, I'm thinking about more than just getting laid.

I really like this girl, but I also need this job, and I'm not sure getting involved with the boss's daughter is the best idea. I'm just about to say to hell with it and head back for my bike when I catch a glimpse of Ana. She's standing with Holly and a slightly older dude who is wearing nothing but jeans and a leather vest. His arms are wrapped around Holly's waist as if he's afraid that at any moment she'll start running. The guy's built, but he's no looker. Holly might be as fucking crazy as a howler monkey locked in a cupboard full of crack, but she can definitely do better than this shirtless douche.

Ana's back is to a fire that's raging in a metal drum in the centre of the yard—why anyone needs a bonfire on a night with a top temp of 26 °C is beyond me, but I guess that's the way they do things around here. She's wearing a peach coloured sundress and the fire's lighting up her head like a halo. She looks like she'd rather be anywhere than watching Holly be mauled by No Shirt Guy.

She catches sight of me and ditches the happy couple. I don't know shit about fashion but I know that Ana in that dress is a sight that'll be seared into my brain forever. Her beautiful tits are bouncing as she makes her way toward me, and the fabric covering her hips sways like a bell when she walks. I feel my dick jerk and thank fuck that the dark hides my bone-a-phone.

"You came," she says, and she's fucking beaming.

"Almost," I whisper. Her brows knit together as I chuckle to myself. "I'm here."

"You're here," she says with a sigh, and it takes everything within me not to throw her over my shoulder and carry her off to my bike. Fuck, this is confusing. It's not like Ana's the first girl to get excited over me showing up to her party.

But maybe she's the first girl that mattered.

"I am."

Wow, this is really fucking awkward.

A few hours ago I was making out with her in the supermarket and now we're edgier than a couple kids with their dad's porn collection. "And I brought beer."

"Great. I'll show you where the eskies are." She leads me through a maze of people, bikers and their old ladies, plus a few more who I've seen in the shop. At least twenty of them give me the evil eye as I walk behind Ana and pretend I'm not checking out her arse. She doesn't make any introductions and I'm guessing that's for my benefit, because I just know some of these guys are dying to grill me about my intentions toward her. And I might even have an answer for them, if I knew what the fuck was going on myself.

As soon as I'm done putting the beer away, an excitable ball of six-year-old boy barrels into my legs and almost knocks me to the ground. That would have made it twice in one day that I'd been bowled over by Belles. Something tells me that, if I overstepped the mark with Ana tonight, then Bob would make it a trifecta, though I'm not sure I'd be able to stand after he was done beating the shit outta me. Maybe not ever. "Elijah, you're here, you really came."

"Yep. I'm really here." I smile at Ana before squatting down to Sammy's level. "How you doin', little man?"

"Awethome now that you're here." He jumps up and down. "You wanna come thee my Mathbox carth?"

"Hey, Sammy, Elijah just got here and Ana Cabana was really hoping she could spend some time with him first—"

"But he thaid he wanted to thee them."

"And he will, just not now."

I stand up and look at Ana. "I don't mind. Really."

"Yeth!" Sammy grabs my hand and bolts for the house. "You hath to come thee my room, Elijah, ith tho awethome."

"I bet it is," I say, as I throw Ana an apologetic look over my shoulder. She's tagging along behind us, looking less than happy that Sammy's whisking me away and a part of me is fucking thrilled she doesn't want the kid monopolising my time.

Sammy leads me up the backstairs, past even more bikers that look about ready to beat the crap outta me, and into the quiet house.

Bob is standing in the kitchen with his wife, helping her carry several dishes filled with salads. He stares at me, at my hand clasped in Sammy's, and at Ana, tagging along behind the two of us.

Yeah, this isn't awkward at all.

"Hey, Mr Belle. Mrs Belle." I offer up the first greeting, mostly just to fill the silence in the room.

"So, I'm Mr Belle when you're in my home, putting the moves on my daughter, but just plain old Bob when I'm at work?" His face is all scrunched up and serious.

"Bob, leave the poor kid alone," Ana's stepmum chimes in. Being called a kid by a woman who's barely out of her twenties is kinda weird. Bob just grunts and carries the trays outside after his wife.

"He's gonna castrate me for this, isn't he?" I mumble to Ana once the screen door closes behind him.

"Are you kidding? That sentence contained the most syllables I've ever heard him utter to someone other than Sammy and I."

Sammy glances up at me. "Whath cathrate mean?"

"Ask your sister, she knows everything."

"But thee'sth a girl?"

"Buddy, if there's one thing I've learned in life, it's that women are always right. Never question it. It's as sure as gravity. Women are always, *always* right."

I spent the next half hour playing with monster trucks in a six-year-old's bedroom, weaving them in and out of the empty beer bottles I'd accumulated. It wasn't at all how I'd seen this night going in my head.

Sammy was a lucky kid. I didn't know much about the woman that Ana called "Dragon", but I knew he was loved. Ana doted on him, and that big bad motherfucker Bob was reduced to a teddy bear when it came to his son. Sammy didn't know it yet, but he'd grow up one lucky son of a bitch.

I was maybe even a little jealous. Not every kid has people willing to do anything to protect them. I just hope he grows up to love his old man and sister the way they should be loved.

Now, as I watch Ana and Holly spin Sammy around to some Beasts of Bourbon song that really should have been left back in the nineties, I can't help but feel a little like I don't belong. Ana may be a teeny, tiny little thing, but her heart's as big as an Ox's.

Yeah, there's a nice visual, I think, and pull another long draught of my beer.

She's been silently coaxing me over, trying to get me to dance, but I don't dance on account of looking like a freaking chimpanzee with two left feet. Some dudes have rhythm with that sort of thing, but me? I save all my rhythm for the bedroom. Give me a blonde with soft curves and a nice rack and I can make her body dance with my hands alone. But on a dance floor? Not so much.

Ana grins like an idiot and makes several weird hand gestures to get me to come closer but I just smile, shake my head and store the memory away for a later date when I might need something pleasant to think about.

"Beautiful, isn't she?" Bob asks from beside me. I wonder how long I've been gawking at his daughter like a total dick.

"Yeah, she is."

"She looks just like her mum did at her age. Got the fire of the devil in her, too. Just like her mother."

"Yeah, I'm starting to see that."

"But she's soft underneath, breakable."

Surprised by the reverence in his tone, I turn toward him. "I can see that about her, too."

"Ana's a good kid. She's suffered through a lot of shit from the kids in this town after that Turner fuck finished with her. I would have broken both his legs already, but I'm on pretty thin ice with the Constable as it is, and I've got my businesses, my wife and Sammy to think about."

"I'm surprised you let that stop you."

"You gotta know when to pick your battles, Son. Sometimes you gotta let your kids sort out their own shit."

"Like choosing who they date?"

He guffaws, "You're a good kid, Cade. I like having you around the shop. But not around my daughter." Bob takes a long swig of beer. "'Course, it's not up to me who Ana dates, and she rarely takes notice of anything her old man tells her these days. But know this: you take her down that road you've been on, drag her down, you hurt her in any way and I'm gonna finish you. I don't care if I have to follow you to the back of beyond. You hurt my little girl and I'll put you to ground quicker than you can fucking blink. Are we clear, Cade?"

"I'm not gonna hurt her, Sir. Ana's about the best thing to happen to me in the last ten years."

He swigs the remainder of his beer and leans in to set it down on the table behind me. "Just make sure you're the best thing to happen to her, too. Ana doesn't need you to be another decision she'll regret." He gives me a long hard look and strides away, over to his wife.

Fuck. He's right. I'm not the best thing for Ana. I'm not even close. I'm just a kid who made some pretty fucked up decisions, who turned into a man who made even more fucked up decisions. The worst of which I did time for. It doesn't matter that I've spent every waking minute since I got out working my arse off and trying to keep my tarnished record clean. It doesn't matter that I've spent every second of my life since trying to be nothing like my father. I'm his flesh and blood and that alone makes me not good enough for her.

She deserves a man that went to uni to get a degree, someone who makes a killing and wears a monkey suit and comes home every night to their big fuck off house full of riches, not some dick who didn't finish high school, works a job "the man" tells him to because his stupid-as-fuck decisions took away all his other options, and who can fit all his worldly possessions on the back of a motorbike, like me. Which then begs the question—what the fuck am I doing here?

I chug the remainder of my stubby and set it down alongside Bob's. *I'm outta here.* I head around to the alley where I left my bike but I don't get much further than the side of the house before Ana calls out behind me, "Elijah, wait. Where are you going?"

"Home," I reply without turning around, and then I laugh to myself, because the motel room where I sleep and store my overnight bag while I work is hardly a place to call home.

"Without saying goodbye?" It's impossible to ignore the hurt in her voice. Fuck. "What did he say to you?"

"Nothing I didn't already know."

"Which means?"

I stop walking, but stand with my back to her. I'm not sure I'm strong enough to walk away. I'm drunk and acting like a complete tool and I can't seem to make myself stop. "Forget it, Ana. Just go back to the party."

"No! I want to know what he said to you."

I whirl around and pin her to the brick wall. She startles, but doesn't try to escape when my arms pen her in on either side. Her chest is heaving, those gorgeous tits are just inches from my hands, from my mouth, and suddenly all I can think about is rolling my tongue around her nipple and teasing it with my teeth. My cock jerks inside my jeans and I'm instantly hard.

"What is this?" I demand.

"What's what?" Obviously Ana has no idea what I'm talking about. I'm guessing she has no idea why I'm so fucking mad about it either, but I don't care. I want an answer to this question so badly that I feel it like an anvil on my chest. I've never been this tied in knots over a girl before and I don't fucking like it. Not one bit.

"This shit between us, what the fuck is going on here?"

She narrows her eyes at me. "You're drunk."

"Answer me," I snap.

A crease forms between her brows. Fuck she's hot when she's mad. "Give me your keys. I'm not letting you drive home like this."

"I'm fine."

"No. You're drunk and being an arsehole," she says, holding out her hand. "Give them to me, or I'll go searching for them."

"Knock yourself out," I say leaning back to allow her room to frisk me.

She's got this determined look on her face as she plunges her hand inside my pocket. I'm not wearing boxers, and the heat from her fingers on my cock as she skims my thin pocket lining is so fucking hot. I want more. She gasps when she realises that her hand is on my dick with only a thin piece of cotton separating us. "See what you do to me, Ana?"

"Sorry," she blurts out, all high and breathy, and yanks her hand away like the damn thing just bit her. The pink in her cheeks is so delicious it makes me want to kiss her. So I do. I push her back against the wall and lean into her, claiming her mouth with my own, my hard on pressing into the soft flesh of her stomach.

"Don't be sorry, darlin'," I whisper, as I break away and trail kisses down her neck. "Just don't stop touching it."

I run my hand down the side of her hip and lift her leg until I'm pressed firmly against her and she has no other choice but to wrap her leg around my own. The space between our kisses is taken up with Ana's breathy moans and my grunts as I thrust between her thighs.

My jeans are in the way and her dress is all crushed up between us. There's too much material between my skin and hers, and yet neither of us seeks to move it out of the way. I just keep grinding into her as she moans my name and tilts her neck so my lips have easier access to her flesh. I know she must be uncomfortable in that position, thrust up against a brick wall with so much of her back exposed in that little sundress, my pelvis smashing into her so hard I can feel the folds of her pussy moulding to my cock, despite the fact that our clothes are in the way.

I know I must be hurting her with how hard I'm pushing, but I'm too selfish to stop. Instead, I run my hand along the back of her thigh and my fingers slip beneath her dress, beneath the barely there lace underwear and slide into her wet heat. She inhales sharply. *Fuck.* She's so hot I feel like my skin might catch fire. I slide the pad of my thumb down into her wetness and circle it over her clit, smiling as I feel her body tremor. She's so responsive to my touch.

I flick my thumb back and forth, move my fingers faster once I hear her breath catch and her hips rock into the rhythm. She's trembling and panting, so close to coming. The need to take her over the edge consumes me. I feel it like a kick to the gut, this desire to please her, own her, and be good enough for her.

It scares the shit outta me.

"Jesus, Ana, you're so damn hot, I wanna bury myself inside you and live there," I murmur against her ear. Ana's whole body stills. Seriously, she went from being seconds away from orgasm to being so still she's not even breathing. My hand freezes. I look at her face. Her eyes are filled with panic. "What's wrong? Where'd you go?"

"Uh … sorry, I think that beer kinda went to my head a bit."

"So then, let it take you over the edge," I say as I continue my assault with both my hands and mouth, but I know the second she puts her palms against my chest that the moment is gone.

"Just … give me a second? I haven't …" she whispers, and I gently remove my hands from her body and take a step back. *No fucking way. That's not possible … Is it?*

Is that why Holly warned me away? Because this walking wet dream of a woman is still a virgin? And here I am, finger banging her up against the side of her father's house. *Fuck!* Ten minutes ago I was walking away from Ana Belle because I'm no good for her; now, that's even truer than before, and yet I'd willingly give my left nut to be balls deep inside her.

"I gotta go." *I gotta get outta here before I fuck this up worse than I already have.*

"Just like that?"

"Yeah, Ana, just like that." I take off toward the alley again.

"Elijah," she says quietly. I hear the hurt in her voice, the disappointment and disbelief, but I block it out. She doesn't follow me and I'm glad. I don't know how many times I can stand to walk away from this girl before I crack.

ANA

"To being single." Holly taps her plastic cup off of mine in a toast and downs the rest of her peach-flavoured wine cooler. I sit my cup back on the table without tasting it and sigh. Her toast would have been much more effectual if she didn't immediately turn around and suck face with Red Hot Rob.

I'm not even sure why we call him that. I mean, his body is kind of nice to look at, but he has this long greasy hair that falls below his shoulder blades and the colouring of a ginger on an emo kick. Now that I think about it, it's like Alice Cooper and Bon Jovi had a love child. Either that or some terrible nineties rock clip threw up on him.

Wow, when did I turn into such a judgemental bitch?

The truth is, I know why I'm cataloguing all Red Hot Rob's faults and staring daggers at my best friend, who is so drunk she's having a hard time keeping Rob's tongue in her mouth. The two are swapping spit outside their mouths and I think I may have just vomited a little bit in mine.

I mean, who does that?

And while I'm thinking of things that people don't usually do—who the hell throws you up against a brick wall and kisses you senseless, not to mention the things he did with his hands, and then just walks away like it never happened? I should show up on his doorstep and demand he tell me what the hell he thought he was doing.

I'm so mad I don't realise I'm even moving until I hear Holly shout, "Where are you going?"

I wave her off like it's no big deal and stalk toward the garage. Two of Dad's friends try to pull me aside, no doubt to lecture me on my sex life, but I shrug them off with a half-hearted line about needing to help the dragon with something inside. Once I clear the front of the house I dive into the garage, strap on my helmet and walk Bespa quietly out to the alley.

I don't hop on and start the engine until I'm on Main Street. I shouldn't be driving. I'm pretty sure that first cup of wine cooler after Elijah left put me over the edge, but that was a good two hours ago and I haven't touched a drop since.

I'm not drunk, I'm just angry. I coast along Main Street toward the motel on the outskirts of town. I really didn't think this thing through, I realise, as the wind batters my bare arms and legs and skates down my back. It's late and oddly freezing for this time of year, but I chalk it up to the fact that I didn't think to grab a jacket before I made my great escape, and wind-chill is a bitch. As if that's not enough, a fat drop of rain hits my back and I almost drive off the road.

The motel looms up ahead, but it starts to pour down long before I pull Bespa into the gravel parking lot. It doesn't matter that I have no idea which room Elijah is in. The Sugartown Motel has been here for years—almost as long as the Sugartown Mill. They built it for the single men who travelled to the mill for work but it mostly sits here with all the rooms unoccupied, unless the odd tourist spends the night instead of travelling through. Personally, I'd rather take my risks on the road, but that's just me.

All of the rooms sit in darkness bar one, right at the end on the second floor. I duck beneath the awning and shake myself like a dog to rid my waterlogged dress from the rain, and then I take the steps two at a time until I'm standing before a green door with peeling paint and a number seven that's been nailed on crooked.

Now that I'm staring at his door I think this probably wasn't such a good idea. I'm freezing, my nipples are probably high-beaming through my dress and I more than likely have panda eyes.

Okay, so no part of this plan was a good idea, but I raise my fist and pound on the door anyway. Several chips of paint flake off and fall onto the ragged looking welcome mat.

Elijah yanks back the door and takes me in with a bemused expression. He's dressed in a pair of jeans. No shirt. No shoes. And, sweet baby Jesus, the tattoos are even more beautiful up close. God damn it! I'm supposed to be mad at him.

"Ana, what are you doing here?" He pokes his head through the door and checks the parking lot, probably worried I brought my dad and his biker friends along for an old-fashioned town pummelling. "Are you wet? Holy shit, did you ride here in the rain?"

"No. I freaking swam, Cade," I hiss back. "Are you going to invite me in?"

I turn my angry, crazy panda eyes on him and he steps aside. I push past into the warmth of his motel room. The door slams behind me. "What are you doing here, Ana?"

"You left," I accuse.

He squares his jaw and narrows those pretty chocolate eyes at me. "Yeah. I did."

"You usually kiss girls and leave them without another word?"

"Sometimes."

"So it's not just me, then? Good to know."

"What do you want, Ana?"

"A towel might be nice. And an explanation as to why you just left me there and ran." Elijah clenches his jaw and saunters into the adjoining bathroom, then hands me a clean towel like he's afraid he might catch something.

I begin patting myself down. When I finally reach my hair I glance in his direction, a prompt for him to answer my question. He scowls at me.

"Look, Ana, you're a real sweet girl, but I'm working for your dad. I know he doesn't like the thought of someone like me dating someone like you—"

"Who the hell cares what my Dad thinks?"

"I need this job."

"What's he gonna do, fire you?" I snap back incredulously.

"You're a distraction. One I can't afford." A look passes over his face. It's like he almost can't believe he just admitted that. He doesn't say anything else and that simple sentence stings more than I care to admit, and so when I realise there's no budging him I put on my big girl knickers—metaphorically speaking, of course—and yank them up so he can no longer read the hurt that I'm certain is written all over my face.

"It was just a kiss, Elijah."

He narrows his gaze, cants his head to the side and I know he doesn't believe me. "Just a kiss? That so?"

I fold my arms over my chest and try to look indignant. "So."

One corner of his mouth tilts up at the side and his certain gaze locks on my wavering one.

Crap, I think he was testing me.

Double crap, I'm pretty sure I just failed.

Elijah stalks closer. I take a nervous step back into the closed front door. Anyone else would be conscious of invading the delicate boundaries of acceptable personal space, but knowing that he has me cornered seems to make him really, very happy. He grins and pens me in with his arms pressed against the door.

What is with this guy and his blatant disregard for personal space?

"You wanna know what I think, Ana Belle?"

"Not really, but I have a feeling you're going to tell me anyway," I squeak.

He leans forward, his mouth brushing the shell of my ear. This small, insignificant touch sends warmth flooding between my thighs and a shiver down my spine. He whispers, "I think you're lying."

"You can think whatever you like, but you're wrong."

"Am I?" He leans in until our lips are inches apart and the moment stretches out in front of us like the beginning of a warm summer day on the road. I breathe his breath, he breathes mine. Our eyes are locked, our bodies move into one another, and then, when his mouth meets mine, it's like we both just come apart. I taste whiskey on his breath. Whiskey and need.

I don't know if it's the same for him, but for me, the whole world could slip away and I won't care as long as Elijah never stops kissing me. His hands are no longer penning me in; they no longer have to. One digs into my hip through the thin, wet cotton of my dress, the other is tangled in the hair at the back of my head. His grip is strong; his frenzied mouth works at mine, so hard it almost hurts, but I kinda like that, too.

The assured way he holds me gives me the confidence to be as free with him as I want to be. Gone is the girl who hesitated as he pushed into me up against my house, and as I break away from him, lifting my dress over my head and letting it fall to the ground with a loud wet slap, I feel a freedom I never thought possible. Elijah's Adam's apple bobs as his gaze drifts over me from head to toe. The dress didn't allow for a bra underneath so I'm standing before him in only a pair of lace knickers. I'm freezing and beginning to feel self-consciousness sneak back in. I wrap one arm around myself, but before I can cover up completely, Elijah takes my wrist and pulls me toward him.

"You're so fucking beautiful." He wraps all six feet of hard muscle around me. I feel smothered and small in his arms but I find I like that, too. Very much. He runs his lips along my neck, across my jaw until my mouth meets his. With his hands he hoists me up and suddenly I'm weightless. I feel the hardness and heat of him through his jeans and I'm more than a little afraid. I know this is going to hurt, but it's not the physical pain I'm worried about, it's knowing I'm going to want more afterward than he's willing to give.

I press myself closer and attempt to steady my rapidly beating heart with slow, even breaths so he won't notice how much I'm shaking. Elijah doesn't notice. He just walks us backward until his legs run into the bed and then there's nowhere else for us to fall.

My breath leaves me in a rush. His weight settles on top of me. *Don't chicken out, you want this, you want him.* While my hormones and my lady parts are certainly on board with handing Elijah my virginity on a silver platter, I don't think my head agrees. It's coming up with excuses as to why I have to flee from his motel room.

Maybe Elijah senses my hesitation, because he pulls back and glances at me with a bemused smile. I must look like a deer caught in headlights. He opens his mouth and I'm sure he's about to comment on how much I'm shaking, but he kisses the tip of my nose instead. He eases his weight off of me, and I'm about to protest when his mouth glides over my collarbone and lower still, until he's kissing my breast and taking my nipple in his mouth.

I arch against him. His calloused hand palms my other breast and then he's trailing his lips over my tummy, licking and kissing his way down until his warm mouth covers me, underwear and all. Elijah shifts on the bed, settling between my legs. His fingers curl beneath the waistband of my knickers and he peels them off, painfully slow, and tosses them somewhere over his shoulder. I'm laid bare before him.

He dips a finger into my wetness and slides it up to my clitoris, circling gently. I want to tell him to stop, or to go faster, or to just wait a minute and let me breathe, but none of that is necessary because all at once his hands are replaced with his mouth and his tongue is gently laving at me. His arms border my thighs. His hands lie flat against my stomach with just a hint of pressure.

My fingers grip the length of his faux-hawk. I've never been more glad that his hair isn't cut in a conventional style; for one, if there was any more I might pull it all out in the throes of ecstasy. Too little of it, and he'd be sporting claw marks on either side of his head.

Elijah's tongue circles my clit, sliding down into my wet heat, until he's buried as far inside me as it will go. His stubbled chin and jaw prickle as he pushes his face into my soft flesh, but it's a sweet pain, and one I wouldn't give up freely. Lifting his head, he lets out a moan. There's a light sheen of moisture covering his mouth and, though I feel like I should be more ashamed, or even a little disgusted, I have to admit I don't think I've ever been so turned on.

He smiles like he knows exactly what I'm thinking and then his mouth is on me again, sucking this time. I feel him take that tiny bundle of nerve endings in his mouth and the sensation lays waste to all other thought, all other feeling than my whole world collapsing in on itself.

I throw my head back and cry out, buck beneath him and clutch at his hair for dear life as he brings me to climax.

Twice.

Or maybe it was one long, uninterrupted surge of bone-melting pleasure. Either way, by the time he comes up for air, he's panting as hard as I am.

Elijah swipes the back of his hand over his chin. He grins. Both dimples pop out. He crawls up the bed and as I watch his predator-like movements, the waning fire inside my belly ignites with new passion. His weight settles over me, his jeans still on. He feels harder now than he was before, if that's at all possible. I look up into those chocolatey eyes and feel myself falling. I know this is more than likely just the endorphins talking because, when it comes to Elijah, I really know nothing about him. How can you love someone you barely know? No. I know I'm not in love with him, but for a moment I let myself believe I am because I can't think of anything more I could want.

I don't know what's going through his head but his dark eyes bore into me as he gently strokes the side of my face. For a split second I think I see him grimace, like he's in pain, but it passes quickly and then his mouth is on mine and he's kissing me deep and slow, and the fire in my belly is so distracting I can think of nothing else. After a beat, Elijah pulls back and whispers, "It's never just a kiss, Ana."

ELIJAH

When I wake, I'm flat on my back with wood the size of Mt Kosciuszko throbbing at my jeans and Ana hovering over my hips. She's still completely naked and completely fucking unbelievable, even though her make-up is smudged and she has one serious case of bed-head.

"Good morning." She gives me a shy smile through a curtain of hair which I brush out of the way in order to see her better. I grip her hips and push them down so I can feel her, so I know she's real.

She has that look about her this morning, wide-eyed and a little skittish, like she's going to bolt. Even though I know that would probably be the best thing for both of us in the long run, I can't let her walk. Just the fact that she's stayed this long in this scummy motel room with someone so undeserving of her time makes me feel things I shouldn't.

She frowns. "Hey, where'd you go?"

"Nowhere," I say, and slide my hand from her waist up her back until I'm gripping the nape of her neck. She's such a tiny little thing. It'd be nothing for someone like me to overpower her, and that scares the shit outta me. It scares me so much I find myself pulling her down until she's wrapped in my arms and our chests are flush with one another's. "I'm right here."

I kiss the top of her head. She offers me her lips instead. It doesn't take long for things to escalate, and within seconds we're both panting hard. Her hips ride my own. It would be nothing to free myself from my jeans and slide into her, but even though it seems like this morning was made for taking her slow and deep, I know that's not something she's ready for.

When I first met Ana, it never even crossed my mind that she could be a virgin. No way had that cherry not been popped. Fuck, if I'd gone to high school with her, I'd have made it my sole mission in life to get this girl beneath me—and obviously, I haven't grown up any.

The second those words came out of my mouth last night as I pinned her up against the side of her house, I knew how wrong I'd been. It's why I walked away before it was too late, before I couldn't. Despite her dating that fucking wanker Scott, it seems like she was smart and never gave it up. Which I'm both glad and ungrateful for. I mean, there's a fuck-load of pressure on me right now. It's not that I've never had a virgin before, but more that I've never been the guy who earned the right to such a gift. I still don't think I'm deserving of it, but she makes me want to be. So I guess that counts for something.

"Ana, baby." I sink my fingers into her hips and hold her there until she can no longer move. Fuck, for someone so inexperienced she certainly knows how to drive me crazy. "Stop. Please."

I shut my eyes. I can't believe I'm saying this. When did I become such a pussy? Oh right, the second Ana Belle walked into my life.

"Did I do something wrong?" she asks, and her eyes dance around the room as if she's looking for an escape. She's terrified that she's said too much.

"No, darlin'." I prop myself up with one hand and take her face in my other so she'll look me in the eye and not down at the bed. "You're perfect, but if you want me to be, you need to stop now."

"I don't know what you mean," she says indignantly, and folds her arms over her chest. I'm not gonna lie, it's really fucking hard to take her seriously when she's naked and straddling my hips and her perfect rack is in my face. I let out a small, good-natured laugh, and it's like a switch is flipped. Suddenly, I'm all too familiar with that temper her dad warned me about last night.

"Ana, how many men have you been with?"

"What kind of question is that?" She scowls down at me before scrambling off the bed and tearing the place apart, searching for her underwear. "I haven't asked you how many women you've been with."

"Too many to count," I respond quickly and try not to grimace at the way her mouth drops open. I can't lie to her when I'm trying to get her to confide in me, so instead I relish in it. Yeah it's a shitty answer, but it's the truth. "Your turn."

"No. It's time for me to leave."

"You're overreacting."

"Overreacting?" she asks. "Screw you, Cade."

"Now, isn't that what we were just discussing before you overreacted and started tearing up my room for your underwear? Which, by the way, you're not getting back." I pull the little lacy knickers from my back pocket and dangle them before her with a shit-eating grin on my face. She makes a grab for them, but not for the first time in my life I'm thankful for my Godzilla status. She'd have to climb me like a tree to reach these babies. That thought rattles around in my head for a bit and suddenly I'm hard again. My voice is low and thick with lust when I say, "Finders, keepers."

"Real mature, Cade. I'll be thinking of you as I freeze my bum off on the ride home."

I tuck them back in my pocket and, surprisingly, she doesn't make a grab for them. Instead, she zips up her dress, the one that she tossed in a heap on the floor last night and—if her nipples are anything to go by—is still soaking wet.

"You're not riding home in that."

"Don't tell me what I can and can't do. You're not my father."

"Thank fuck for that! This'd be one twisted daddy–daughter relationship if I was."

"This isn't a relationship, it was a mistake."

"Baby, this is the furthest thing from a mistake."

"No? Obviously trying to hand you my virginity all tied up with a big red bow was a stupid move on my behalf. You don't want it.

Why would you be interested in some small-town, doe eyed virgin when you've clearly had so much better?"

"Shut up," I say, just to throw her off the mental path she's heading down. If she thinks about it for more than a minute she might realise she could do way better than some fucked up man whore with a shady past and nothing to his name but a motorbike and a string of bad decisions.

It looks as though she may have already figured this out because she opens her mouth to say something but I thrust my hand into her hair and pull her toward me, smothering her mouth with my own. For half a second she doesn't kiss me back, but when I scoop her up into my arms she wraps her legs around my hips and melts into me, her kisses as fierce as my own.

I all but throw her on the bed. Her breath catches in her throat, and she leans up on her elbows. I nudge her knees apart with my own and lean my weight into her so she can feel just how truthful the next words out of my mouth are. "I want it. More than you know, but you can't just hand it to me on a silver platter. You should make me work for it, make me earn it."

She looks confused. Confused and aroused. I don't blame her. I'm both of those things, and yet I've just guaranteed that my balls will be blue for all eternity, because there's no way that I could ever deserve a girl like this. Not in this lifetime. Maybe not even in the next.

"We can't go five minutes without wanting to tear one another apart," she whispers, and her eyes dare me to deny it. I don't. It's the truth, after all.

"So we'll tear one another apart and put each other back together, piece by piece." I slide my hand over her hips, down the damp fabric of her dress. While my room may be warm already, it's not so warm that she won't end up sick if she keeps this thing on. I ease up onto my knees and pull her with me so she's doing the same. My hands snake around her waist to the zip at the back of her dress. She shoots me a questioning glance as little by little I tug the zip down, my fingers grazing her smooth flesh.

"I thought you said I needed to make you work for it?"

"Darlin' there's a million other things I can do to your body without shoving myself inside it."

She's covered in chills as I pull the fabric over her head and I desperately want to erase them with my tongue, but Ana's shaking on the bed before me and finally, I remember why I removed it in the first place.

I ease off the bed and open the cupboard, pulling out one of the hangers I never use. I hang the dress in the window, where it's in full sunlight. I know I should probably close the curtains, but when I turn and see her naked body spread before me, sunlight gleaming off her snow white skin, I can't bring myself to do much of anything but shed my jeans and cover her body with my own.

For a long time we do nothing but maul each other with our mouths and roll around on the bed, and then I slide my hands between us and make her come in about two seconds flat, and yeah, I'm not gonna lie, the fact that I can get her off so quickly makes my heart swell with pride—shut the fuck up, it's a guy thing.

My heart's not the only thing swelling. But for now I'm content to leave it at that as I watch her bask in that freshly fucked glow, because in all my life I don't think I've ever seen a more spectacular sight.

She cracks an eyelid and whispers, "Stop staring at me, it's weird."

"Eat me," I reply and scoop her up until she's lying on top of me. She sits herself up and I can't resist trailing my hands over her gorgeous tits. She wriggles a little, as if she's suddenly ticklish. My cock jumps around excitedly like it's going to see some. Fuck. I've been in a state of perm-a-wood ever since I met this girl. She spears her bottom lip with her teeth and says, "Okay" before trailing her mouth down my neck and chest. She hovers over the tattoo on my left pec. Surprise twists her face as her eyes zero in on the name written in cursive, hidden there amongst an eerie moonlit cemetery. I tense.

Don't ask me about it. Not now.

For a moment I think she's going to, and then she lowers her gaze and brings her mouth to my stomach, licking, kissing and sucking all the way. I breathe a sigh of relief.

When she reaches my navel I grab her wrist, stopping her from going any further, "Ana, you don't have to do that."

"And if I want to?"

Fuck me! Does she have any idea what that does to a man? It looks like she might, because she smiles this sneaky little smile and dips her head lower, taking me into her mouth. Her hand follows her lips up the length of my cock and back down again.

Oh fuck.

I've never had a problem staying the course, but holy mother of nun cunts, am I about to lose my shit like a twelve-year-old at his first glance of pink bits in Playboy. I fist my hand in her hair, gently at first, and then harder. The urge to push her head back and forth until I'm defiling her beautiful mouth is so strong that I force my hand to go limp, so I won't hurt her.

I've played this game too many times to count. The players are different, but the rules never change. Until now. Until her. All the rules are different now, and I'd do anything not to fuck it up. This is what I think about as her delicate little mouth milks every last drop of come from my cock. I just had the most incredible woman sucking me off and she's got me so fucking tied up in knots that I forgot to enjoy the simplicity and base nature of it all. I missed the whole goddamn thing.

Ana smiles coyly up at me, and then crawls up the bed and tucks herself in under my arm. I automatically pull her closer and kiss the top of her head. She lets out a contented sigh, and I feel her relax further into me. We lie in the patch of sunlight streaming in across the bed and she traces the tattoos on my arms and chest until she falls asleep.

I'm too wired to sleep. My brain is buzzing from the high and a million thoughts swarm my head. Despite the morning's workout, my body is itching to move, to get up, to run. Instead, I hold Ana while she naps. I stare at the ceiling and wonder what the hell I've done, and what I'm going to do now. It doesn't matter which way I look at it: when it comes to Ana Belle, I'm completely fucking screwed.

ANA

The minute I set foot in the house Dad is on me. "Where the hell have you been?"

"Excuse me?"

"You up and disappeared, without a word, Ana. Not to mention the fact that you drove while drinking."

"Okay, first of all, I wasn't drunk. I'd stopped drinking at least two hours before I drove anywhere, and I told Holly where I was going—"

"Holly is not your father!"

"Why are we even having this conversation? I'm an adult, Dad. It's time you started treating me like one."

"You're not an adult. You might be nineteen, but that doesn't mean you know what's best for you."

"Oh, and you do? Okay, let's talk about what's best for me. Is it dating one of your biker friends, waiting by the window for my old man to come home after he's finished screwing club whores, like the rest of the old ladies do? Is it staying in this shitty, fucked up town, marrying one of the dickheads I went to school with and running the pie shop for the rest of my life? Hey, you know what? Why not throw in raising Sammy, too, since you and your whore of a wife seem too busy with your biker club to take care of the kid she spat out of her gaping vagina? Why not just throw the kid in and hammer that last nail in my coffin?"

"You watch your tone, missy," he hisses.

"No, Dad. You watch yours," I spit back.

"Let's get one thing straight. While you live in this house, you live by my rules. You come home at a decent hour, not the next day, wearing the same clothes you had on last night. That's how shit gets started in places like this, Ana. You want more of those rumours floating around that you're the town bike? You want me to get hauled back to the station for punching out some other fucker that's been running his mouth?"

"Are you done insinuating that I'm some giant fucking whore?" I fold my arms over my chest. "You wanna know where I was all night, Dad? At Elijah's motel room. And since you're so damn concerned about it, my virtue is still very much intact."

His eyes go saucer-wide, like he cannot believe I just said that. Come to think of it, *I* can't believe I just said that. Call me crazy, but the fact that my dad thought I was a slut, along with the rest of the town, broke my heart into a million tiny pieces. As angry as I am with him, and as grown-up as I claim to be, I'm still his little girl, and it cuts to the bone to hear how low his opinion of me really is.

"Yeah, Dad, still a virgin. But thanks for your vote of confidence." I throw my keys on the table, grab a hair tie from the phone caddy on the bench and yank my hair back into a messy bun. "Now, if you'll excuse me, I have to spend the next eight hours of my free time making pies for this town that thinks so highly of me."

Dad's lips turn down in the corners, his eyes are full of remorse, and his shoulders slump. His mouth is working but no words are coming out. Sticking it to him like that should have made me feel better, but it doesn't. It makes me feel just as ashamed as when he'd insinuated I was a whore. That's the thing about guilt; it always leaves you feeling cheap.

"Ana …" he begins, but I wave him off and head for my room.

"Forget it. I have to get to work." I close the door and allow myself a minute or two for the tears pricking my eyes to fall.

I have ten pies lining the countertop when I hear Elijah's bike pulling in around back. I smile to myself, thinking of the better part of the day when my dad wasn't accusing me of being a whore and I was instead partaking in activities where I could perhaps still be considered one. I marvel at how small I felt in his hands and at how quickly he was able to blow my world apart for the third time today when he pushed me up against the cool shower tile.

I'm still smiling as I pour melted chocolate into the recipe base for the pie that Elijah inspired, and I'm halfway to creating another recipe in my head when I hear the front door bang back on its hinges and my dad come tearing out of the house and across the gravel walkway toward Elijah. "CADE!"

Oh crap! I throw the spatula down on the bench and run for the door. My dad has Elijah by the collar of his jacket, holding him up against the back of the shop and, despite being younger, taller and musclier than Dad, Elijah's hands are up in surrender. "I know what you're thinking, but I didn't pursue her, I swear. It just happened."

"So you think that makes it okay? Because she came to you? She's nineteen, she doesn't know what the fuck she wants."

"Dad!" I snap and the two of them glance at me. Dad backs off, but only enough so that there's maybe an inch or two more space between them, and he's no longer holding onto Elijah's collar.

"Bob, your daughter's old enough to know what she wants." Elijah runs a hand over the back of his neck and then looks at me a little sheepishly. "For God's sake look at her. Have you ever seen a more put together nineteen-year-old? Look, you're my boss. I respect you immensely. I respect your family and your family's reputation in this town, but your daughter? There aren't enough words to describe how much I think of her."

"Oh, I know exactly what you think of her. You and every other young prick in this town."

My father is getting riled up again. His face is beet red and he practically has steam pouring out his ears. I wedge myself between them and gently push at his broad chest. "Dad, back off. What happens between Elijah and I is none of your business."

He puts his hand over mine and looks down at me, "You're my little girl; everything you do is my business."

I shake my head and give him a sad smile. "No. It's not. I can't be a little girl forever, Dad. I'm not a little girl. I haven't been since Mum died."

"Aww, hell, kiddo." He sniffs, and then, I guess to prove he's not a complete pansy—because the definition of a "sheila" in my father's eyes is a grown man who cries—he turns away from me and spits on the ground before taking a step back towards the house.

I glance at Elijah, making sure he's not already planning to run for the hills. He gives me an odd but warm smile, and then his eyes widen when he sees my dad turn around again.

"Hey, kiddo, I'm sorry for what I said earlier. I didn't mean it. I *don't* mean it."

I smile, because despite the fact that he can be a big and scary beast of a man at times, underneath he's like a puppy dog—albeit one with a mean bite—but mostly, I smile because, in my entire nineteen years, this is the first time I've ever heard my dad say sorry, to anyone. "Don't worry about it, Dad. I know you're just trying to look out for me."

He nods like he's satisfied with that answer and then points a finger at Elijah. "You remember what I said last night. You think on it long and hard before you make any decisions that affect her or you'll be seeing the wrong end of a shotgun. You got it?"

Oh god, please tell me he didn't just threaten to have Elijah killed if he broke my heart? And suddenly Elijah's speedy exit from the party last night makes perfect sense.

It's Elijah's turn to nod. "Yeah, I got it."

"I'm gonna need you at work bright and early Monday mornin'. You good with that?"

"Yes, Sir," Elijah replies and Dad walks back up the stairs and inside the house.

I snag my lip between my teeth and glance awkwardly at Elijah. "Hi."

His smooth chocolate eyes fasten onto me and his lips tip up in the corner so that I know exactly what he's thinking. "Hi."

"What are you doing here? I wasn't expecting to see you until tomorrow."

He moves closer, until we're standing toe to toe and I'm close enough to feel his warm breath on the top of my hair. "I kept thinking of you, all alone in that big old kitchen making pies. Then, naturally, I thought of how good your pie tasted and how I wanted to taste it over and over again."

Somehow I don't think we're talking about pastries, anymore.

"That so?" I squeaked.

"Mmm, that's so." He runs a finger up my arm, over my collarbone and cups the nape of my neck in his hand. He leans in as though he's about to kiss me and there's a moment of terrible, delicious torture as I wait for him to bring his lips down on mine, but he presses them into my cheek in a soft, slightly wet kiss instead. "Plus, if I have to choke down another cardboard microwave meal, my stomach's never gonna forgive me."

"And who says I'm going to let you taste my pie again?"

"Baby girl, five minutes alone with me and you're gonna be begging me to taste your pie."

"Well, I guess it was pretty brave of you to show your face in front of my dad after I spent the night in your motel room. Surely you deserve some kind of reward for your heroism? You get that he's hurt people for a lot less, right?"

He chuckles and pulls me through the kitchen door. "Yeah, I got that."

"And you understand that you're not getting a free meal here, right? I mean, if I have to work, then so the hell do you."

"Wait, you really want me to help you cook pie?"

"No, I want you to stand there like some Greek Adonis looking all ridiculous and cute. Of course you're going to help." He looks as though he's about to protest again so I arch my brow and say, "So help me god, if you say anything about a man's place not being in the kitchen I'm going to kick your ass, Cade."

He puts his hands up in mock surrender. "Wasn't gonna."

"Good." I rifle through the drawer and pull out two aprons. "Now, do you want the pink, or the yellow with cupcakes? Personally, I think the pink is really more your style.

ELIJAH

$\mathcal{S}$omeone was pounding on my door and that someone was about to get their head kicked in. I was sweaty, my head felt like it'd gone a couple of rounds with Tyson and I ached from head to friggin' toe. Ana's kid brother had come home from school last week sporting a nasty case of a zombie virus and had since shared it all around. Because sharing is caring. I'd tried to keep my distance, but seeing as Ana spends half her time with Sam and I spend the majority of my time with her, I'd ended up being one of the infected, too. Oddly enough, this damn flu had hit everyone in her family, but Ana seemed immune.

The pounding in my head and on my front door continues until I finally roll out of bed, snatch up the half empty bottle of Johnnie Walker on my bedside table and take a hefty swig. It burns like a bitch the entire way down and feels even worse sitting in my empty stomach, but if it'll help to burn out this flu then I'll down the whole bottle now just so I can feel better and get back to work.

Still nursing the bottle, I stumble over to the door, wrapped in a blanket and a pair of trackies. I pull the door back, and Ana's face is the one that greets me, so I have to rethink my plan of pounding in her head because that would just suck. Plus she looks like a fucking goddess in those jeans.

"Hey. How you feeling?"

I just stare at her. I'm sure my sweaty, glassy-eyed, crackhead appearance says it all. "You look awful."

"Feel it, too. You shouldn't be here, babe, you're gonna get sick."

"I never get sick and I got Holly to cover my shift for me so," she holds her hand out for me to shake and says in a breathy, sexy voice that has my Johnson twitching in my pants, "hi, I'm Ana, and I'll be your nurse for the rest of the day."

"Oh good, 'cause I have this ache in my pants that could use some TLC." I smirk and take another swig.

"Nice try. How about you give me the bottle—" she reaches out to take it but I hold it above my head.

"How 'bout you get drunk with me, instead?"

"Give me the bottle, Elijah, before I hurt you." She's serious, too. On any other occasion I might have taken her up on that offer, but in my current state I've probably got all the coordination of a newborn baby, and no man wants to emasculate themselves in front of the girl they have perm-a-wood for. I hand her the bottle and surrender myself over to her care.

"Good boy, now go and lie down." I waggle my eyebrows and she gives me her serious face before a laugh escapes. Even though my ears and nose are full of crap and my hearing's reduced by about 50 per cent, her laugh is still the best fucking sound I've ever heard. "I made you some soup with dry toast. I have tissues, cough medicine, throat lozenges and every *Fast and the Furious* movie ever released on DVD."

"Baby girl, what are you doin' with a guy like me?"

"The same thing you're doing with a girl like me." My head is too fucking messy to work out what she means by that, so I trudge back to bed and watch her fine arse in those jeans instead.

Within minutes Ana is beside me, fluffing pillows and forcing medicine down my throat that tastes far worse than whiskey ever could. Then she feeds me dry toast and the best chicken soup I've ever had—come to think of it I can't remember a time when I ever ate chicken soup before this, but I'm sure even if I had, it was never this good. She slips a DVD in the player when I'm done and settles into the crook of my arm.

About twenty minutes in I remember she hasn't eaten anything, and when I say as much she replies, "I ate before I came."

I press my lips into her hair, slide my arm a little higher up her waist and whisper, "Say it again."

"What?"

"Came."

She laughs. I run my hand over her perfect tits and tilt her chin up to kiss her. I know I shouldn't, but she's here watching the ultimate guy movie with me and she made me chicken soup and forced medicine down my throat—and yes, she took away the whiskey but that was probably for the best, too—and it occurs to me right then, in my fever heady state, that I've never had anyone take care of me before the way she does. I could get used to having her care for me.

Too used to it.

My heart pounds uncontrollably. *Fuck, when did I become such a complete pussy?*

"Oh my god, you're like some twisted little sex fiend when you're sick." She sits up and climbs over me until she's straddling my waist. I lift her hips and seat her back down over my cock, which has been rock hard since she curled up next to me.

"Darlin', nothing about me is little."

She lets out a breathy laugh which is one part humour and all parts desire. "I can see that."

She rocks back and forth gently over me. I can feel the heat of her sweet, hot pussy through her jeans and I sink my fingers into her hipbones, but it isn't enough. I tug at her waistband.

"Off," I grunt. "Everything off."

"You're kinda bossy when you're sick, too," she teases. "I like it."

"Yeah?"

She bites her bottom lip. "Yeah."

"Then take these damn clothes off and I'll boss you around all you like."

"Yes, sir." She slips off the bed, careful not to take her eyes off me as she undresses. Once her t-shirt is off I know why: her bra is completely sheer. Seriously, there's like the thinnest scrap of ... whatever the hell they make women's underwear out of between her full, beautiful tits and the world, and all I want to do is run my mouth over the fabric and tear it with my teeth. She smiles like she knows exactly what I'm thinking and slowly peels off her jeans, revealing a matching see-through-as-fuck G-string that definitely has a date with my teeth.

"Jesus, baby girl. Are you trying to kill me?"

"What, you don't like them?"

"You're shitting me right? The only thing I like more is seeing you in nothing at all and writhing underneath me."

And speaking of.

I tug at the waist of my pants but Ana climbs back on the bed to help me. I must look pretty damn pathetic because she takes a hold of my hand and says, "Let me."

She gently pulls them from me and throws them over her shoulder onto the floor, then leans back, reaching behind her to unclasp her bra. I sit up, reaching out to stop her. "Leave them on."

She pushes on my chest so I'm lying flat on my back, and then she takes me in her mouth, her hand gently cupping and squeezing my balls while the other milks my shaft. My eyes roll back in my head. I slide my fingers into her hair and tug, probably harder than I should. She makes a sound, but it's muffled by my cock, and I'm not sure whether it's one of pain or pleasure. I do it again.

Definitely pleasure.

Whaddya know? My sweet, innocent Ana likes it rough. I did not see that one coming. And my brain isn't quite sure how to process the information either. On one hand it excites me. Really fucking excites me. But on the other, it means I'm at an even greater risk of falling in love with her and that scares the ever-loving shit outta me.

Ana shifts on the bed so that she's straddling my thigh. Her perfect arse is sticking up in the air and the thin elastic of her G-string follows the curve and disappears into her crevice. I trace the fabric with my finger and then I sit up and hook my arm underneath her waist, lifting her off of me. She giggles and shoots me a questioning glance before I set her back down so that she's still straddling me, but now she's facing the opposite direction and her glorious pussy is in my face.

I run my hand over her arse but I can't resist the urge to bring my palm down upon those beautiful, smooth cheeks. Some arses are just made for slapping, you know? Ana cries out. Her mouth is still wrapped around my cock, so once again the sound is muffled, but she rocks her hips back into my hand and I know I've done something right.

"You like it rough, baby girl, is that it?" I feel her hesitate. The steady rhythm she'd been keeping with her hand and mouth falters and she goes tense all over. "Hey, you're safe with me. You know that right?"

I feel, more than see, her nod, and her voice has the sweetest quaver to it when she says, "I know and I think sometimes … I like it rough. I mean, it's not like I have a lot of experience with this sort of thing, but I … well, I like everything you've done so far."

"And if you don't like something that I do?"

"I'll tell you to stop."

"And you believe I will?" I'm not challenging her, just trying to feel out how far her trust in me goes.

"I trust you, Cade."

"Good." I slide my hand over the red welts I've left on her arse and I feel her relax as she settles back into her own rhythm of exploring my cock with her lips and tongue. I pull her underwear aside and slide my finger from her arse all the way down to her clit. Ana squirms beneath my touch and I trace my finger back the way it came, pausing for a moment to play in the wetness of her opening. I glide my finger over the puckered flesh of her arsehole, circling the sensitive skin. Ana's whole body goes ramrod straight.

"Yes or no, baby girl?"

"I don't … I've never—"

"Yes or no?" She pushes her arse into my hand. "That a girl."

I dip my thumb into her pussy and glide it back to that sweet little hole and gently, slowly, ease in. Her grip is so tight it hurts, and even though her mouth is no longer bobbing up and down on my dick as she explores these new sensations, I almost lose my shit right there imagining what it'd be like to push my cock inside. *Fuck me!* I've never seen a woman more responsive to touch than she is.

"Okay?"

"Uh-huh," she whispers.

The urge to flip her over and fuck her senseless is so great it could bring me to my knees, but I made her promise to make me work for it, and getting her off a handful of times doesn't mean I've done jack shit to earn that right yet. So, for now, I busy myself by plunging my middle finger into her pussy and allowing my tongue the chance to explore everything else, from her clit to the inside of her thighs.

She hasn't resumed her sucking. In fact, aside from the places where our bodies are connected, she's not touching me at all and I couldn't care less. My Johnson's not happy about it, but he fucking should be considering I'll never need a new mental image for my spank bank ever again. Seeing the way Ana writhes against my hand, the way her hips buck and shudder, hearing the breathy moans escape that ridiculously fuckable mouth of hers as she comes for me is enough to make me never want to look at another woman again, much less fuck one.

With all the shit I've done, the hurt I've caused people, some I barely knew and others I knew too well, for all the worthless hours I've spent wandering through this mess I call a life, looking at this girl before me—who is so perfect and innocent, and downright trusting in every way—I know that, somewhere along the line, I must have done something right for her to want to let me in.

I also know that I'm completely fucking screwed.

ANA

"Come on. You have to give me more details than 'it was nice'. I mean, why the hell haven't you strapped him to the bed and impaled yourself on his enormous cock yet?" Holly whines.

It's not that I'm not used to her being this vocal about my sex life—or up until recently, my lack thereof—it's the fact that she's sing-songing it throughout the diner when my kid brother is sitting at a booth nearby, and so is Sugartown's one and only homeless resident, who carts around stray cats in his trolley and always smells like pee. He's harmless. A little crazy, but he's never been a threat to anyone. Ordinarily, Crazy-Eyed Callaghan would meet us at the back door at the end of the day and we'd offload any leftover pies into his eager hands. Today, for some reason, he's a paying customer and has just as much right to be in here as anyone else.

I grab Holly by the arm and yank her behind the counter. "Would you keep your voice down, please?"

"What's the matter? Don't want Crazy-Eyes to hear all about your boyfriend's big cock?"

"I didn't say it was big."

"Honey, you didn't have to. Have you seen the guy? He's a freaking giant. A sexy giant, but a giant no less. If he's not big, then there really is no god."

"Oh my god, you are so sick." I laugh and throw my cloth down on the counter and trade it instead for the pie I made Elijah. "I'm just going to run this over to him, really quick."

"Oh, speaking of sick, is he into kinky shit? You know, cuffs, paddles, anal?" I feel my whole body flush head to toe, and I almost drop the pie. Holly's eyes widen with excitement. Even Crazy-Eyed Callaghan has never looked this nuts.

"GET THE FUCK OUT!" she shrieks, and Callaghan starts shaking his head and muttering to himself as he gathers his ratty plastic bags together.

"Holly," I whisper-yell before turning to him to apologise. He doesn't hear me, on account of her carrying on like a banshee.

"Oh my god," she shrieks. "You have to tell me everything right now!"

I hightail it out from behind the counter, snatch up Sammy, who is looking about as freaked out as I am, and bolt for the door. And, just as I'm thinking it might be time to find a new best friend, Holly throws back the shop door and screams, "That big, kinky giant of yours isn't going to save you from me, Ana Belle. I know where you live, girlfriend, and I WILL find you!"

"Ana Cabana?" Sammy asks, as he shoots daggers at Holly over my shoulder. "Wath kinky mean?"

I really have to learn to keep Holly away from my kid brother.

"I'll tell you when you're older," I say, and set him down on the footpath. He disappears into the shop. As I approach the garage, I can hear the sounds of flirty feminine laughter and the occasional clang of a wrench banging around. Dad took off with the dragon to some club meet thing earlier, so I know Elijah's here alone finishing things up. Correction. *Was* here alone.

"And when I'm older, Anath's gonna tell me what kinky ith," Sammy states proudly, and I hear that stupid whore with the flirty laugh giggle again. The sound grates on me and I have a really weird sense of Déjà vu. I know that laugh, and I wasn't wrong about it belonging to a skanky whore. Nicole White.

"Aww, he's so cute. Is he yours?" she asks. *Oh for the love of god, that bitch knows exactly who the kid belongs to. The same girl who she stole her last boyfriend off.*

"Naw, he's just my wingman." Elijah hauls himself out from under the stupid cow's Mazda 3 and fist-bumps Sammy. "Ain't that right buddy?"

"Hellth yeah," Sammy replies while he smashes his little fist into Elijah's, and I can't help but laugh.

Elijah's gaze meets mine and a silent greeting is exchanged between us. His is possibly a little more friendly than mine.

"Sorry to interrupt," I say, though I'm really, *really* not sorry at all, and if my tone didn't convey as much, the look I give him sure does. I hold the pie out for him to take. "I thought you might appreciate this after a hard day's work."

"Oh my god, you actually made him a pie. That's so cute," Nicole says, and I swear I hear a hint of jealousy in her patronising tone.

Elijah gives her an odd look and then turns his attention back to me before yanking me toward him and taking the pie out of my hands. His other hand slides down my arse and cups my cheeks.

"Ana makes me all kinds of things," he says, squeezing my bottom for emphasis and my heart swells so much in that moment that I kinda love him for putting Nicole in her place. In fact, I'm not even sure that line was for her benefit at all.

"Oh, I didn't realise the two of you were together," Nicole snipes.

I throw her a look over my shoulder. "Would it matter if you did?"

"Oh come on, Ana. Surely that nasty Scott business is in the past?"

"Oh, it is." I turn and smile at Nicole and Elijah pulls me back against him. I press my hand to his cheek as he tucks himself against my neck. My grin grows to proportions that could only be called psychotic. "Absolutely."

Sammy runs in from the courtyard out the back, drops a handful of toy cars at Elijah's feet and adds his two cents. "Scotth's an arthface with a sthinky weiner."

"No arguments there, little man," Elijah says, and mock punches Sammy's shoulder before setting his pie down on the workbench. "We'll still need to do some more work on the Mazda, Nicole. So, if you leave me your number, I'll call you tomorrow when it's done."

Elijah fishes out a piece of paper and a permanent marker and puts them down on the bench in front of her but instead of using them, the way any normal person would, Nicole picks up the marker and sidles up to him. She takes his hand and scrawls her name and number across his palm. I'm about to go ten rounds with this bitch right there in front of Sammy, and something tells me Elijah knows it, because he shoots her an annoyed look and says, "Right, well, I'm about to close up shop. Ana and I are babysitting the kid tonight."

"Ooh, romantic," she quips.

I swear to god, if she doesn't shut up I will club her with a monkey wrench.

"I'm noth a baby," Sammy protests.

"Of course you're not, little dude. I don't know why they call it that. It's kinda stupid really." Elijah turns back to Nicole. "Anyway, I'll have Bob call you tomorrow when the car is done."

"Oh. Okay, sure," she mumbles and then turns to me with one of the fakest smiles I've ever seen. "Ana, we should totally hang out one day."

"Yeah," I say then mumble under my breath, "so not going to happen."

"Well, thanks, Elijah," she says, and she just can't resist touching his arm one last time before she walks away, deliberately swaying her hips as she leaves.

I stare daggers into her back until she disappears from view, but the sound of Elijah's laughter has me whipping my head around so fast I think I may have actually pulled something. "What's so funny, Cade?"

"Nothing, just never picked you for the jealous type."

"Yeah well, I am. So bite me."

"I didn't say I didn't like it." He lifts me up and sets me back down on the workbench, edging his way between my legs.

"Are you gonna kith my thister again, cauth dude, thath tho grossth."

"Hey Sammy, do me a favour?" Elijah asks. "You know how the whole courtyard is covered in stones?"

"Yeah?"

"Well, earlier I dropped a dollar coin out there and I really, really need that dollar, but I just can't see it because I don't have awesome x-ray vision like you do. You think maybe you could find it for me? It's really important that I get that money back."

Sammy folds his little arms over his chest and gives Elijah his best discerning stare. "Whath in it for me, Cade?"

"I'll split it with you."

"Pleath. I get more than that for getting out of bed in the morning."

"God, you Belles' drive a hard bargain."

I shrug. "He learned from the best."

"I have no doubt."

"Alright, you find me my dollar and I'll give you this shiny ten dollar note."

"Are you serious?" I baulk. "For ten bucks, I'll go and find your dollar."

"Uh, uh, uh." He gently pushes my shoulders back to get me to stay put. *"You* will be otherwise indisposed."

"Sammy, I'll throw in ten, too."

"Alright, I'll do it," Sammy says and hightails it outside.

"If I didn't know any better, I'd think you had experience blackmailing small children, Cade. You don't have one of your own stashed away somewhere, do you?"

Elijah's still watching Sammy's hasty retreat, but I swear I see pain mar his features before he turns his warm chocolate eyes back on me. "Nah, not exactly father material."

Okay. Is it just me, or did he totally just turn fifty shades of guilty?

It occurs to me then that, despite all the time we've spent together lately, I still know nothing about him or his past. And there's a million and one things I've wanted to ask him, but I haven't, at the risk of sounding like some overenthusiastic creeper. Where did he grow up? What do his parents do? Does he have any brothers and sisters? Is he close to them? And then there's the most nagging question of all—why does he have the name Lilly tattooed over his heart? It's not like it's emblazoned across his chest in neon pink or anything, it's very cleverly and very artfully worked in amongst black and grey thorns and what looks like a gothic graveyard scene, but the fact that another girl's name is permanently inked on his skin still makes my insides churn in that oh-my-god-what-if-he's-still-in-love-with-someone-else kind of way.

Still, it's not like I can ask him outright. Not only would it make me seem totally insecure—which I am by the way, I'm aware of my downfalls and I'm completely okay with this—but it would just be so insensitive to come out with, "Hey, Elijah, you know that girl's name that's tattooed on your chest along with the graveyard? Is it because she's actually buried in the ground, or is she just figuratively dead to you?"

No. I definitely can't ask him. Not yet, anyway, although at this rate, we'll both be buried in the ground before I even pluck up the courage to ask him his favourite colour.

Elijah's snaps me out of my mini meltdown by saying, "By the way, what's this about me being a big kinky giant?"

"Urgh! Holly doesn't know how to keep her big mouth shut around my little brother. She's pounding me for information."

"As long as I'm the only one pounding you for … other things. Actually, scratch that. Two hot chicks pounding into one another is a sight I'd like to see."

I pull away from his embrace to stare him down. "You think my best friend is hot?"

"I think your best friend is psychotic, but come on, you can't say something like 'she's pounding me'—" His voice goes all high-pitched and, what I assume is supposed to be girly, but really makes him sound like a baby-voiced nymphomaniac, which is just wrong on so many levels. "—and not have a man go to his happy place."

"Hey, for your information, I do not sound like a sexed-up Teletubbie."

"Okay, so you don't sound like that, but baby girl, when you come, there isn't a sound in the world to rival it," he whispers in my ear before pressing his lips into my neck. "It's pure fucking magic. Making me hard just thinking about it."

"You're always hard." I playfully shove at his chest and he slides my hips closer to the edge of the bench so that I can feel just how true that statement really is.

"Exactly," he says, and nips my ear lobe. "How long do you think we have before Sammy finds—"

The sound of whooping comes from the courtyard and Sammy races in shouting, "Eat it thuckerth, you owe me twenty buckth."

"Hey Sammy?" Elijah says. "I'll give you twenty more if you leave us alone for ten minutes."

"For real?"

"For real, brother." Elijah takes out his wallet and hands Sammy a twenty. He slaps another on the bench and says, "That bad boy is all yours, once you've served your time."

"Cool." He's out the door quicker than I've ever seen him move and Elijah wastes no time in pulling me to him.

"Just ten minutes, huh?"

"Baby girl, there's a whole lot of orgasms you can fit into ten minutes."

And what do you know? He was right.

ANA

"Where the hell are we going?" I scream, though I know it's likely he won't hear me, given that we're going 110 km on the highway and in the process of overtaking a Mack truck.

I feel Elijah's waist shudder beneath my fingers and realise he's laughing at me. He's not going to tell me. I knew that much before opening my mouth. I've been pestering him since he busted into my room this morning and demanded I get dressed because he was kidnapping me for the day, and he still hasn't budged. Then he'd started rifling through my underwear drawer, picked up a pair of frilly pink knickers and inspected them, as if they held the answers to all life's questions.

"Okay, I hate to be the one to break this to you, but I really don't think those are your size, Cade," I'd mumbled as I'd tried to tame my bedhead without appearing obvious.

"Why haven't I seen these on you yet?"

"The day's still early," I remarked caustically and he waggled his eyebrows at me and tucked them into his back pocket.

"You own a swimsuit?"

"I live in subtropical climate. Of course I own swimmers."

"One-piece? Or bikini?"

"Are you going somewhere with this?"

"Where is it?"

"Top drawer on the left."

He yanked open the drawer and rifled through until he found what he was looking for. Producing my yellow string bikini he held it up in front of him and whistled. "Holy shit! I knew this was gonna be a good day."

Then he'd shoved me out of bed by dumping half my wardrobe on me and promising me ice-cream if I got dressed and came quietly.

The downfall of riding bikes is that, even on a warm summer day, you still have to factor in wind chill. It makes dressing for days like this difficult, because Australian summers are merciless and jeans and leather are the last things I felt like putting on my body in 40 °C heat. I'd just prayed he was taking me somewhere cool enough that string bikinis were considered acceptable attire.

Elijah slows the bike and turns off the highway. It's quieter now, but instead of pestering him again about where he's taking me, I tuck my head in against his back and watch the trees fly by in a haze of brilliant greens. Another ten minutes sees him pull the bike over at a tiny shoulder in the road marked out with bollards. There is room enough for three cars, but we're the only ones inhabiting the space.

"Admit it, you brought me to the woods to off me." I ease off the bike and begin working on my chin strap. All around us is bushland, but the ground beneath my feet is mostly made up of grass and sand, and I can hear the gentle lull of the ocean nearby. In front of us lies a small winding track surrounded by more trees. "Aww, and you haven't even had the chance to see my bikini yet."

"Ah, but this way I'll have the chance to do both. They don't call this place Shark Bay for no reason."

Elijah was already off the bike and taking out the ammo cases that he stored his belongings in while he was on the road. He'd quite cleverly crafted his own way to carry his belongings through the use of a custom made sissy bar that housed them. I smile down at him as he chocks up the side kickstand with a small wooden block so it won't sink into the soft ground.

"You know, if you rode a Vespa you wouldn't have to chock your bike up with kindling. They have these amazing new things now called centre stands."

He stands and snakes his arm around my waist, pulling me into an embrace, only instead of kissing me he takes my chin in between his thumb and forefinger and gives me his sternest face. "Do not mock my baby." He pulls away and strokes his palm over the seat. "She was my first love."

"Well, your current … er … girl, is getting jealous with all the attention you're paying your first love, and *she* has orifices you can stick things in without having your boy bits burnt off."

He pulls me into him again and his mouth goes to work on my neck. "Fuck I love it when you talk dirty."

"Come on, before we get arrested for roadside indecent exposure."

"Yes, ma'am," he replies and leads me to the path.

The beach was beautiful, pure white sand, calm crystal azure waters and not a single soul in sight, but Elijah wasn't happy stopping near the track. No. He made us walk for another kilometre before choosing to plonk down our belongings near a huge paperbark tree that had long since succumbed to dune erosion and was now firmly embedded in the beach.

He unrolls the picnic rug he'd carried and sets it and an ammo case down before us.

"What's in the case?"

"Breakfast." He sets out some grapes, apple juice and a few white takeaway bags, the kind that hamburgers usually came in. They're sodden and the oil has soaked through, but I couldn't care less. This impromptu picnic is singlehandedly the most romantic thing a guy has ever done for me.

"You brought me on a picnic?" Tears were springing to my eyes, which was so unbelievably stupid and girly.

Elijah glances up at the quaver in my voice and baulks. "Shit, baby girl, don't cry. It's just a couple of soggy egg and bacon rolls and the beach on a beautiful day."

"I love soggy egg and bacon rolls," I say and plonk myself down on the Tartan blanket, knowing all the while that I mean infinitely more than loving greasy breakfast hamburgers. I know next to nothing about Elijah's past. It drives me crazy, knowing that in a small way I have him, and yet the secrets that he keeps ensure I'll never really have him at all, not until he learns he can open up to me and trust me the way I want him to. Despite all his secrecy and the fact that I haven't really had anything else to compare it to, I think I'm in love with him. Each day I feel myself falling a little more, and I don't really know what that means for either of us. Sure, he's here with me now. And yes, he seems content living in Sugartown and working at the shop with my dad, but for how long?

Elijah wipes away a tear and cups my cheek. "You okay?"

God, I'm such a head case. He'd probably start running for the hills if I said the words I'd just been thinking out loud.

"Yeah." I nod, and set about schooling my features into something that doesn't resemble a sobbing, snivelling crazy person. "It's just, every time I think you couldn't possibly get any more perfect, you do something that surprises me."

He laughs and then seems to sober a little when he realises I'm serious. "I'm far from perfect, darlin'."

"No you're not. Not to me." I crawl across the mat towards him and take his face in my hands, kissing his lips softly. He lifts me up and sets me back down in his lap so I'm straddling him.

"You're incredible." I pepper his face with kisses as I say, "You're generous, sweet and unbelievably accommodating between the sheets."

He chuckles and tucks a strand of hair behind my ear as he says, "You're unbelievably easy to accommodate."

"You're beautiful." He raises a brow and I roll my eyes and add, "In a very rugged, manly sort of way. And the way you are with Sammy? He's special, and a lot of people don't see that, but you do. Plus, you said you like my pie."

"Darlin', there isn't a man alive who wouldn't like your pie," he mocks, and I give him a playful slap across the arm.

"Face it, mister. You're a catch and I'm not letting you get away."

"Then it's a good thing I'm not going anywhere," he says and falls backward onto the soft sand, kissing me senseless.

After our soggy rolls and a swim we lay on the blanket, wrapped in one another's arms, despite the heat. I trace the tattoos over his chest and say, "Tell me about these."

"What do you want to know?"

Everything. But namely why another girl's name is emblazoned on your heart, and is there a reason why you haven't had it removed before now when you're clearly not together?

I can't say that, though. I have to ease my way into questions with Elijah because his instinct is to shut them down by distracting me with bone-melting orgasms. Which is not necessarily a bad thing, but it does make it difficult to get to know him better.

"Who's Lilly?"

Crap. So much for easing into it.

He makes this scoffing sound in the back of his throat, like a derisive laugh, only it's laced with anger. "Somethin' on your mind, Ana?"

"I think it's a fair question, considering you had her name permanently etched into your skin. And over your heart, no less." Even as I'm saying the words, I'm still not sure why it's all that important. I don't know why I'm being so irrational about it. I mean, it's a bit of ink, for god's sake, just five little letters that could have belonged to anyone. It could be the name of his beloved pet pooch, but my blood feels like it's simmering inside my veins no less.

Elijah shifts out from under me and begins gathering together our things.

"What are you doing?"

"I think we should head back. You've got some work to do at the shop, and I've got some things to take care of."

"Seriously?" I stand up, too, so that he's not doubled over talking to me like I'm a naughty child. He's incredibly intimidating when he towers above me like that. Even if I wasn't 5'2, he'd be intimidating regardless, but at least this way I'm able to look him in the eye. Kind of. "You'd seriously rather run than have a conversation about your ex?"

"She's not my ex."

"Then who is she?"

He looks me dead in the face, and the rage I see swirling in those pretty dark eyes makes my stomach clench. "No one you need to worry about. She's dead."

I know that. Or at some point I'd guessed as much, but I still feel like crap when I hear the words flee his mouth and see his anger turn to sadness. Irrationally, that just makes me angrier.

"You don't talk about your past. In fact, you go out of your way to change the subject, like you're ashamed of where you come from."

"I am ashamed!" he bellows, and I snap my head back as if he's just struck a physical blow. I spin on my heel and start heading for the path, though I have absolutely no idea what I'll do when I get there. I'm not crazy enough to hitchhike—I saw *Wolf Creek*, people—but I'm not sure I want to spend the next hour on the back of the bike snuggled up to Elijah, either.

"Ana, get back here," he growls.

"Screw you!"

"Where you gonna go, baby girl?" he singsongs, and because I can practically feel him breathing down my neck, I pick up the pace. The next thing I know I'm airborne, and Elijah flips me over his shoulder like a goddamn cave man.

"Put me down, arsehole." I kick and scream and pound on his back with my fists. I think I may have even got in a shot to the side of his head with my knee.

"You keep strugglin', baby girl. I can do this all day."

I believe him, too. The boy's probably got enough stamina to stand there for several days, but the minute I stop acting up he unceremoniously dumps me onto the blanket and crouches in the sand before me.

"I'm sorry. I shouldn't have yelled, I just …" He exhales loudly and looks down the empty beach before meeting my gaze. "I guess there isn't a whole lotta good to talk about, you know? The shit I've seen. The shit I've *done*. I'm not proud of any of it."

"I've done things I'm not—"

"I've done time, Ana. Twice."

I feel my eyes widen in surprise. He'd hinted as much the night of our "date" but I thought it was all just for show. I didn't believe that he'd actually been in jail.

"Yeah, not so perfect now, am I?

"You hurt anyone?"

He shakes his head solemnly. "Just my future and any shot I might have had at a real career. I fix bikes because I'm good at it. I've been taking engines apart and putting them back together since I was ten years-old. Sometimes I think I have oil running through my veins instead of blood. I make enough to get me from one town to the next, but it's not any kind of life. Sure as shit not enough of one to drag someone like you into it."

"Someone like me?"

"Baby girl, you could have any man you want and instead you settle for a broke ex-con."

I wasn't sure I wanted to know the answer to my next question. In fact, I was pretty sure I'd really rather not know, but I had to ask all the same. "What did you do?"

"The first time?"

I nod.

"Stole a car with some buddies of mine, took it for a test drive and wrapped it around a telegraph pole. Sean ended up with a concussion and a broken arm, Luke had a cracked rib and Brent and I walked away unscathed—at least until they found out I was driving. Then they marched me straight into juvie and spat me out three years later."

"And the second time?"

He swallows, hard. "Part of my release on good behaviour is that I can't talk about it."

"Well, that's convenient," I deadpan.

"It's the truth." Elijah swipes a hand over his face. "Look, I should have told you this a lot sooner—"

"No shit."

"I've kept my nose clean since I got out. I don't plan on ever going back. That shit's done with. There are parts of my life that I can't talk about and others that I won't. If you think you can handle that then great, if not, then we end this thing right here."

"What is this *thing*?"

"You tell me."

Easier said than done. Yes, I was falling for the guy, but holy crap, how do you fail to mention something this huge to someone you care about? And does he really care about me, or am I just a way to pass the time between this town and the next?

I finally meet his gaze and I'm surprised by the anxiety I see there. It softens my anger, just a little, enough to understand why he'd keep this a secret from me. Aside from the fact that it's been court ordered, that is. "Does my dad know?"

Another solemn nod. "One of the stipulations of my release is that I have a job to go to before I move on anywhere. I have a parole officer who rides my arse if I'm more than an hour late to check in with both her and my new employer. If I break parole I go back inside, hard time and no hearing."

"And he's okay with this?"

"When he gave me the job, he was, but when I met you—hell no! Why do you think he fought so hard to keep me away from you? He wanted to string me up by my balls after he found out you'd spent the night with me."

"Well, I kinda know how he feels."

"I'm sorry, Ana." He tentatively cups my face in his hands, as if he's afraid I'll pull away. I don't. I lean into his touch instead. "It didn't feel right, telling you before now. I'm working hard to keep that shit buried, you know, but sometimes it all just resurfaces and kicks me in the nuts."

"I get it, I do. But if you lie to me again, Cade, it won't be my dad you'll have to watch out for."

"Shit, baby girl." Elijah ducks his head and his dimples come out swinging. "You're pretty bloody scary when you wanna be."

"I learned from the best."

"No arguments there."

ELIJAH

You'd think having a kid along on a date would seriously cramp any chances I had of getting his older sister naked beneath me by the end of the night, but whenever Ana saw me treating her kid brother like my six-year-old best mate, it's like her maternal instincts went into overdrive. At nineteen, she may not have been aware that her body clock was already switched to "soccer mum", but it was as plain as fuck to me. She'll make an incredible wife and mother someday, and I feel a pang of stupid jealously that I won't be around to see it.

I can feel her eyes on Sammy and me as our dodgem car careens head first into a couple of little punks that'd been out for blood since the ride began. She leans against the wire fence, her cheeks flushing as she spears her bottom lip with her teeth. I can practically feel the lust emanating off her. A couple of guys stop to check out her arse and a swell of pride and possessiveness rolls over me. *That arse is mine*, and in just a few short minutes I'll show everyone by slipping my hand into the back pocket of her jeans and squeezing it until she yelps. For now, I'll avenge the beating we're taking from these little Justin Bieber lookalike dipshits.

Sammy lets out a squeal of a laugh, his head thrown back as another little turd ramrods us in the rear.

"You okay, buddy?" I ask and he nods. "Whaddya say we hit these fools where it hurts?"

"Do it!" he screams and flies back against the seat as I hit the pedal to the floor. Christ, he's so bloody little, I'm surprised the jolt doesn't break him in half. We take off after the fuckers, side-slamming both their cars into the guardrail at once.

Ignoring the signs about remaining seated while the ride is in action, Sammy jumps up on his seat and gives them both the finger. "Eat thit fuckerth."

I laugh before catching sight of Ana on the sidelines. I can practically see the steam pouring out of her ears. She's ranting about something, though the candy-coated shit they call pop music is grating at my eardrums and blocking whatever the hell it is she's raving about.

"Dude, sit down. You're totally cock-blocking me right now!" I yank Sammy back down in his seat.

"Whath cock-blocking?"

My eyes go wide with horror and then I laugh. "Ask your sister."

The end of some tragic bloody Lady Gaga song signals the ride's end and, before I can stop him, Sammy's up in his seat again and screaming at his sister, "Ana, Elijah thaid to athk you what cock-blocking meanth."

Every person within fifty metres turns their head to gawk at us. I throw Ana a sheepish grin and her returning glare is both a thing of wonder and the kinda shit nightmares are made of.

"Both of you get your bums over here, now!"

Aww shit, I am never getting near that pussy again.

"Thee lookth mad." Sammy stares up at me as we make our way over to the gate.

"Here's twenty bucks." I fish a note out of my wallet and slap it in his little hand, "See that fairy floss stand over there?"

He follows the line of my pointed finger. "Go get us a couple bags, okay? I'll handle your sister."

The man opens the gate for us and gives me a brief lecture about standing up while the ride is in progress. I assure him it won't happen again and nudge Sammy forward, before turning to face the firing squad.

"Sammy, get back here!" Ana screams after her brother but I pull her toward me to stop her from going after him. The fairy floss stand is less than five metres away and I'm keeping a close eye on him, but she's not satisfied with that and struggles in my grasp.

"Let go of me."

"He's fine. I sent him across to get us some sugary goodness. You look like you need it."

"What the hell happened back there, Elijah?" God, she's so fucking hot when she's fuming. "I leave him alone with you for five seconds and already he's swearing like a sailor?"

"Come on, baby girl, it was an accident."

"Yes, because I can totally see how the words cock-blocking slip out when you're conversing with a six year old. You have to be careful around him, Elijah. Kids are like sponges, they absorb everything they see and hear. What the hell am I going to do when he repeats something like that in class?"

"Hey, would you relax?" I rub my hands up and down her arms. "Kids say all kinds of shit these days."

"Relax? Is that what you're going to be, *relaxed*, when my dad's castrating you for teaching his son what cock-blocking means?"

"That depends. Will you come and nurse me back to health?" I kiss her lips and begin trailing kisses down her neck, careful to indulge that sweet spot that she loves so much just beneath her ear.

"Maybe." She's still not happy with me, so I dart my tongue out and lap at the soft skin. Fuck she tastes good, like vanilla and cookie dough. Her breathing becomes heavier, her eyelids close and her mouth opens in an "O". "Okay, yes."

"Ewww, groth," Sammy pipes up. He's standing behind Ana with a tower of cellophane bags full of fairy floss.

Ana spins around and baulks when she sees his cargo. "Geez, Sammy, why not buy the whole stand?"

"I tried. He thaid I didn't have enough."

"Come on, kids, I think the monster trucks are about to start." I take the bags from Sammy, tucking them under my arm before they end up all over the ground. I slip the other around Ana's waist and slide it into her back pocket, where it belongs.

*O*n the drive home, Sammy stretches out across the front seat of Bob's Chevy, his head on Ana's lap, legs tucked into a ball and feet dangling off the edge.

Ana is quiet; but I know she's not still pissed at me. I made sure of that by kissing her stupid outside the giant jumping castle while Sammy bounced around, head-butting other kids. I glance over. It's hard to see clearly because of the lack of street lights, but she looks like she's waging some sort of internal battle.

"You okay, baby girl?" Her terrified eyes meet mine and I almost veer off the road. "Ana, what's wrong?"

"I love you."

Then I do veer off the road, just onto the gravel shoulder, but it's enough to jolt Sammy awake, enough that Ana cries out and clutches him to her for dear life. I have a brief disagreement with the steering wheel and then guide the car back onto the road. Sammy's back asleep before we even leave the bloody shoulder and I stare straight ahead while my heart thrashes around in my chest.

I haven't a clue how to deal with this situation. Seriously. I'm trembling, the blood is whooshing in my ears and I've got a white-knuckled grip on the wheel. *The last person to say those words to me …*

Lilly.

My chest cleaves open as the unwelcome memory rapes my mind. *"Be good for mum, okay Lil?"*

"I will." She beams. *Her dark curls brush against my face and her little arms squeeze like a vice around my neck. I don't think I've ever seen her this bloody excited.*

"I love you, E."

Those were the last words she ever said.

Fuck! I should have walked away from Ana before now. I should have told her the truth: that getting into bed with me means having more than just her heart compromised. It could mean her safety, too.

"Are you going to say something?" she whisper-yells, careful not to wake Sammy, and god help me she's pissed again. Probably more so than I've ever seen her.

I panic and blurt out the first thing—no, the only thing—that's going through my head. "The last person to say that to me was Lilly."

Her brows shoot skyward and I see tears prick her eyes. "Oh."

I know what she's thinking, and I hurry to chase away the hurt I see written all over her face. "Lilly was my kid sister."

"Oh." She nods and looks out the window, as if the view is particularly interesting. It might've been, if it wasn't pitch black outside. "Was?"

"Yeah, was," I say solemnly.

"I'm sorry. You don't have to tell me anymore if you don't want to."

"It's okay. I can see how much you want to know."

"Elijah—"

"You gonna shut up long enough for me to get a word in?"

She nods gravely and chews her bottom lip. I can see already how much this is affecting her, and I know why it has her on the verge of tears. She's so soft-hearted that way, a part of me resents having to tell her this wretched truth for fear it'll hurt her.

"She was all excited about going away with my mum for a girl's weekend. They were getting out of the city and taking off to some horse ranch where Lil was going to learn to ride. She was obsessed with them, horses. Had them plastered all over her room, though she'd never even come face to face with one." I shake my head as I remember all that crazy plastic My Little Pony shit I used to trip over in the hallway.

Ana's voice is a whisper, as if she's afraid I'll stop talking if she speaks too loudly. "What happened?"

"They never even made it past the front gate."

"Why not?" Her eyes are wide with horror and glistening. The tears spill down her cheeks and I look away so I don't run us off the road again.

"Lil wrapped her arms around me, she was so damn excited she forgot for a minute to be embarrassed by her big brother. She said 'I love you, E.' I strapped her in the car, kissed Mum goodbye, and turned and walked back to the house. The next thing I know there's a big motherfucking explosion, and parts of our four-wheel drive are raining down all over me. There was nothing of them left to bury."

She's sobbing now, so hard that I'm not sure how it doesn't wake Sammy on her lap; maybe he's slipped into a sugar coma after all that fairy floss.

"Jesus, baby girl. Don't cry." I swipe at my eyes with the back of my hands.

"How can you stand it?" she sobs quietly. I can see the effort it's taking her to quit crying, to try to be strong for me. "How are you even a functioning human being after something like that?"

I shrug, but the truth is, I've had a long time to think about this and here's the only answer I can come up with: "The world doesn't stop because a couple of people die. Families die every day."

I glance over at Sammy. His head rests in Ana's lap. Her fingers absently stroke the side of his face as she cries. I'd give anything to trade places with him right now. "At first, you're not sure how you'll survive something that crushing, and then one day you get up and you go about living again. Or, in most cases, you just get through, one day to the next."

"I'm so sorry this happened to you." Her tears have eased up a little, but she's still at risk of drowning her kid brother. I tell her as much and she shakes her head and presses her palms to her eyes.

"Where was your dad in all this?"

White-hot rage burns through me at the mention of that worthless piece of shit. "Dead."

Ana stops rubbing her eyes and gapes at me. "Oh, Elijah." She reaches over and brushes my face with her tiny hand. I take hold of it with my own and place a kiss to her soft flesh. "I'm so sorry," she whispers, and the tears start falling again.

More than anything, I want to pull the car over and hold her. I want to kiss and touch her until all the pain of that stupid, shitty life melts away, but I don't. I stare ahead at that white line, the only thing that's kept me grounded and away from trouble these past few years. I stare at it until it blurs and burns into my mind the string of mistakes I've left behind me. I stare at it and wonder if it's time to start following it again until it runs out completely.

Pulling the front door shut behind me, I race across the gravel alley and into the back of the shop. Holly's leaning over the front counter, fogging up the glass with her breath.

"You know I'm gonna make you clean that, right?" I say, and toss her a rag.

"Ana." She whirls around, completely guilty. Her eyes practically pop out of her head when she takes in my outfit. The shock is not completely unwarranted, because I'm wearing skinny jeans, fuck-me boots and my fitted black leather jacket, zipped low with nothing but a bra beneath it. "Holy shit, woman! Where is he taking you, again?"

"Lantern Parade in Lismore. Do I look okay?"

"Are you kidding me? Cade is gonna bust a nut seeing you in this outfit."

"That's the idea. I think."

A highly irritating laugh comes from the booth closest to the window. It sets my teeth on edge and kinda makes me want to punch someone's face in. *Nicole White.* I glance in her direction and see her bitchy partner in crime sitting opposite. *God, has there ever been a more pathetic sight than former high school queen bee bitches, still carrying on their hierarchy bullshit long after they've graduated?*

Perhaps the only thing worse is seeing their pinched up, constipated faces pressed to the glass of my pie shop as they outright ogle the fresh meat out the window. I follow their gaze and realise they're staring across the road at a shirtless, grease-stained Elijah.

My Elijah.

A tsunami tide of jealousy swells inside me. It's irrational, but there all the same.

"How long have Slut and Sluttier been here?" I whisper to Holly.

"About twenty minutes."

"And how long has my boyfriend been parading around without a shirt?"

"About an hour," she replies, dreamily. I whip my head around to glare at my supposed best friend and she shrugs. "What? There's a kinky sex god half-naked across the road. Sorry, girl, but a body like that deserves to be worshiped."

"He gets enough worshipfulness from me, his girlfriend by the way—in case you'd forgotten who you're ogling."

"Oh, I haven't forgotten. Haven't forgotten you promised me more details either."

"You're such a perve."

"You know it. And honey, you have nothing to worry about. Anyone can see he's mad about you." She smiles and then throws me a wink. "Plus, even if I wanted to hit that, my hands are bound by the code: Hoe Hoes before Bros."

"That's too bad, because Elijah *loves* restraints." I poke out my tongue and Holly's mouth falls open.

"You dirty little slutsky. One of these days you're going to remember I'm your best friend and tell me everything."

"One of these days I'll tell you every little insignificant detail, and it'll be so ingrained in your mind, you won't look at either one of us the same again. Then you'll have to move towns in order to escape all those devastatingly gruesome mental pictures."

"Ha! Like that'll ever happen." She leans over the counter and begins fogging it up again, then draws explicit pictures in the residue. "Ana, girl, you and I are gonna be stuck in this sad excuse of a town for the rest of our lives."

"Maybe. But I'm beginning to wonder whether that would be such a bad thing." I stare longingly out the window at my man. He wipes down his bike with smooth, even strokes and, with a giggle from the front booth, it's apparent that I'm not the only girl in the room appreciating the sight of his muscled torso straining beneath his tanned, tattooed skin. His phone must ring because he straightens and stares at the screen before running a hand over the back of his neck and answering it. Then he disappears inside the shop and I take it as my cue to leave. Holly has other ideas and pulls me back to her side.

"You're in love with him," she accuses, but on her face is a huge, megawatt smile, and I can't help but grin awkwardly back. Holly wipes a pretend tear from her eye. "Aw, my little girl's all grown up. When are you going to let him stick it to ya?"

That's my best friend for you; sadly there's never been a filter between her brain and her mouth. Which, come to think of it, is probably why she's always got someone's penis in it.

"I was thinking tonight."

"OH MY GOD! You're letting the sex god nail you tonight and you're only telling me this now?!" she screeches, and I so desperately want to hide beneath the counter because both Nicole and her bitchy sidekick, Renee, are glaring at us. Holly remains steadfastly unaware of the mortification she's inflicting upon me and jumps up and down, clapping her hands. "Okay, okay, okay. Knickers?"

"The white G-string you helped me pick out."

"White? That's good. Virginal. He'll be reminded this is a first for you and hopefully won't just impale you on his pork sword." Holly doesn't see me scrunch up my nose in distaste at that imagery. Her mind is working a mile a minute and she has a glazed-over look in her eyes that I'm beginning to feel nervous about. "Matching bra?"

"Of course."

"You know it hurts like a bitch the first time? Sometimes the second, too."

"Yeah, I'm really not looking forward to that part."

"You'll be fine. You're obviously in very good hands."

"Really not as comforting as you'd think," I deadpan.

"Hey, it's better than being with a then fifteen-year-old Chris Johnson who couldn't figure out which hole was which and ended up prematurely ejaculating before he'd even rolled the condom on the whole way."

"You're never gonna let him live that one down are you?"

"That experience scarred me for life."

"And yet you still turned around and tried again the next weekend."

"Yeah, and some friend you are. You really should have stepped in and prevented that. All I can say is, thank god your hot cousin Jackson came to town a month later; otherwise I might have never ridden another pony again." She waves off my belligerent look. "Anywhoo, enough about me. You remember how babies are made, right? You're covered, or he will be?"

"Yes, Mum. Unlike some, I paid attention in PD/Health class."

"That a girl." She slaps my arse hard and sends me on my way. "Now, go bring that tattooed, motorcycle riding, kinky sex god to his knees, and don't come back until you're walking funny."

With a chuckle, I hurry to the front door of the diner, a bundle of nervous energy and excitement. Just as I reach for the handle Nicole slides out of the booth and steps in my path.

"Hi Ana."

"Er, hi?"

"I just wanted to thank you for not making a big deal about me sharing Elijah the other day."

"Come again?"

She giggles and Renee whispers under her breath, "Wasn't that what he said?"

I glare at the two of them.

"You know, the other day when he dropped my car off to me? I thanked him myself, of course, many times, but I just wanted to let him know how grateful I really am."

Oh no she didn't.

"Then you should tell him yourself. You've only been eye-raping him for the last half hour, what's a bit of harmless flirting between friends?"

Her responding smile is dripping with venom, though her voice is airy and filled with laughter. "You're so funny, Ana. I really can't understand why we weren't closer in high school?"

Probably because you stole my boyfriend out from under me, you two-faced home-wrecking whore, I think, but I don't give her the satisfaction of hearing those words out loud.

Holly comes up behind me. "Well, don't stand around chit-chatting all night, you've got a hot date, remember?

"Right," I mutter, and fling open the door. Now I'm an anxious mess for an entirely different reason.

"How long have they been together?" Renee asks Holly, and as I'm exiting the diner I bend down and pretend to fuss with the zipper on my boot.

"Ana and Elijah?" She feigns nonchalance. "Oh, they've been banging one another's brains out since he first rode into town. Guess he doesn't need that motorcycle anymore, now he just rides her."

"That's not what I heard," Nicole says.

"No? Then you haven't been in the room next to them when they really hit their stride. It's like someone opened all the cages in the zoo and the animals are having a free-for-all."

I cringe at that last statement, quit playing with my boot and begin marching across the road to meet Elijah. Though she always has my back, and my best interests at heart, sometimes I wish Holly would contract a flesh eating throat virus that would render her speechless for the remainder of her life.

lijah has the front door to the garage pulled down, so I slip in through the side door. The shop is shrouded in shadow, and I'm just about to call out to him when I hear him talking on the phone in the bathroom. "You listen to me, you worthless piece of shit. You hang up the phone and you lose this number."

"I don't give a shit what you say to the club. Tell them I rode the bike off the edge of a cliff. I've got a good thing going here, and I will be fucked if I let you waltz back in and ruin everything I've worked so hard for. This conversation alone is enough to send me back to the slammer. Zero contact with club affiliates, did you forget about that condition of my release?"

There's a pause, and then he roars so loud it rattles the drywall of the tiny bathroom. "I AM NOT YOUR SON! I stopped being that the day your retaliation got Lil and Mum killed!" There's a loud yell and the sound of plastic thwacking against the wall and shattering across the tiled floor.

I'm frozen to the spot, caught between breaking down the door and demanding an explanation or running in the opposite direction. Elijah mutters to himself, "Pull it together arsehole."

While I'm contemplating my retreat, he wrenches the door open. I know the guilt of overhearing his conversation is written all over my face so I'm not sure why I try to pretend like I'm in the dark, but I smile sweetly. "Hi."

"How long you been standing there, Ana?"

"Not long, I just got here."

"Oh yeah?" He eliminates the distance between us and slides his hands around my waist. Then he lifts me up and sets me back down on the workbench, easing his way between my thighs. He's shaking slightly and I can feel the caged violence in him, and the effort it takes to be gentle with me. "You're a terrible liar, you know that?"

He tugs my zipper down an extra inch until my boobs are practically falling out of my jacket. Then he slips his hand inside my bra and rolls my nipple between his thumb and forefinger. "Nice outfit. You got a hot date tonight?"

"Yeah, actually I should get going. Scott's picking me up in a minute," I joke, just to relieve some of the tension between us, but it has the opposite effect. Elijah growls and tugs hard on my nipple, causing my breath to catch in the back of my throat and a shot of fiery pleasure to arc between my breast and my already drenched crevice. "Now is really not the time to be putting images of you with other men in my head, Ana."

"You wanna talk about it?" We both know I don't mean the ridiculous idea of me with other men.

"No," he says, a little too quickly, and then presses a hard kiss to my lips.

"Elijah—"

"I don't wanna talk about it. I wanna put you over my knee and spank you til your arse is raw. And then I wanna flip you over and eat you out until that beautiful pussy can't come any more." He peppers my face and neck with kisses, then slides a hand between my legs and begins working me into a frenzy. The seam of my jeans rubs against my clit with every stroke until I'm a sighing, shuddering mess of a woman. "Then I wanna fuck your mouth until you drain every last drop from me."

I have my own ideas about that last one. As much as I love going down on him, I'd much rather he fucked me than my mouth, but I'm not prepared to admit that little detail yet. Besides, I'm under no illusions that if he took me now while he's in this dark—and frankly, kind of scary—mood, I wouldn't be walking for a week. As hot as that makes me, it's really not the way I think my first time should go.

Not that it matters at this point. A few more strokes of his hand and I'll consent to anything as I'm riding that delicious post-orgasmic high. I think he senses this, too, because he withdraws his hand and tilts my face up to his. I'm panting, desperate and *aching* for him to finish me off, but the wicked glint in his eye tells me he has no intention of doing so. I let out a ridiculous whimper that shames me beyond the point of no return, which says a lot when you consider who my best friend is. Elijah laughs, low and so sexy that it sends a fresh frisson of yearning through me.

"What's the matter, baby girl? Cunt got your tongue?"

"You're cruel," I whine and slap playfully at his chest. He catches my hand in his and brings it to his lips.

"Ah, but I promised you a date."

"And it couldn't start *after* my orgasm?"

"Usually that happens at the end of the date." Elijah carefully zips me back into my jacket and leads me out through the side door before locking up after himself. He falls into step beside me and slides his hand into my back pocket, then he leans down and whispers, "If you're a very good girl, I might even tie you to the bed and take more from you tonight than just your orgasm."

I freeze midstride. *Does he already know that this is where tonight is leading? Is it written all over my face? Did he somehow hear Holly from across the street? And is he kidding me with this whole bondage thing, or have I bitten off much more than I can chew?*

All these questions run through my head as I watch him jump on the bike and turn the key in the ignition, though the questions I should have been asking Elijah have nothing to do with losing my virginity.

Why do I get the feeling that the answers to the questions Elijah's so eager to avoid are the ones that will ruin everything?

ELIJAH

The streets are lined with people; adults and kids, voices, music and the smell of fried food is everywhere. People jostle one another for space in order to get a better view of the parade. Several big-arse lanterns pass us by, ships and dragons and something that looks like a giant fertility goddess, each more elaborate than the first and most requiring four or more people to carry them.

We stand across the road from a pub, huddled in with the other spectators. There's several big biker dudes drinking and making a raucous outside the pub, though no one but me seems to be paying them any mind. I'm not sure why my eyes keep sliding from the parade to them. I don't recognise a single face, and they certainly don't know me from any of the other coat-clad revellers here but these days, anyone wearing a cut instantly forces my hair to stand on end.

I wrap my arms tight around Ana's waist and pull her into the warmth of my jacket. She's got to be freezing. Earlier, the sight of just a sheer lace bra beneath her jacket nearly had me tearing off her knickers and nailing her on her father's work bench, and wouldn't that be fun to explain to her old man come Monday once he'd seen the security feed footage? But I made a promise to myself that I'd never touch her in anger and, after talking to that scumbag of a father of mine, anger didn't begin to explain what I was feeling. Ana deserves more than that, she deserves more than some angry ex-con shithead just looking to get his dick wet.

And speaking of shitheads … one of the guys across the street must feel my eyes on him because he meets my gaze, makes a show of checking out Ana and then salutes me with his beer. He's big, about my height actually, and equally as ripped, but I reckon I could take him because he has about fifteen years on me. I can't take him with his biker boyfriends standing around, though. Audience or not, they'd have me on my knees and crying for my mummy in seconds.

"You need to be wearing more clothes," I gripe as I tug her zip up to the hollow between her collarbones.

"Alright, who are you and what've you done with my boyfriend? Because he seemed to lurrrrve my outfit earlier."

"Baby girl, every man with eyes loves you in that outfit. That's the problem. I'm gonna wind up behind bars defending your honour."

Ana has some witty reply, but it's lost on me on account of the group across the road. It's grown in the time I've been distracted with her, and now there are six sets of eyes on us, and only four sets of those are unfamiliar.

Fuck!

My heart thunders inside my chest. For a moment, I'm frozen where I stand while I watch recognition set in. The two new additions know my face just as well as I know theirs, and several heartbeats pass in the time that I glance between their eyes and their Hell's Angels patches. Patches I should have been wearing, and the lack of those patches will more than likely mean the end of me.

Fuck, fuck, fuck, fuck.

Ana lets out a delighted little squeal as a pair of drummers begin beating out a rhythm, and a troupe of belly dancers twirl and twist in front of us. I glance from the dancers to the bikers, and it's as if our standoff suddenly shatters.

"Time to go," I whisper and yank on her arm.

"But the parade hasn't finished yet," she protests, but hurries along behind me anyway.

My bike's parked down the road and around the corner, but we'll never make it there without being seen by the group that's pursuing us, and I know without having to look behind me that they're pursuing us. I know because I can hear the protests from the crowd and the parade affiliates as the guys cross the road to come after us.

"Oh my god, are you seeing this? Those guys just—"

"Ana." I grab hold of her shoulders and give a gentle shake. "Is there a back alley we can use to get to the bike?"

"What? It's just around—"

"Yes or no?"

"Yes." She shakes her head in disbelief. "Elijah, what's going on?"

"I'm gonna need you to run."

"What?"

I don't take the time to explain, because if I did we'd both be dead. Instead, I yank her along with me and we take off running, pushing past the throng of people. I gotta hand it to her; she may be the only woman I've met who can run in heels and still look fucking sexy doing it.

"This way," she yells and we slip into an arcade that I wasn't even aware had been there until we were running through it. We come out the other side into a dark alleyway; no street lights, no people. I don't think they've followed us, but that doesn't mean they won't find the bike before we do. And, though the license plate was changed the minute I got out of prison, it's still the same bike my grandfather handed down to me, and there really aren't a lot of 1979 Moto Guzzi California's in Australia.

I should have traded the thing in, or at least let her gather dust in storage for a few years. Instead, my simple decision to cling onto the one thing I truly loved from my past could cost us both our lives. And maybe I even deserve to go out like a rat, to be strung up by the balls and beaten bloody, but Ana sure as shit doesn't deserve to be anywhere near that.

We come tearing out of the alleyway into the empty street. We're alone. For now.

"What the hell was that about?" Ana's standing beside me with her helmet in her hands, but she's not moving.

"Put on your helmet," I command and find my patience stretched to its breaking point when she stands there demanding an answer. "Ana, put on your god damn helmet and get on the fucking bike!"

"What the hell is wrong with you, Elijah?"

"Ana, baby girl, if you don't get on this bike right now, you're going to get us both killed," I plead, and my fear must finally resonate with her because she hurriedly straps on her helmet and jumps on behind me. The engine roars to life and I twist the throttle and gun it down the road. We're almost to the town limits when two single headlights appear in my side mirrors.

My head is pounding, my heart racing, veins running cold with fear. Not for what they'll do to me. Sure, it's gonna fucking hurt like a bitch, because that's what we do to traitors. We take them apart, slowly. We poke and we prod and we strip them of their cuts and burn off their marks and we hurt the ones they love—not because we're sadists, but because once you patch in, the club doesn't just become your family, it becomes your whole fucking world. And once you fuck with a good thing, that good thing fucks with you.

When it comes to taking someone's old lady it's never personal, it's just the quickest way to rip out a man's heart and force him to watch it beating in his hands. Even though I was merely just a prospect when my arse was carted off to prison, I grew up in the club. My dad is sergeant-at-arms, I've been privy to what goes on in those darkened rooms beneath the clubhouse countless times and I'll be dead before I let Ana see the inside of them.

I shout to Ana to hold on and thrust the throttle all the way. The bike shudders and lurches forward. I check the speedo and feel a weird swell of pride that my little baby's still got some kick in her. Ana has a death grip around my waist, and for once I'm thankful that we can't communicate freely on the bike, because I know she's dying for answers that I'm still not ready to give her.

The headlights in my side mirrors are rapidly gaining on us and fear has my balls disappearing inside me. I should have left Ana behind, somewhere she'd be safe until Bob or Holly could come get her. Instead, she's holding tight to me as if I could protect her, as if my stupid decisions won't get her killed.

Ana points to a turn-off up ahead and I slow the bike just enough to take the corner without gutting the underbelly. Once we're flying down the straight I breathe a bit easier because my vision isn't hindered like it was in the winding hills outside of Lismore. I can see exactly what lies ahead of us, and at the moment it's nothing but cattle fields and straight bitumen. The relief is short lived, though, because I'm already pushing the bike as far as she'll go and the two Harleys are no longer in my rear view. Instead, they slide up beside us playing some kind of fucked up game of pong where we're the ball, caught dead in the middle, drifting back and forth across the road between them.

"Pull over!" one of them yells above the roar of our engines.

I shake my head at the Angels' VP, Rocker—nicknamed that because he's completely off his—a man who scared the shit outta me as a kid and still does. "Fuck you!"

"Come on, Moose," Kickstand says—yeah, you guessed it, his road name came from the fact that he forgot to put his kickstand up while taking off in front of a bunch of über hot girls one day. And mine? Well, it's kinda self-explanatory.

Kick and I were close, both made prospect at the same time. We're both the same age, and both came when the club called because we'd never known any other family than the one our dad's had indoctrinated us into. I glance at his cut and realise he's now a fully patched in member, which is exactly what I would have been if I hadn't taken the fall for him and been ordered to run. "We just wanna talk, man."

"Got nothin' to say!" I shout back and give the throttle one more sharp twist, praying like hell she'll pick up speed and not die under us. Ana clutches my waist as we lurch forward. I wish I could say something to comfort her, but my energies are better focused on getting us the fuck out of here. Up ahead there's a crossroads, and though I know it's ridiculous to think we might get away from our tail, it's all I can focus on. If we can somehow get ahead of them, it might not be hard to lose them along the road between here and Sugartown.

If I thought heading in the direction of the nearest police station would help, I would, just to keep Ana safe, but I'm not fool enough to believe the badges would make even the slightest bit of difference. After all, you can't hide out at a station forever.

As we approach the crossroads I don't slow like I should. Instead I quickly pat Ana's arm so that she knows to hold on tighter and attempt to take the corner at holy-fuck-high-speed when, from out of nowhere, some arsehole with no headlight decides on a game of motorcycle chicken. I almost didn't see him, but as I swing hard to the left and the bike slides along the gravel shoulder, I realise that was the point.

We're airborne in seconds. I reach out to grab her but she's so much smaller than me, she flips through the air and lands on her side in the gravel. *Fuck*. I hit the ground just as hard. My leg tremors. At a glance, it's torn up pretty badly. Blood pours from my head. A single tooth rattles around in my mouth and I spit it onto the ground with a wad of blood and dust. Disorientated, I unstrap my helmet to make sure there are no more teeth dancing around inside my mouth that might choke me.

"Ana?" I yell, as I attempt to climb to my feet. I settle for crawling my way to her because my leg won't take the weight. Dazed, she rolls toward me. There's a small cut on her forehead that's bleeding like a bitch. She's clutching her arm to her chest and there's a patch on her upper arm where the gravel ate through her jacket and sliced up her bicep like a cheese grater.

"I'm okay," she mumbles and then lets out a scream. That's when I feel the foot in my back pressing me down against the asphalt. Someone cocks a gun and shoves it into the back of my neck.

"Don't move, motherfucker."

"Hey, Rocker, ease up, okay? It's Ethan."

"Ease up? Prez wants this fucker's head on a platter and you want me, his VP, to ease up?" he punctuates each word with a jab of his gun into the back of my head. "He fucking sold us out, Kick. He's a rat!"

I glance over at Ana, who's being forced onto her stomach as I lie here, helpless to do anything but watch. I don't know the man holding her down but I could tear him apart with my bare fucking hands for the way he's touching her arse as he searches her body for a weapon. He wears a cut with a Wolf on it. *Not an Angel, then.* There's no relief in that thought because this is the guy that was ogling her like he wanted a taste just a half hour ago. He doesn't know dick about me, he's not invested in my betrayal, not like Rocker and Kick, and yet he's here anyway. Which means whoever these Wolves are, they're either running drugs or guns with the Angels.

Fuck! We are so fucking screwed.

"Get up." Rocker hauls me to my feet, his gun now thrust up under my chin. "We been lookin' for you a long time, boy."

"Been runnin' a long time."

"You been shackin' up with this pretty bit of pussy, here? You always could pick 'em, Son." He whistles low, and the guy holding her on the ground slides his hand over her arse and then thrusts it between her jean-clad legs. Ana lets out a startled cry. Her whimpers are swallowed up by the empty night around us. She's shaking hard, and I know she's in shock.

"Touch her again and I'll rip your fucking face off!" I sneer at him.

He laughs and yanks her to her feet. He unbuckles her helmet and throws it to the ground and then pinches her cheeks together, tilting her head to get a better look at her face. Then he looks at me with a shit-eating grin. "You mean like this?"

He tugs her zip down so her jacket falls open, exposing her big beautiful tits and turns to face her. He reaches out a hand that she flinches away from, but he grabs her arm and yanks her hard towards him before burying his face in her chest. "Don't worry, baby, Maggot's gonna take real good care of ya."

Ana struggles in his grasp. She cries, hard, wracking sobs that rattle her little frame. Her eyes meet mine and the pleading in them twists my gut until it feels like I'm coming apart. I try and lunge toward the bastard who's mauling my woman from tits to arse but Rocker yanks me back into reality by cocking the gun under my jaw.

"Uh-uh-uh."

"Leave her alone. Your beef is with me, not her. Let her walk and you can deliver my head to the prez yourself. I won't fight, just let her go."

Maggot pops open the button on Ana's jeans. She struggles and lashes out with her injured arm, and she manages to get in a few solid hits to his chest and face before he pulls the gun from his waistband and pushes it to her temple. "Hold still, bitch. I can just as easily get in your pants with a bullet in your brain."

"Rock, are we sure about this? This is Ethan, man, the only person other than Tiny you trusted enough to fuckin' glance in the direction of your bike, much less fix it." Kick, who's been awfully fucking quiet this whole time, steps into my peripheral.

"He ain't Ethan, he's a motherfucking rat!"

"We don't know that for sure. Till now, no one's seen the bastard since he was released."

"Been runnin' like a rat, hasn't he? What does that tell 'ya?"

"I didn't sell out the club. I got out on good behaviour. Saved a cop from being shanked in the middle of a riot. Part of my condition of release was to put the club behind me. That's why I've been running, I can't go back in or I'm toast."

"Bull-fucking-shit!" He nods in Maggot's direction. Maggot pulls Ana into him so that his chest is against her back. One hand cradles the gun against her head and the other slips inside her jeans.

"Bitch is fucking wet," he slides his hand further into her pants and, from the way she cries out in pain, I know his fingers are inside her. "You got some kinda rape fantasy, sweet cheeks? 'Cause I am totally fucking down with that."

I see fucking red. No word of a lie, everything is tainted with the swell of rage inside me. I jam my foot down on Rocker's instep. He cusses and loosens his grip on me. I drive my elbow back into his face with a solid hit to the nose and I feel him drop like a tonne of bricks. I don't have time to see how Kick's going to deal with this situation—I must trust the bastard enough not to shoot me in the back, because he's all but forgotten as I scoop up Rocker's gun and aim it at Maggot as I run toward them.

He has a kicking, screaming Ana bent over at the waist and he's attempting to shove his dick inside her. I shoot him once in the hip and he drops to the ground with a scream. I fire off an entire round into his head and chest, screaming out the remainder of my rage when my bullets run out. I reach down into the mess of blood and bone and take his gun before firing more bullets into his dick.

Ana's been stunned into silence. Her jeans are down around her ankles and she's shaking so bad her tremors look like convulsions. I take a step towards her and she flinches.

"Baby girl—" I begin, but the sound of shots ringing out behind me forces me to remember we're not alone. I spin around with the gun aimed and ready, but it's just Kick staring back at me with a wide-eyed expression, his gun held aloft, his other hand held up in surrender. Rocker is still on the ground, only now he's sporting two clean bullet wounds to the head.

I keep the gun aimed at Kick's head and jerk my chin toward his weapon. "Put it down!"

"Easy brother," he says eyeing me nervously.

"I'm not your brother. Now, put the fucking gun down, Kick."

"Yeah, okay." He slowly eases the pistol down to the ground and steps away.

"Back it up." I keep my weapon firmly trained on his head as he cautiously walks backward. I lean down, scoop up the gun, click on the safety and shove it in the back of my pants. "Down on your knees and place your hands behind your head."

"Come on, Moose. I just killed a brother for you." His voice catches on that last word as the weight of his actions sink in. "I just killed my VP for you."

"And I spent three years in prison for you, now we're even."

"What are you gonna do, Ethan? Shoot me?" Kick's shaking now too, strands of his blond hair tremor ever so slightly, and not from the wind because the night is as still as it is violent.

"I'd rather not, but I don't see another way around it."

"I won't breathe a word, brother, I swear it." His eyes dart all around us, looking for a way out. There isn't one. He'd be dead before he reached his bike and he knows it, because he knows me.

"Don't know if I'm willing to take that risk, Kick."

"Come on, man, I just killed our fucking VP—"

"Your VP. I never made patch on account of me being behind bars."

"You really think I'm gonna rat you out? If it gets out that I killed a brother me and everyone I've ever met is as good as fucking dead."

"You gonna run instead?"

"You gonna let me?"

I shake my head. "You run and they're gonna know you had something to do with it. The way I see it, you got only one option. Bandidos have a chapter in Byron Bay. Fake an ambush."

"There'll be retaliation, from Angels and Wolves."

"Not my problem."

He opens his mouth, hesitates, licks his lips and says, "You'll have to knock me around a little, otherwise they'd never believe it."

"Oh, I'll knock you around, alright. It'd be my pleasure."

After checking on Ana—who is still shaken enough to let me help her get dressed and hold her in my arms for a moment before shrugging out of my grip and falling to her hands and knees to throw up—Kick and I work quickly to make the scene look like a set-up.

When it comes time to rough him up, Ana watches me like a hawk. I hate that she's seen what she has tonight. I hate that I completely lost control around her and gunned down a man not three feet from her side. I hate that she's seen this side of me—the side that proves my degeneracy. But, most of all, I hate that another man has had his fingers inside my woman, and that if I hadn't acted quickly it could have been so, so much worse.

I turn toward her. She's studying me like I'm someone she doesn't know, which I guess is partly true, but still, her eyes volley back and forth between Kick and me like she's waiting for another fight to break out. I know that isn't the case. Kick is dead unless we do this, and he knows it, too. "Baby girl, look away."

I slam my fist into the side of Kick's face while his attention is still on her. He rocks back on his heels, but I don't allow him time to recover. I beat him again and again until he lies motionless on the ground. I'm pretty sure I've broken his nose, fractured his cheekbone and cracked a few of his ribs, and while I may have relished that first punch as if it would give me back the three years I spent inside after taking the rap for him, I didn't revel in any of the rest of it.

At one time, Kick had been my only real friend. A part of me missed him. A part of me resented him, but no part of me wanted to do him grievous bodily harm. He had, after all, killed a brother for me, and if the club ever found out what had really gone down here, they'd make him an example. And let me tell you, you don't ever wanna be the example. You'd pray for the devil himself to take you before the Angels had their way with you.

ANA

The nurse gives me an uneasy smile as she leaves the room with a promise to return with more bandages. All our other wounds have been tended to. My fractured forearm would be in a cast for another six weeks, and the cuts on both our foreheads had only been superficial, but the gravel rash on my arm was bleeding like crazy. My jacket had to be cut away because blood had dried and fused my skin to the leather, and I wore a paper hospital gown while the nurse pried the remaining bits of gravel and debris from my skin.

Elijah grabs my hand and squeezes as he mutters for the millionth time since getting off the bike in front of the hospital, "I'm so sorry, baby."

I squeeze his hand back, limply—on account of the painkillers, or the fact that something has broken inside me tonight, I'm not sure. I don't say anything in return. I don't want to, and I don't have time, because the nurse comes back wielding bandages, and begins sluicing more fluid over the wound, and extracting more pieces of road from my arm.

Elijah—no, *Ethan,* because despite the insanity of what happened on that road, I hadn't missed the fact that they'd called him that, several times—rises from his seat beside me and says, "I'm just gonna go make a phone call, tell your folks we're okay."

He was calling my dad? Was he completely freaking nuts? I give him a horrified look, at least I think it was horrified. The Endone the nurse had given me probably makes me look like a schizophrenic koala bear. Elijah/Ethan/Moose shoots me a meaningful look, smiles at the nurse and clasps my face in his hands. I don't have time to react, but I think I probably would have pulled away if it weren't for the drugs clouding my brain. "You must have hit your head harder than you thought, baby girl."

I think he's angry I'm putting a chink in the armour of his precious ruse. When we'd hobbled into the emergency room he'd sprung into this story of how we'd been out for a carefree night ride and hit a pothole and come off the bike. He'd made no mention of being run off the road by a group of vicious biker fucks who'd tried to rape me and torture him. He made no mention of the fact that he'd blown a man's head off and beat another within an inch of his life. The way the lies had rolled off his tongue had made me sick because he was so damn good at it. He'd been lying a long time, it seemed.

As he stares at me, waiting for his words to sink in, I suddenly remember the phone call. How stupid of me to forget. He's not calling my dad; he's just calling "the club" with an anonymous tip that one of their boys is broken and bloody and tied to a motorcycle in the middle of nowhere. I smile and nod and play along because I know there's something off about him right now, as if that isn't the fudging understatement of the century, and I'm worried that he might not step outside and make that phone call after all and right now I really, really need to be away from him.

"Be right back," he says to the nurse and shuts the door to my room behind him.

Once I'm certain he's gone, I reach out with a shaking hand and grab the nurse's arm. I look at her name badge and her friendly, sweet face. "Jane, does that door have a lock on it?"

"No, but I can alert security if you need me to?"

I shake my head. If Elijah can't get to me through security he'll likely freak out and start thinking with his fists and, as far as I want to be from him right now, I don't want him going back to jail. "Do you think we could shift rooms?"

"Are you in danger, Miss Belle?"

I ignore her question and rummage through my bag for my phone. "No. I'd just really rather not see him right now."

"Do you have someone else to come and pick you up?"

I nod and Jane places a wide sticky bandage over my arm and gently pats it into place. "You're all set here."

"Thank you."

"I'll switch off the lights and tell him you've gone in for a CT scan. That's the most I can do without calling security."

"Thanks."

I hit the call button on my phone and after three rings she picks up, sounding breathless. "You had better be calling me with details or the next time I see you I'm going to club you over the head with my battery-operated friend here."

"Holly, I need your help."

We pull out from the parking lot and head toward the town's exit. The same road I travelled on with Elijah just a few hours ago. *Funny how so much can change in such a short amount of time.* After all my paperwork was signed and I was given the hospital's okay to leave, Jane had snuck both Holly and I out of the service entrance. We'd climbed into Holly's Peugeot and hightailed it out of there without being seen. Or, at least, I thought we'd gone unnoticed, but if I was correct, the headlight tailing us belonged to Elijah.

"Okay, I don't want to alarm you but I think we're being followed," Holly said glancing between her rear-view and my stoic face.

"I know."

"Should I pull over? Make him grovel on his knees?"

I shake my head and stare out the window. "Just drive."

"What the hell happened? Two hours ago you were pledging your love and preparing to hand over your virginity with a big red bow and now you're avoiding him?"

"We didn't have an accident."

"Yeah, I got that much. What's with the super secret squirrel act?"

"Elijah used to belong to the Hell's Angels."

For a moment I think she hasn't heard me properly but then her screech of, "GET THE FUCK OUT!" fills the car and I want to cry, but I think the Endone's numbed my brain cells, too. Suddenly, all I want to do is sleep away this nightmare and wake up healed and as far as possible from the shit storm Elijah's dragged me into.

"We were chased and sideswiped, held at gunpoint. One of them tried to rape me."

"Are you fucking kidding me? Are you alright?"

"I wish," I whisper, and feel tears finally prick my eyes until I'm sobbing again like I was on the side of that road.

"Ana, what should I do?" Holly asks and I almost laugh, because in the fourteen years we've known one another I've never heard her sound so serious and afraid.

"Just keep driving."

"You wanna go home?"

"No. Dad will flip if he sees Elijah and I fighting on the front lawn with me looking like this. Take me to your place, please?"

"Of course." She looks at my shirt, the one Elijah had taken off once my jacket had been cut away and insisted I wear home. I can almost hear the wheels turning in her head. "You said tried? They didn't, did they?"

"No. Elijah stopped them."

"Of course he did," she mutters and then clearly, after she's thought some more about it she asks, "How?"

I turn and give her a look that pretty much says, "Don't ask" and she doesn't.

Elijah follows us all the way to Sugartown. He never once tries to overtake, or force us to pull over by cutting us off. He drives straight past his motel and follows us down Holly's street all the way to her driveway where he disappears as the automatic roller door slides down behind Holly's Peugeot, separating us from the rest of the world.

"You head on up to my room." Holly gives me a fragile smile. "I'll sort him out."

"Thanks," I say, and wipe at my tears before opening the car door and standing on shaky legs.

Holly's house is newer than mine and built in a much nicer neighbourhood. It also has a garage adjoining the house and, as I climb the stairs, I'm thankful I don't have to walk outside and right past him. I'm not sure I'm strong enough to keep running from him tonight. I don't know what that says about me, but it's the god's honest truth. I'm afraid I'd melt into a puddle the minute he placed his hands on me, so I hurry up the stairs and duck into Holly's bedroom where I gently slide open the window overlooking the front lawn.

Thankfully, Elijah had the sense to wait for one of us to come to him and hasn't tried banging down the front door to get to me, but he's certainly not quiet when he says, "Where the hell is she, Holly?"

"You can't be here."

"I'm not leaving until I see she's okay."

"What the hell makes you think she'd be okay after something like that?"

"She told you?"

"Yeah, dumb-arse, she told me. She tells me everything. Including the fact that she was about to cash in her V-card tonight for your sorry arse."

He sighs and squats down on the driveway, lacing his hands behind his head. His voice is haunted when he says, "I gotta see her. You gotta let me talk to her."

"No. You're lucky I'm not calling Bob, you shithead." She sighs and grasps the collar of his jacket, yanking his face back to hers. "You have to go home and let her deal with everything she's seen tonight. If she wants to talk to you after she's had time to absorb it all, then Ana will come to you. Until then, you back the fuck off and leave her the hell alone."

"Yeah, okay," he mutters, but I wonder whether he's really absorbing anything she just said. He runs a hand over his face, hangs his head and stares at the pebbled drive. He looks so lost standing there, like a little boy. I lean forward in the darkness and, for a minute, I swear he sees me because he stiffens and then lets his head fall back with a shaky exhalation.

"Holly," he says as she's walking away. "How's her head?"

"Her head is fine, Elijah. It's probably feeling clearer than it has in weeks." She backs up towards the house and says, "It's her heart that's been broken into itty bitty little pieces."

ELIJAH

For an entire week, Ana has avoided me. She's disappeared every time I set foot inside the diner, so every time I'd be left with her very scary, tiny best friend breathing down my neck until I walked right back out that door. She hasn't answered any of my calls or texts, though I've been blowing up her phone for days. I'm convinced she isn't going to talk to me, ever again.

When I'd set foot inside the garage Monday after the accident, Bob had bailed me up against the wall and hit me square in the face for driving like a fool. Apparently, Ana had given him the same story I'd given the nurses at the hospital. I don't know why she was protecting me but I knew if Bob ever found out what had really happened on that back road, I'd be a dead man.

Bob had lived the life; he'd escaped with his balls and his family intact. Unlike Ana, he'd known about my affiliation when I first came to work for him. He knew why I'd been sent to prison, he knew about the events that led to my release, and he also knew I was running as fast and as far away from that life as possible. If he knew I'd let that shit come within a foot of his daughter, of his family, he'd waste no time handing me over to the Angels, and I wouldn't blame him.

After it became apparent Ana wouldn't see me, Bob had pulled me aside to pump me for more info regarding our wild Saturday night. I'd fed him some bullshit about being a stupid insensitive male and he'd laughed it off, and said if I didn't try to pull his daughter out of the bitch-fit mood she'd been in since she dumped my sorry arse he'd dock my pay. I'm not fucking kidding. The bastard would do it, too.

That's how I wound up here at ten am on a Saturday, watching Sammy's Little Rugby League team dominate their competition. I would have been barracking from the sidelines but his sister doesn't know I'm here yet, and I don't want to frighten her off before I get the chance to speak to her.

When I sidle up beside her I cup my hands over my mouth and shout out to my little mate anyway, "GO SAMMY!"

Several parents give me dirty looks and I feel like flipping them off, but I know that won't help my case with Ana so I ignore them and wave at the awkward six-year-old who's waving madly at me from the middle of the field.

"You shouldn't have done that," Ana mutters. "He'll be distracted now that you're here."

"Can I talk to you?"

"I don't think that's a good idea."

"Come on, baby girl, you gonna shut me out forever?"

"Maybe." She looks at me with so much hatred that my heart hurts. Then she drops her voice to a whisper, "It depends how long it takes me to get rid of the image of you slaughtering a man inches from my face."

I glance around. No one was close enough to hear that, they're all focused on the game, but I'm not taking any more chances out here in the open. I grab her elbow and cart her off to the brick building housing the public toilets. Even from the outside they smell like shit, and there's graffiti everywhere and a couple of condom wrappers littering the ground. I press her against the wall. "What the fuck is going on with you, Ana?"

"What's going on with me? I had a gun held to my head last week. I had a guy trying to rape me because I was caught in the wrong place with the wrong person, and you wanna know what the fuck is wrong with *me*? What the fuck is wrong with *you*, Elijah? Or should I say Ethan?"

I feel myself frown at the mention of the name. I hate the sound of it on her tongue, like it belongs to another man. In a very real way, it does.

"Oh, you didn't think I heard that part, did you?"

"Ethan Carr is my birth name, I changed it when I got out to help me disappear. It's awfully fucking hard to pretend you don't exist when you're still carting around ID with your family name on it."

"I don't understand why you'd have to disappear in the first place? Why were you sent to prison? And why did those men think you were a rat?"

"You wanna know what got me sent away?"

"Yeah, I wouldn't mind knowing the reason why I was almost killed last week."

"Before Kick and I could patch in we had to make it through our initiation. Some DA had information that the club needed. We had to go and rough her up for the info—"

She narrows her eyes. "Rough her up?"

"Assault, Ana."

"You beat a woman because your *club* told you to?"

"We were supposed to. None of it sat right with me, or Kick, but we had people waiting outside to make sure we'd go through with it. Once we entered the house we were supposed to tie her up and make her talk, then the boys would come in and take care of the rest. But we tripped some kind of alarm. She was sleeping with a cop who drew on us. I bought Kick some time to get away."

"Why?"

"Because that's what the brothers do for one another. He had three priors, I had one. He was my best friend. Stupidly, at the time, I thought it made more sense to protect him than to protect myself. So I got three years in a cell for breaking and entering and battering a police officer and Kick walked free.

"While I was on the inside, the club came to see me. They said once I got out, I'd be patched in. They asked me to do things to some of the other prisoners, small acts of retaliation. I never got caught, was never even suspected, then one day a riot broke out because I made the wrong hit."

"The wrong hit?"

"I attacked the wrong guy. During the riot I was trying to save my own arse and managed to save a prison guard in the process. My time inside was almost up and I would have headed straight back into the waiting arms of the club, but the judge who'd sentenced me somehow caught wind of my heroic feat—" I make air quotes with my hands to let her know how ridiculous that is, because the truth of what happened with that prison guard was so much uglier than that. "—and he set my release six months early for good behaviour, no affiliation with the club and I had to disappear off the grid, change my name and remain in regular scheduled contact with my parole officer.

"The club had several deals go south. Their other contact on the inside had to be the rat, but with the timing of my release and my disappearance, the weight of the club's deals blowing up in their face fell on me. I knew better than to rat on the club. You rat, you die. My dad had instilled that in me from birth."

"So we were almost killed because of a misunderstanding?" A line forms between her brows. She's so fucking cute when she's mad, and I laugh a little at the stupidity of that thought because Ana brings new meaning to the words hell hath no fury. "Oh, you find this funny, do you?"

She shoves at my chest and I gently catch her cast in my hand before it can do me serious damage. "No. I don't find any of this shit funny. Nothing about being away from you is funny." I trace my fingers over the plaster cast and then down over her hand. "How's the arm?"

"It's in a cast, Elijah, how do you think it is?" A whistle blows, sounding the end of the game, and Ana yanks her arm free and begins the walk back to the oval.

"I'm sorry, baby girl. I fucked up."

"Yeah, you did."

"So that's it? No second chances? You're just gonna walk away from this clean?"

She backtracks and doesn't stop until she's right up in my face, or as in my face as she can be, given how short she is. "You think I'm walking away clean? I'm a fucking mess, Elijah! I can't close my eyes without seeing that arsehole's face, without feeling his hands on my body, inside me. He held a gun to my head and you watched—"

"And I killed the motherfucker, didn't I? I blew his face apart until he was no longer recognisable, Ana! Jesus. Fucking. H. Christ! What more do you want from me?"

Fuck. I know this isn't the way to speak to her. I know I should be calm and speak quietly and I'm trying hard not to lose my shit here, but she just makes me so fucking crazy. Crazier than any woman has ever made me.

She sobs, and I take a step forward, desperate to comfort her, to wipe away her tears and hold her in my arms, but she backs away, holding her arms up to keep me at bay. "Nothing. I don't want a goddamn thing from you, Elijah."

Ana disappears around the corner of the brick building and I have to fight the urge to follow her. She's been through enough shit with the people in this town and doesn't need me making a spectacle of her at her kid brother's footy match so instead, in the privacy provided by the toilet block, I pound my fist into the brick until my knuckles are bloody and the pain settles in, bone deep. I'm not letting her walk away from this. I can't.

ANA

*I*n the three weeks since my run in with Elijah at Little League Rugby, Holly has been glued to my side. Not that I'm not grateful. I am. I'm also indebted. If it weren't for her helping me out on a Sunday with the baking, the pie shop would have sunk with this stupid cast on my arm.

She's done more than that, though. Elijah still insists on coming in every day for lunch and, every day at the same time, I take my lunch over to the house to avoid him.

If Holly's beside me he won't even try speaking to me, he knows it's a lost cause. But it's when she's not around, when I'm at my lowest, that he chooses to spark up a conversation with me. Every time I see him it's like a blow to the gut and I don't know whether it's the same for him but the more he attacks at my defences, the more I feel them coming down. And I hate us both for it.

That's why I agreed to come out with Holly tonight. She's been so good to me for so long that I thought it was time to be a good friend back. Only, as we enter the pub and the noise of the band and the crowd assaults us, and the realisation sinks in that I'm wearing a red dress that's way too short and way too tight across my boobs and I probably look like a complete arsehole with too much make-up on and my hand still in this god dammed cast, I want to turn and run straight back out that door. And when my eyes slide across the room and fix on the pair of chocolate ones staring intently back at me and then onto Nicole White practically straddling the pool cue beside

Elijah, I feel it like I've been punched in the face. Which is why, when Scott and his idiotic friends come strutting over to us like they own the place, I decide to do something I promised I never would again. I talk to him and make out like every word that comes from his mouth doesn't make me want to throw up.

Nicole chooses this moment to play up the fact that she's yet again sinking her claws into my sloppy seconds by laughing like a complete whore and running her fingers down the side of Elijah's face.

"Looks like our exes are getting friendly," Scott mumbles. He sounds about as happy as I feel.

"Buy me a drink, Scott," I say, as I grab his collar and lead him towards the bar. "It's the least you can do after the crap you pulled in high school."

"You got it, Blondie."

*H*olly has a thing for the new bartender. He's a city kid that clearly comes from money and is certainly pretty enough to look at. He has that tortured musician thing going on: sinful lips, sleep mussed hair and broody stares. He studies everything like he intends to write a hit song about it. And the weird thing is, I don't doubt this guy is going places. We don't normally have the luxury of live bands playing at the Sugartown Hotel, but the new guy somehow convinced Dave that music would get more patrons in the door, and so far it appears to have worked.

Holly and I make a show of dancing. We both agreed it was the right thing to do to support the new guy's band theory. Best intentions aside, I know we're both just trying to gain the attention of the two hottest men in the bar. I make the mistake of seeking out the gaze of one of those hot men and earn a stab to the heart because of it. Elijah once said he couldn't imagine anything hotter than Holly and I together and, as the band blasted out a very sexy and slightly emo cover of The Divinyls' *I Touch Myself,* Holly practically molests me in her effort to get the new guy's attention. It looks as though Elijah is one step away from jumping the pool table and molesting the both of us.

Scott jumps right on in behind me and I feel my spine turn to slush when I think about the last time a guy got that close. Then I remember the way Elijah had reacted to that scenario and, with a quick glance in his direction, I excuse myself and head for the bar. He doesn't make a move toward me, but I feel his eyes burning a hole in my backside until I'm sitting safely on a stool.

Holly stays on the dance floor and I'm okay with that, because it gives me a chance to suss out the new guy and see if he meets the best friend seal of approval.

"Thirsty work, huh?" He leans over the bar. His eyes sparkle as he winks at me. He's got a very Adam Levine kind of vibe—sex on a stick and just as cheeky, too. "What can I get ya?"

"Johnnie Walker, blue label, neat."

"Ooh, top-shelf? Either you're in for a big night or you're buying for the guy in the corner who's been tossing them back like lollies and hasn't taken his eyes off you all night."

"Let's go with the first one," I say and slap a fifty-dollar note on the bar. I gulp down the shot. My stomach threatens a mini revolt and I have to choke it down again before it makes an embarrassing reappearance. After the burn settles all I can taste is Elijah, and my heart hurts all over again.

"Tonight, I'm drinking for Australia," I declare and tilt my glass toward him in a salute.

"Thatta girl." He refills my glass and shakes his head when I slip my credit card from my clutch. "This one's on me."

"Thanks." I smile and sip the shot slowly, and then, because the scent is so familiar I hold the glass beneath my nose and inhale. When I open my eyes sex on a stick is watching me with a half-smile and a knowing glint in his eye.

"How long has it been?"

I don't know if he's talking about the last time I got laid—which sadly has been never—how long it's been since I had a drink—I am sort of acting like a raging alcoholic—or how long since Elijah and I broke up, but I find myself answering the latter, anyway. "Four weeks."

"I think from the death glares he's sending me right now that it's safe to say he wants you back."

"It's complicated."

"Yeah?" New guy grins. It's one of those sexy rock star smiles that disintegrates a room full of knickers in the blink of an eye. "So is life."

"No shit."

"The two of you girls dancing," he says, glancing over my shoulder at the dance floor. "Was that all for him?"

"Mine was," I sigh. "Holly's though, hers was all for you."

"And this Holly, is she complicated?"

"Surprisingly not." I lean back to get a better look at him. It's kind of an odd question for a guy who doesn't know her from a bar of soap, and I feel a flutter of excitement for her when I realise he wants to get to know her a lot better. "Holly's a great girl. She calls it like she sees it, she doesn't like to be undermined, patronized or interrupted when she's ranting. She's loyal to a fault and she's been a bossy, nosy bitch since kindergarten."

He laughs and shakes his head. "Wow, that's really a stellar recommendation."

"She's the best woman I know. I hear she's also fireworks in the sack, though that little titbit came from her, so don't blame me if it turns out not to be true." I swallow back the rest of my drink and slide off the stool I'm occupying. "Will you tell her I left? I don't want her to feel like she has to take me home when there's someone else waiting for her."

"I'll tell her," he grins.

I swing around and face the room, my eyes automatically searching out Elijah's, as if they're on autopilot. Disappointment washes through me when I don't find them anywhere. Maybe he went home, or maybe he's in the bathroom taking a pee. That thought automatically makes me need to go myself so I turn back around and say, "Oh, and if you break her heart I'll hunt you down and rip out yours." And then I strut away to the ladies.

I'm still laughing at the look on his face when I stumble into the bathroom and freeze in my tracks. Propped up against the wall is a young couple fucking one another's brains out. Crude, yes, but there's really no other way to describe it. His jeans are down around his ankles displaying a firm arse and two long muscular legs, one with a very detailed tiger tattoo. Her legs are wrapped around his hips. One of his hands supports her weight while the other palm is slammed flat against the tile, and his thrusts are hard enough to nail her to the goddamn wall. He groans with each one and the sound rings in my ears—primal, animal, it calls to some baser thing inside me yearning to be let out of her cage.

The moment seems to stretch on for eons.

Neither one of them has noticed me yet. Her eyes are tightly closed, and the noise of the door banging shut is swallowed by her moans.

"Oh, fuck me harder," she cries out and I find I'm equal parts aroused and revolted. Also, I can almost pinpoint the second when my addled brain catches up to what my eyes are witnessing and my heart shatters in two. I can't look away, and yet I'll never be able to look at him the same way again. In this moment, all the bullshit that had transpired between us before seems like just that, bullshit.

But this?

This is the sort of betrayal I can never forgive him for, because no matter what the excuse, he knows how I feel about him. He also knows how I feel about her and he knew there was a chance I would find the two of them like this, and the fact that he's willing to hurt me for the sake of a quick fuck makes me hate him just a little.

I'm not an idiot, though. It's obvious he's enjoying himself, too. That's evident by what he says next as he hammers into her, "God, you feel so fucking good."

Nicole lets out this ridiculously high-pitched giggle and opens her eyes. They widen in shock and then narrow down as she registers that I'm standing there, watching. A smile spreads across her face, wide and victorious. And then she grabs his arse with her long taloned hands and drives him into her faster.

It isn't long before he's finishing hard and fast, exactly the way he never could with me. And that cuts deeper than anything I've seen so far in this disgusting bathroom. He leans against her, spent. He doesn't kiss her; there's none of the tenderness of our post orgasmic moments, but that hardly matters. The truth is, he still fucked a girl up against the bathroom wall knowing I was in the very next room.

Nicole bends down to whisper into his ear, "Looks like we've got ourselves an audience."

Elijah freezes and then he turns his upper body to face me. Only his upper body, because I'm assuming the lower half is still buried in that whore. "Ah, fuck."

I don't say a single thing in return, though there are many, many words on the tip of my tongue. I simply convey all of the hurt I'm feeling with one look before calmly stepping through the door.

Once I'm in the hallway with that mind-fuck of a mess behind me, I take a deep breath and bolt outside. My plan is to run all the way home. It's just a few short blocks, and the bathroom incident has sobered me enough to ensure I won't wind up stumbling and passing out in someone's front yard. That's the plan, but life hardly ever goes according to one.

"Ana!" I hear his footsteps pounding the pavement behind me, but I don't bother to turn around, I just run faster and pray he doesn't catch up. Apparently I'm not that lucky though. Elijah reaches out and yanks me back into the curve of his chest. "Baby girl, would you just stop and talk to me."

"Don't you dare call me that!" I kick and try to lurch away from him but he holds my arms down by my sides, rendering me completely useless. "You just had your dick buried in another girl and, no less than five seconds later, you're calling me baby girl? Fuck you, Cade!"

He spins me around so my back is pressed into an alcove created by an empty storefront. "What do you want me to say, Ana? You broke this shit off, not me. So why do you give two fucks about who I'm buried inside?"

"I don't."

"Bullshit. You jealous? That it?"

"Oh completely," I sneer, "because I've always wanted to be nailed to the wall of some dingy toilet that hasn't been cleaned in over a century."

"I forgot you were such a purist."

"Fuck you!"

"Wish you would've." He leans forward, pinning me against the glass with his massive frame, his eyes all molten chocolate, his voice pitched low and gravelly. "It'd be the fuck of your life, darlin'."

"This is sick." I attempt to move past him, but he places a meaty paw in the middle of my chest and gently pushes me back against the glass. "Let me go."

It's only then that I realise just how drunk he is. He smells like whiskey and need and sex, and knowing the latter is because of someone other than me makes me want to throw up.

He begins pressing sloppy kisses into my neck and, god help me, it's been so long since he touched me that I find myself revelling in the feel of his hot mouth on my skin. So much so, that a small moan escapes my mouth before I can rein it in.

"God, I miss that. I miss the sounds you make when you come. I miss the way you come alive beneath my hands." He runs his hand up my dress, slides my knickers aside until his warm hand is cupping me. His finger glides into my wetness while his thumb strokes circles around my clit. Despite my better judgement, I feel myself leaning into his touch, and the more his fingers work against me, the more my thoughts flee and my body takes over until I'm panting and aching for more. "Yeah, just like that, baby girl. Fuck, I miss you."

That revelation brings my orgasm to a crashing halt and I press my hands into his chest and plead, "Stop."

He doesn't. Instead, he doubles his efforts and acts as though he hasn't heard me. Warmth travels up from my toes and floods the centre of my belly. I rock my hips into his hand.

"Come for me, Ana," he whispers.

"No." But even as I say it, I'm breathless with need. My legs are trembling beneath my weight and I'm shaking from head to toe, and it's sure as hell not from fear. One more circle of his thumb and then I completely come apart in his hands, clawing and scratching and pulling him closer as wave after delicious wave of my orgasm sluices through me, even though I'm appalled and repelled by what he just did.

He leans in and whispers, "I love you, baby."

I freeze against him. Finally hearing those words should make my heart soar. Instead, it shatters that last fragile shard of dignity I have left and I completely lose it. I shove him back and punch him right in the jaw with the fist of my fractured arm. I cry out, because it stings like a bitch. Clearly, I've just ruined whatever good progress I'd made with it these last few weeks because it hurts just as much as it did the night I first injured it.

Elijah rubs his jaw and then turns angry dark eyes on me. "Fuck!"

"Yeah, I can see that you love me, Elijah. What with the way you were fucking Nicole up against the wall. I can see you missed me real bad."

"Jesus Christ, Ana, she's filler!" he roars, getting all up in my face again. "Fuck! That girl in there has nothing on you. And yeah, I fucked her. I fucked the shit outta her because I thought for one minute, just one single fucking minute, I might be able to bury myself in someone else and forget about you."

"Is that supposed to make me feel better? That you have to screw other women to forget about me?"

"Honestly, darlin', I don't care how it makes you feel. It's the truth."

"Like you're an expert on the truth."

"God, you're so fucking self-righteous. You didn't seem to give a shit about the truth when I was getting you off with my hand just now."

"I told you to stop."

"And I would have, if I thought for even one second that you really wanted me to."

I don't have any response for that because it's true, I didn't want him to stop, not really. When it comes to the way Elijah touches me, I never want him to stop. But that was the kind of thinking that had led me into this cluster-fuck in the first place, so I simply shake my head and close my eyes, wishing I could walk away. Wishing I didn't let him get to me. Wishing I didn't still love him so much.

"This shit between you and me isn't over, Ana. No matter what you and I do it's never gonna be over, you got that?"

"You're wrong. This shit between us was over the minute you decided to start lying about your past."

I wrench myself out of his grasp and walk away, and this time he lets me. I'm maybe fifteen feet away when he says, "Ask yourself why you care so much, Ana. When you lay your head down tonight, ask yourself why you're so mad at me for fucking another girl, when you're the one that let me go. Ask yourself if you still love me."

"Of course I still love you, arsehole." I stomp back toward him and shove him again. This time he stumbles a little, but manages to trap my hand to his chest so I can feel the harried beating of his heart.

"Then stop fucking torturing me, baby girl. Please … Just stop torturing me."

Tears roll down my cheeks. He lifts his hand to wipe them away but I wrench out of his grasp and start running toward the house. He doesn't follow me, and I'm both thankful and torn up about it. It doesn't matter whether or not I still love him. Nothing matters but forgetting this whole mess ever happened, including hearing those three little words I'd waited so long to hear from him.

ELIJAH

I pull up outside her house. It's near dark on a Sunday so I know exactly where to find her, though as I stare at the light coming from the back door of the shop it occurs to me that she might not be alone. I never thought to ask if she'd needed help baking her pies when her arm ended up in a cast—I think I just took it for granted that she was doing fine. Our argument last night proved that I don't know shit.

I'm still wading through the alcohol haze of the previous night. I have no idea what I'm doing here, other than that I miss her like I'd miss the fucking air to breathe if it was taken from me. I fucked up. Bad. I don't know what the hell I was thinking, doing Nicole. Sometimes you just need to fuck a woman, you know. To forget? To remember? Hell, if I knew, but there's a base instinct to burrow yourself inside a woman when both your heart and head can't take any more fucking misery. It's a stupid as fuck excuse, but there it is.

I walk over to the open door and lean against the jamb. Holly and Ana are inside, some hugely popular R&B band is blasting from the stereo, Mackerel More something or other, and Holly's talking animatedly about getting lucky on the bar at the Sugartown Hotel after hours. I'm not darkening the door for long before Ana turns and sees me standing there. Her good mood falters, she frowns and she lets out a sigh. I shove down the hurt, and smile, even though it's the last thing I feel like doing.

Holly stops midsentence and swivels toward me. "The fuck?"

I ignore the tiny, scary redhead and speak only to Ana, "You got a minute?"

"Are you fucking serious?" Holly demands, then stalks toward me and starts ranting and raving about how I should leave Ana alone and how I'm turning into the worst kind of stalker and that, if I'm not careful, I'll find myself up shit creek without a paddle because there may suddenly be a witness emerge to give their story on the events of that night with my biker brothers. I let her go on, even as my heart hammers in my chest with fear because someone other than Ana and Kick has the ability to put me away for a very long time with a simple phone call. Even as I think about throwing the ranga midget over my shoulder and depositing her on her arse outside, I don't, because I deserve everything she's saying and more.

"Holly," Ana says. "It's okay."

"Yeah? For how long, Ana? Til he runs his mouth again and you decide to lash out with your injured arm, forcing me to drive you to the hospital to have your cast refitted again?" I glance at Ana in confusion and see that she's sporting a brand new fluoro pink cast. I'd known she'd hit me pretty hard last night, I was still wearing the evidence of that, but I hadn't realised she'd done more damage to her arm. "Or maybe this time you'll run your mouth and he'll hit you—"

"Now hold on just a goddamn minute," I begin.

At the same time Ana says, "Holly!"

"You know what? Fine. Duke it out, scream and yell until you tear one another apart and get this shit out of your system for good. You don't belong together. And this may be hard to hear, Elijah, but Ana is way too good for you and you're all kinds of wrong for her. If you're smart, you'll stay away from one another, because this little thing between you is toxic and it's going to tear both your lives apart." Holly unties her apron and throws it down on the counter. She looks only at Ana when she says, "Call me when he's gone and I'll come back and help you finish up."

She doesn't say a thing as she passes me. She doesn't have to, because all the hatred she feels for me is as clear as day in her eyes.

The squeaky screen door bangs back on its hinges and then closes with an audible slap. Outside, I hear the roar of an engine and breathe a sigh of relief once I hear it drive away.

"You really hurt your arm?"

"Yep. Another four to six weeks in this crappy cast. At least the last one was white and I didn't have to worry about what the hell was going to clash with it, but this fluoro pink thing? Yuck!"

"You're rambling."

"Yep, I guess I do that when I'm nervous—"

"I know," I say, both because it's a trait of hers that I'd always found adorable and because I want her to know that I know all of her idiosyncrasies, even the ones she wasn't aware of. "I'm sorry I hurt your hand."

"Well, to be fair, I didn't have to punch you in the face."

I laugh humourlessly. "Yeah, you did. I was a complete dickhead."

"Yes, you were," she whispers and then swallows hard before glancing out the shopfront window. "You broke my heart, Elijah."

Tears spill down her cheeks. I move to wipe one away with my thumb and she flinches and shifts out of reach. I've never had a woman push me away before and I'm certainly-as-fuck not about to let it start now with the only woman who's ever mattered. So I follow her to the other side of the kitchen and corner her until I'm close enough to be her shadow.

I place my hands on her waist and she lets herself be lifted onto the bench, and then I ease myself between her legs and cradle her face in my hands. She closes her eyes. I don't know whether she's savouring the moment or wishing she wasn't in it, but I hope to fuck it's not that last one.

"I fucked up, baby girl," I whisper. She nods and more tears roll down her face. I smooth them from her skin with my thumbs. "Tell me how to fix it."

Ana gently shakes her head. "I don't think you can."

"Yes I can. I can fix this," I say resolutely. "I'll put us back together with my bare hands, just don't walk away. No more secrets, no more mistakes."

"Elijah." She grasps my hand and gently pulls it from her cheek. "Holly was right. We can't go five minutes without fighting or trying to tear one another's clothes off."

"That's normal—"

"That's not healthy. For either of us."

"Don't do this, Ana," I warn, but my words fall on deaf ears. It's written all over her face; she has no intention of backing down this time. I shake my head and send her a pleading glance. I'm not above getting on my knees and begging her to give me another chance, but I can see in her eyes that the time for grovelling came and went, and I was buried balls-deep in another woman instead of falling to my knees in worship.

"Ah, fuck!" I rub at my chest to ease the burn in my heart. "This is bullshit, baby girl. The way I feel about you, the way you feel about me, that shit doesn't just up and go away. I know I'm not worthy of someone as fucking spectacular as you. I know it. This whole fucking town knows it. But I'll be a better man. I'll change. I'll do fucking anything you ask of me, just don't do this."

Ana presses her hand to the centre of my chest and I capture it with my own the way I did last night, only now I bring it to my lips and kiss it all over. I feel her defences melt a little so I decide to knock them over completely, until there's nothing but the dust of her resolve left. I cup her face and force my lips down upon hers. I watch surprise flit across her face and then I close my eyes and throw myself into proving that she's wrong, that though we're not fine right now, one day soon, we will be.

She kisses me back, tentatively at first, and then, as I fist my hands in her hair and push myself further into the space between us, her legs wrap around my hips and I pull her off the bench in order to feel her small body wrapped around me. She tastes of salt and need, and damn if I don't want to fulfil every single one of hers. She lifts her t-shirt over her head and throws it to the floor, and then she claws at mine until I'm no longer wearing one either. I slam her up against the refrigerator and she arches into me, her big beautiful tits at the perfect height for sucking. I claim a nipple with my mouth and gently bite down until it peaks against my teeth and tongue. Ana cries out so I do it again, harder this time. The end result is a thing of beauty; she pushes herself against me and reclaims my mouth with her own. There's nothing tender or tentative in this kiss; she's a squirming, clawing wildcat, and I'm revelling in every second of her newfound confidence.

"You're so fucking perfect," I say as I rock my hips into hers. My cock strains against my jeans as I push into the soft fabric of her yoga pants and I feel her lips part around me.

Fuck me! I almost blow my load right there. She's soft and soaking wet and so completely fucking all-woman that I feel like I could just melt into her warmth.

I rock into her again, harder this time, until I'm certain she can feel just how fucking hard I am and how much I want her. The fabric barrier between us is driving me insane; I want to tear off her pants and push myself so deep inside that her pussy won't ever forget how good we are together, even if her heart's determined to.

Ana moans. Her breath comes out in hot little pants against my cheek and I know that, just like me, she's close to coming.

"God, you feel so fucking good," I mutter as I drive myself faster, pushing as deep as our clothes will allow, but she doesn't react the way I expect her to. Instead, she's completely frozen. And then tears spill down her cheeks, and I have no choice but to gently set her down on her feet.

I don't have the foggiest idea of what's going on but something tells me, without even knowing what went wrong, I've fucked this up royally.

"Hey, come here." I cradle her head to my chest and wince as her tears spill onto my stomach because I don't know what the hell they mean.

We stand like that, with her head cradled to my chest and her arms flung around my waist for too long, and then, when not a sound can be heard but our breathing and the gentle hum of the fridge, Ana wrenches herself out of my arms, dries her eyes with the back of her hands and says, "Go home, Elijah."

"You're my home, baby. Don't take that away from me. Please?"

"No. I'm not. If I were, you would have told me the truth. And you certainly wouldn't have fucked another woman right before you told me you loved me."

"Ana—"

She swipes at her eyes, bends and picks her shirt up from the floor and puts it on. She turns to face the bench and goes back to awkwardly rolling out a lump of pastry with her left hand. "We can't do this anymore. We need a clean break or we'll just end up hurting one another."

Is she fucking kidding me?

When it becomes apparent that she's not, and that she's done beating a dead horse I press a kiss into her hair, taking one last chance to breathe in her sweet, vanilla scent.

"We're already hurting, baby girl," I say and leave the kitchen a fucked up, heartbroken mess.

ANA

An entire month after my break up with Elijah, I'm still just as miserable as I was the minute he walked out of my kitchen for good. After he'd left that day I'd cried until Dad came home from a club meet and found me passed out on the floor. He'd picked me up, carried me to my room and that's where I'd stayed for two days before Holly came a calling to kick my lazy, heartbroken arse out of bed.

A month on and she's still dragging me around to places I don't want to go. Tonight, it's a harvest hang-out. I don't know how many of these things Holly and I have attended, but they always begin with a bunch of idiots gathering in a newly harvested cane field on the outskirts of town and end with a bunch of drunk idiots running from the cops before they get arrested for drinking in a dry zone and lighting bonfires during bush fire season.

Tonight the crowd is mostly old enough to know better, and yet here we are: a bunch of high school leavers too afraid to admit we're not ready for adulthood and more terrified still to leave our safe little town for the big, bad world.

Before Elijah, I would have given anything to get out of this place. Afterwards, I'm thanking my lucky stars for the job security that comes with being the pie shop owner's daughter, because it means I don't have to face what all my school colleagues are going through; where they should study, where they should live, and that all-important period of self-discovery you go through after you're given the weighty title of being an "adult".

Thanks to my mother and father's dreaming, my future is securely mapped out for me. I'll work in the diner until I'm too old to remember the recipes, I'll more than likely still be cleaning up after my kid brother until he's forty, and then I'll die alone with a thousand cats who won't hesitate to eat me once the kitty chow runs out, and all without ever having left Sugartown.

I should be more upset about my future prospects being so bleak but I just can't seem to give a crap these days.

Holly groans, "Would you at least try to look like you're having fun, please?"

"But I'm not having fun, Hols. I'm watching a bunch of bogan dickheads chugging beer-bongs to avoid witnessing you be mauled by your boyfriend. No offense, Coop."

The boyfriend in question is Cooper Ryan, the hot bartender from the Sugartown Hotel. He's recently become a permanent fixture in my best friend's life which is fine by me because he's sweet, he treats her right and he gives me Holly-free time enough to wallow in my misery. He swings his head out from the hollow of her neck and smiles at me. "None taken. I do maul. I should really cut back but I'm just a stupid, beer-chugging dickhead unable to resist her charms."

"Well, they say awareness is the first step." I smile back, but it's as weak and horribly disingenuous as they always are lately.

"Aww, Cooooop." Holly reaches up on tiptoes to kiss him. "Do you have any idea how much I want to tie you up and screw your brains out when you say things like that?"

"I have some idea," he mutters into her ear.

I roll my eyes. "Would you two get a room, already? You're making the other bogans nauseas."

"Ha! Now you know what it was like when you and Eli—" Holly begins, but her eyes double in size as she realises she almost named 'he who shall not be named'. "Shit, Ana, I'm sorry."

"It's okay, Hols. I'm going to go grab a drink. Why don't you two go grab a room, or the backseat of Coop's car, or any other semi secluded place to … um … get busy, and I'll meet you back here in fifteen?" I tease, but I'm only half joking about the sex. At least if they get it out of their system now, we won't be run off the road because Holly decides she'd rather jump on Coop's gearstick than get us home in one piece.

"Ana?" Holly starts.

I shrug her off with a wave. "I'm fine Hols, just thirsty."

"I love you my little slutsky!" she yells, just loud enough to draw the attention of everyone around us, in true Holly fashion.

I laugh and make my way over to the bonfire, which oddly enough is where the eskies with all the combustible liquor are. *Because nothing says inconspicuous like an illegal twenty-foot bonfire that can be seen from space. Idiots.*

I pull out a bottle of Stella Artois and think of Elijah. I wonder where he is and if he's thinking of me, too. Earlier, I saw Nicole and her evil minions, so at least I know he's not fucking her up against a wall somewhere. My heart aches all over again when I think of him inside her. I hate him so much for making me witness that because never in a million years would I wish the same fate upon him. I love him too much, which makes me think that, despite his declaration, he didn't love me at all.

I flip the bottle cap off my beer and take a long hearty swig, which almost comes straight back up when I open my eyes and see Scott standing before me.

"Hey, Blondie." He smiles down at me with one of his stupid boy-next-door grins. "Rough night?"

"And it just got worse."

"Ouch." He raises his own beer in a toast and gives me that stupid half-smile that used to turn me to complete mush but now kind of makes me want to punch him in the face. "You really know how to wound a guy."

"So I've heard."

He reaches into the nearest esky and pulls out two more Stellas. "You wanna take a walk with me?"

"Why would I do that, Scott?"

He shrugs. "Payback for drinking all my beer?"

"Sorry, I didn't know it was yours," I mutter, as I avoid meeting his eyes. Though I despise him, his eyes are still kind of pretty to look at. In fact, all of him is pretty to look at. Not as pretty as Elijah, but pretty, none the less.

Annnnnd now I know I've had too much to drink.

I run a mental tally in my head—one vodka and cranberry at Holly's house and one and a half beers since we arrived. It's not much, but it's enough for a lightweight like me. Still, I'm in a reckless, poisonous mood, so despite the buzz I have going, it's not enough.

Weirdly, Scott must pick up on that because he says, "Come on, I have some hard stuff in the car and you look like you could use a stiff drink."

"What kind of hard stuff?"

"Tequila."

"To-kill-ya! Awesome! Lead the way."

Scott smiles, stuffs two beers in the pocket of his hoody and walks me over to his giant, dual cab, fifty-thousand dollar Toyota HiLux—which is just what every idiotic nineteen-year-old needs to be driving, especially when there's alcohol involved—and fishes out the bottle of tequila before handing it to me. I'm so relieved I could kiss him, but I'll settle instead for not punching him in the face.

Scott leads us to a small ravine, far enough away so we can no longer hear the noise of the party. He slides down the embankment and sits on a patch of soft grass. I follow suit, though my descent is a little more awkward and I end up stumbling a few steps before backing up and plonking myself down next to him. We're looking at nothing but row upon row of cut cane fields and there's no other light but the moon—and yes, I am here with the McDoucheNozzle that basically told the whole town I was a giant slut, but it's peaceful, and Scott always was good at distracting me from reality.

I twist the cap off the tequila and take a hearty sip. It burns like nothing else going down but once it's finally settled the warmth spreads through my tummy and it feels sort of nice, so I take another.

"Easy, tiger." He takes the bottle from me and swallows back some of the contents. It must go down the wrong way, because he coughs and splutters and beats at his chest like a gorilla. "Holy shit that hurt, I now know why you call it to-kill-ya."

"Don't tell me you're a virgin, Scott?"

He turns to me with his brow raised and an incredulous look upon his face. "You do know I went out with Nicole for a whole six weeks, don't you?"

"Not the kind of virgin I was talking about, but thanks for the painful reminder of the fact you ditched me for boob-a-skank," I say, and snatch the bottle back.

"Yeah, well, I was an idiot."

"No argument there."

"So, what's the deal with you and gigantor?"

"Who?" I feign innocence, or ignorance—I can't remember which, because I'm drunk, remember?

"You know, prison-tattooed, scary-arse gigantic motherfucker?"

"Oh, *that* gigantor." I shake my head and sigh. "No deal. We broke up, he fucked Nicole and broke my heart."

Scott raises the bottle and says, "To fucked up exes!"

"To home-wrecking sluts!" I salute as I take a swig.

Scott takes back the bottle and waves it in the air. "To wankers who don't know a good thing when they have it."

I snatch it back and say, "And to arseholes who break your heart," before shooting him a dirty look and taking a long pull from the neck of the bottle.

By now my head is swimming. I'm pretty sure my fifteen minutes is up and I know I should get back to the party so Holly doesn't worry, but I don't feel like making the trek. I don't feel like doing much of anything, actually, so I lie back on the grass and stare up at the stars.

"I like your to-kill-ya, Scott." I hope he doesn't notice how much I just slurred that sentence, and then I wonder why I care whether he knows I'm blind drunk or not. This fucker broke my heart, too. Granted, not as badly as Elijah, but he still did it. My inebriated brain at least has the sense to tell me that I didn't love Scott like I love Elijah, and that just pisses me off and hurts my heart all over again. So I tell my heart to shut up by pulling Scott down beside me and pressing my mouth to his with a brutal, messy kiss.

It doesn't take him long to catch up. In fact, within seconds he's pawing at me and pulling me on top of him. His hand skims up under my shirt and palms my boobs. For half a second I close my eyes and pretend it's Elijah's hand. There's one very noticeable difference though: either Elijah possesses some innate, supernatural ability to instinctively know how to please women or he's had an awful, awful lot of practise, because Scott's hand pushing and prodding at my boobs feels more like a breast exam than anything Elijah ever did.

I go with it, though, because it's better than thinking about how miserable I am or how much I miss him or that it's been a month and the pain still hasn't lessened any and I don't expect it ever will.

Scott's mouth covers mine with a sloppy insistent kiss, and suddenly I want to gag. He's rock hard, pushing his pelvis into mine with bruising force, holding my hips against him with one hand at the small of my back and my head with his other. I yank away, gulping in air as I raise myself up to a sitting position, but Scott's stronger and he pulls me back down on top of him and then effortlessly rolls us so that I'm pinned to the ground beneath his body. I'm starting to see what a horrible idea this was. I'm also beginning to realise just how much I must hate myself to have absolutely no regard for my own safety or self-preservation. In fact, if Ted Bundy had of walked up to me wielding a cute smile and a bottle of spirits, I likely would have tagged along behind him, too.

"Wait," I say, as I attempt to sit up once more by shoving at his chest, but he pushes me down with a heavy palm splayed between my breasts. I'm lightheaded and the pressure of him on top of me makes my tummy do weird flippy things, and not of the good variety. "Scott, stop. You're hurting me."

"Relax," he whispers, nibbling on my ear.

Bile rises in my belly. I shove at him, more forcibly this time, and when he doesn't move I lash out with my hands, gouging my nails down one side of his face. "I said stop, you arsehole!"

He sits back on his knees and presses his hand to his cheek. He's bleeding. His eyes blaze with desire and hate, but I don't give a crap. I waste no time getting to my feet and climbing up the embankment.

"Ana, get back here!"

"Fuck you!" I scream back. No sooner have the words left my mouth than I feel his arm slip around my waist and drag me backwards, down the embankment. His other hand covers my mouth and, even though I bite down on it as hard as I can, he gasps but doesn't let go. I thrash and kick against him, all the while screaming into his palm as he lugs me further down the hill.

We're not in the same spot as we were before. There's no grass here, only a rocky patch of hard-packed earth. If we were in the same spot I'd consider using our abandoned tequila bottle as a weapon, but I can't even see it—I can't see anything on account of the dizziness and moonlight. I kick him hard and break free. I run as fast as my uncoordinated body will take me. It's not far enough. Before I can reach the embankment he grabs my arm and pushes me to the ground. I hit the unyielding earth with a thud. Breath whooshes out of my lungs and my head lands hard. I'm stunned, and sick to my stomach.

My vision goes dark. My skull pounds as if it's been caved in. Scott hovers over me. I attempt to lift my head, but find I can't. I can't move without this roiling wave of nausea threatening to choke me. His weight settles on top of me and he whispers, "I let you get away once, Ana. I'm not letting you get away a second time."

"No," I protest, but the blackness swallows me up completely.

I don't know how long I'm out. It can't be long because I wake to the tearing, searing pain of Scott pushing himself inside me. It's so severe that for a beat I'm stunned. Then I begin to thrash—though I learn quickly that it only makes it worse. One hand is clamped tightly over my mouth and the other holds my arms down at the wrists as he unmercifully drives himself deeper and deeper inside me. I kick out with my legs, but there isn't a whole lot I can do without causing myself even greater injury, so I merely lie there and wait for the right time to fight back as tears roll down my face to mix with the dry earth.

Every thrust inside me is a knife buried to the hilt. The burn and sting of tender flesh tearing, the crushing weight of his body against mine, I feel it all, until a short time later his rhythm lags. He must be close to coming because he grunts and his eyes roll back in his head, and I take that opportunity to use mine, like I should have in the beginning. I head-butt him. Pain reverberates through my skull.

"Fuck!" Scott tears his hand away from my mouth and cries out in a rage, "You fucking bitch!" I scream for help. I buck and try to unseat him but he holds me down and grins, "You're gonna regret that."

He slams his elbow into my cheek and once again everything fades to black.

I've been switching channels for well over an hour. The motel doesn't have Foxtel and what I can see of the screen is mostly just static fuzz, but I'm still watching it like it's the most enthralling shit ever. I reach for the bottle on my bedside and swig back a mouthful of Johnnie Walker. Last week I spent so much goddamn time drinking at the Sugartown Hotel that, when I wandered in earlier today to get some takeaways, publican Dave just handed me a bottle, took two hundred dollars from my wallet and I rode home with my new best friend Johnnie to make some bittersweet memories.

Somewhere between the microwaved meal and some fucking stupid Kleenex commercial with puppies, that weirdly reminds me of Sammy, I think about Ana, and how much I miss her. It hurts to know that while I'm at work she's right across the street from me and I can't bring myself to cross the road, fall to my knees and beg for her forgiveness. I love her so goddamn much it hurts. I hate that she won't give this another chance. I hate that up until now, I'd never met a woman that'd had me sitting around in my room on a Friday night pining for her like a fuckin' lost puppy.

This is bullshit, I think as I pull on my jeans and yank my jacket from the chair. Ana has made it clear she doesn't want me. She made that perfectly fucking clear, and the only thing that brings me even the slightest bit of relief is burying myself inside someone else and pretending like Ana Belle doesn't exist and my every waking thought isn't consumed by her.

I run a hand through my hair and thumb my keys, hoping I don't look too shitfaced to get laid. It's 11.30 pm, but there's still another half hour before the pub calls last drinks—that's a whole twenty minutes to find someone to fuck.

I'm pretty sure it's safe to say Ana won't go back to the pub for a while. I've been there every night for the last three weeks and I've never seen her so much as set foot in the place. Not that I blame her; it's not really where I want to be, either, with the memories of that fucked up night etched into the walls. It's just that Bob hasn't been real friendly since I broke his daughter's heart and the pub is really the only other place I can go to hold a conversation with another adult. Plus, anywhere with liquor is my favourite place to be these days.

Just as I'm reaching for the door I hear a soft knock from the other side. I open it and look at the girl standing on my doorstep, but what I'm seeing doesn't make sense because Ana is standing in front of me looking like she got attacked by a fucking zombie horde.

Her blonde hair is dirty, one side of her face is swollen shut and her clothes are bloody and tattered. My heart hurts just looking at her. My head is spins, trying to put together a puzzle without any of the goddamn pieces.

"What the fuck happened?"

"I didn't know where else to go," she whispers looking up at me with big round eyes full of hurt.

I can barely breathe. I'm shaking with rage. *I'm gonna kill someone. I'm gonna tear their fucking head clean off their shoulders.*

I pull her across the threshold. She falls into my arms, and then she falls apart. She sobs into my chest and all I can do is hold her tighter than I ever have and pray that I'm wrong about what I think happened. I've seen her cry before, I've been the cause of her tears too many times, but I've never seen her broken like this. She sounds like a wounded animal, and it's killing me that she's not talking.

"Ana, who did this to you?" I'm having trouble keeping a lid on my rage. I'm not good with tamping down my anger, and right now I wanna rip out someone's fucking heart. Ana doesn't answer, she just sobs harder.

I'm going fucking crazy wondering what happened to her, wondering who did this and how far they took it, wondering whose skull I have to beat in as payback.

"You gotta talk to me, baby girl," I plead. "I'm going outta my mind not knowing what happened to you."

And then she speaks. She tells me everything and I begin to wish she hadn't. Every last detail, except for the name of the scumbag that did this, and my heart hurts so much you'd think I was the one who'd been held down and stripped of my virginity and my dignity.

"No. No. No," I whisper, and slide down the end of the bed. I land hard on the floor with my back pressed against the ratty ensemble and bury my head in my hands as tears sting my eyes.

I know I should be holding it together better than what I am. I should be strong for her and take her in my arms and tell her that I'll find a way to fix this, too, but I can't. I haven't seen her in weeks, at least not up close, but I quickly come to the realisation that this is my fault. That if I hadn't fucked up so badly she would have been here with me instead of shitfaced at some party with the fucker who did this.

Ana's in shock, trembling so badly I'm afraid she's going to fall down. She doesn't sit, she just stands alone in my room looking like a broken little girl.

"Give me a name," I croak through a throat that scrapes like sandpaper.

That snaps her out of her daze. Her gaze slides down to mine and her face contorts. Panic. I've seen that expression before, just as I blew some fuckers face off that had been trying to rape her. Fuck! I hadn't been there to save her this time. Instead I was here, getting fucked up on a bottle of whiskey and feeling sorry for myself. "No! You have to promise me you won't go after him. Promise me. I can't have anyone know about this, especially not my dad. You can't—"

"We need to tell the police. You need to go to hospital; you need a rape kit and the morning-after pill."

"No!" She shakes her head, and covers her mouth to quiet her sobs. "No one would believe it. People saw me leave with him, willingly. This whole town thinks I'm a slut, Elijah, they'd never believe I didn't want it."

"What about the shiner on your face? You ask for that, too?" I exhale loudly and try to soften my tone, pleading with her. "They can get DNA proof, Ana. But only if you do it soon."

"I'm not going to the police. My dad can never find out about this."

I ball my hands into fists, itching to hit something, anything. Desperate to destroy, maim, and hurt that motherfucker so bad he'll wish he was never born. "This is bullshit! Why are you protecting that little piece of shit?"

"I'm not!"

"You let him walk, he's just gonna turn around and do it to another girl," I say through clenched teeth, getting to my feet because I can't sit idle. "He needs to pay for what he did to you."

"I'm not protecting him. I'm protecting me!" she screams and backs away from me, heading for the door, but I make it there before her, slamming myself between her and the exit. "Get out of the way, Elijah."

"No."

"Move," she demands, tugging on the handle beside me.

"Where you gonna go? Huh? Can't go home lookin' like you do."

"I'll go to Holly's."

"Holly lives with her parents," I reason. "You go walking in there like that and the first thing they'll do is call the cops. And the cops will call your dad."

She flinches and releases the handle. I take her face in my hands, careful not to apply any pressure to her cheekbone.

"Stay here tonight, please? I won't force you to do anything. I won't tell anyone. I promise, just don't leave." I lean in and press my forehead to hers. Tears wet my cheeks. My throat is all tight and itchy, and I can't swallow properly. *Fuck*. I haven't cried like this since Mum and Lil died.

I know she can feel me shaking with rage. Right now I wanna tear this room apart. She won't tell me who did this, but she doesn't have to. I know exactly who that little fucker is and I'm gonna take great delight in castrating him. Ana wipes the moisture from my cheeks. I catch her hand and press it to my lips. "I'm so sorry, baby girl. I should have been there. I should have—"

"Shh." She tilts her head up to face me and presses her lips to mine. There's something defiant in the way she kisses me, like she wants me to lay claim to her mouth again. "Help me wash him away."

I think this is a fucking terrible idea but I can't let her down again, not now, maybe not ever, so I nod and sweep her into my arms and then carry her into the bathroom. I run the shower and help her peel off her clothes.

When she's stripped down to her underwear, she hesitates. I gently ease her hands out of the way and unclasp her bra, the scrap of lace falls to the floor. There's a purple mark over her left nipple; the flesh is raised, but not broken. She flinches when I touch it, and I slowly draw my hand away when I realise where it came from. The son of a bitch bit her. I close my eyes before I can stomach seeing the rest of the marks he left on her body.

"You don't have to stay, I can take it from here," she says, and I know from the expression on her ruined face that she's ashamed of the way she looks.

"Hey." I tilt her chin up so she can read the sincerity in my eyes. "There's never been a woman more beautiful than you, Ana." I press my lips to her forehead and smooth my thumb over her cheek to catch her tears. "There never will be."

Running my hands over her hips, I slip my fingers under the elastic of her underwear and gently pull them down, past the bruises on her thighs and over her dirty feet. They're soaked with so much blood that it turns my stomach, but I hold her close. It's all I can do not to bolt through the door and tear this town apart to find that little shithead.

He doesn't deserve to breathe the same air as Ana, doesn't deserve what he took from her. No one will ever be deserving enough of Ana Belle, least of all me, and yet here she is, trusting me with her heart, her secret, her safety.

I lift her into the shower and grab a washer from the towel rack. Stripping off, I join her under the stream, letting the hot water needle out the tension in my body as I hold her. I do as she asks and, with gentler hands than I thought I possessed, I help her wash away the stain he's left upon the woman I love. I hold her in my arms and we cry together until the hot water runs out, and then I dry her off and carry her to bed. I hand her some sleeping pills and some Panadol for the pain and fold myself around her body until she falls asleep. Quietly, I tiptoe back into the bathroom, take the grate off the air vent and feel around until my hand comes to rest on the cool metal inside. Then I use Ana's phone to make a call.

ELIJAH

Five minutes after I ended the call with Holly her car had come tearing through the motel car park. She'd parked diagonally across two spaces, pulling up so hard she'd almost toppled me on my bike.

I told her what he'd done. She cried and sat down heavily on the bitumen in her fluffy bunny PJs. She looked like she wanted to throw up. She wasn't the only one. I'd had longer to deal with this information, but my rage hadn't lessened any. Holly had given me shit about going after him. She screamed and ranted so loudly I thought she might wake up Ana, but whether it was the shock or the pills she was dead to the world, just the way I needed her to be. Holly had been bordering on hysterical when I'd started my bike, but she'd agreed to watch Ana until I got back.

Now, I sit staring up at that fucker's house, watching, and waiting. It's still pitch dark outside, but it won't be if I stay here much longer. I flip the kickstand down and quietly make my way around to the back of the house. What I'm about to do will get me sent away for a long time, possibly the rest of my life, but there's no other option here.

Pulling out my lock pick I slide it into the back door off the kitchen. I'm a little rusty, but after a minute the lock gives way and the door swings open. I pray like hell they don't have an alarm system because if they do, I'm toast.

I step inside and ease the door closed behind me, then I slowly make my way up the stairs. At the top, I glance at the three closed doors and thank mums everywhere for buying stupid signs that read: Scott's room, like the one I'm staring at right now.

I creep over to the door. It's at the very end of the hall, so I have to bypass his parent's and one other bedroom on my way, and I hold my breath and hope like hell this doesn't end before it even gets started.

I breathe a sigh of relief when my passage goes without a hitch, and another one still when I carefully turn the handle and I'm met with no resistance. I ease into the room and quietly shut the door behind me, taking a minute for my eyes to adjust to the darkness.

It's obvious he's here and not out abusing some other woman because he's snoring softly. For a moment I just watch the rise and fall of his chest as he sleeps. I try not to think about what it will be like for his parents to wake and find their son dead in the morning, but of course as I stand in his childhood room surrounded by footy trophies, high school memorabilia and a poster of a half-naked woman bent over a V8 that looks an awful lot like my Ana, I can't help but feel a twinge of guilt for his family at what I'm about to do to their precious, sack of shit, rapist son.

Walking to the bed, I pull the gun and a strip of Duct tape from inside my jacket and place the tape over his mouth as I press the barrel against his forehead.

His eyes spring open immediately. He screams, but it's muffled. He's not stupid enough to try wrestling the gun from me and I'm both thankful and disappointed for that. It takes everything I have not to blow his fucking head off right now, but I want him as shit-scared and fucking humiliated as she was, so I'm committed to seeing this through for Ana's sake.

"Remember me, arsehole?" I whisper. It's an effort not to scream in his face, but that really wouldn't help my situation any.

The scumbag makes some desperate pleading noise in the back of his throat. His eyes are shining with fear and I shift so I'm sitting on his chest and staring down into his pretty boy face that I want to fuck up every which way from Sunday.

"You took something from someone tonight," I begin and he shakes his head vigorously beneath my gun. I decide he can't feel it enough and press it into his forehead a little harder which gets his full attention. He stills beneath me, except for the shallow breaths he's taking and the sob that wracks his chest. "That wasn't a fucking question you fuck-rag. I know what you did, you know what you did and you're gonna fucking die for it."

"Did you know she was a virgin?" I ask. I can see by the way his eyes widen slightly that he didn't. Not that it matters, really. Rape is rape. It's still brutal and unwarranted, no matter what the circumstances, and men like him deserve to be strung up and castrated. He starts yammering again behind his gag and I pull back my elbow and slam it into his face. He screams like a little girl. It feels good to have an outlet for the rage so I do it again, harder this time. Then I press my hand down over his nose so his cries don't gain any unwanted attention.

"This the first time you stuck your cock in a pussy that didn't want it? Think carefully before you answer, you little fuck, because I will know if you're bullshitting."

He closes his eyes and very slowly shakes his head.

"You sack of shit," I mutter and clench my jaw together tightly in order to keep from filling his groin full of bullets. "You're lucky I don't cut it off and nail it to your parent's door."

His eyes widen and he starts screaming again. He's making too much noise so I punch him in the face to shut him up. Then I climb off of him and stand beside the bed with my gun aimed squarely at his groin. "Take off your pants."

He shakes his head and I lean down so our noses are almost touching. "This 9mm may be small, but it'll still blow a hole in your head. Now, imagine what something like that could do to your Johnson." Scott's eyes widen in terror. His nostrils flare wildly as he sucks in air and tries to plead with me from behind the duct tape. "So this is how it's going to work: I tell you to do something, you do it. I won't ask again, I'll pull the trigger instead. Are we fucking crystal clear, or do I need to start shooting family members for you to get that point through your thick skull?"

He nods and, with trembling fingers, pulls his pants down to his ankles. I lift the knife from my belt and watch the fear slide over his face. It's equal parts beauty and horror all at once. I move toward him and catch my reflection in the window above his bed and it occurs to me that I've never done anything with this much premeditated brutality. I've killed men in self-defence, once on the inside and once on the out to save the woman I loved from the same fate that this scumbag delivered to her tonight. I've done a lot of fucked up shit and left an awful lot of unhappy people in my wake, but I've never carved up a man's junk and put a bullet through his brain while his parents were asleep in the next room. And, as I stand there glaring at my reflection, I see that if I go through with this, if I put a bullet in this fucker's brain and splatter him all over his bedroom walls, it won't make me any fucking different from him.

Would Ana forgive me for ending his life? Would she forgive me for letting him walk free? Would I? I don't know the answers to any of these questions, and that scares the shit outta me.

A musky acrid scent hits my nostrils and I snap out of my thoughts and glance down at the piece of shit before me. He's so fucking terrified he's pissed and shit all over the bed. I wrinkle my nose, take a step closer to his head and bring my fist down on his cheek so hard it whips his head to the side and knocks him out cold. Then I pull up a seat beside him and waste no time making sure the outside reflects the ugliness on the in.

It's not fucking pretty, and several times I gag and retch and worry his parents are going to walk in on me impersonating Jack the Ripper, but it isn't long before it's finished. My gloves are covered in blood—my knife too, obviously. I pick up the end of the sheet and wipe my hands and the blade on the clean white bedding.

Then I calmly walk over to the desk, tear off a sheet of paper from a notepad and write a letter to his parents:

Tonight your son raped a nineteen-year-old girl.

This is to make sure it never happens again.

I set the note in the middle of Scott's chest. He's out cold, but the rise and fall of that piece of paper eases some of the anxiety inside of me. I came here tonight to kill him and I didn't. A part of me hates myself for being such a goddamned pussy, but the other part knows I did the right thing.

He destroyed my girl tonight and I destroyed his chance of ever doing this to another woman again. We're not even close to even but I'll settle for it anyway, because it may just keep another naïve girl from having her life destroyed by that fucker.

Two kilometres from the Turner household and I have to pull the bike over because the shock of what I just did sets in, and I start spewing before I've even pulled off the road. I spend a good twenty minutes outside the Sugartown Primary School heaving up my guts, and then I climb back on my bike and drive to the nearest payphone where I report a break in at 24 Pine Tree Road.

Across town, I hear the wail of police sirens cut through the quiet early morning air and I jump back on the bike. I drive right past the motel, about 10 kilometres past it actually, and hurl the gun off into a cane field. I bury the gloves by the side of the road and clean myself up as best I can with some wet wipes I keep in an ammo case, then I speed back to the motel to spend as much time with Ana as I can before the men in blue come for me. And they will come. I have absolutely no doubt about that fact. In a way, I'm counting on it to keep me in line, because I could still very easily turn around and put a bullet in that kid's head.

Once I slide my key in the door Holly is right up in my face, demanding answers. I pull her into the bathroom with me and quietly close the door to keep her from waking Ana.

"What the hell did you do?"

"I took care of it."

Her eyes widen. "What does that mean, Elijah?"

I run my hands under the hot tap to clean away a spot of blood on my wrist and curse these old pipes for taking so long to heat up. My knuckles are bruised and, despite the leather gloves I'd been wearing, the skin is still all torn up from slamming my fist into Scott's face. I desperately want a shower so I peel off my jacket and shuck off my boots but then it occurs to me that Fanta-pants has no intention of leaving until she gets her answers.

"He's still breathing," I say. *Not that he deserves to be.* "He's had some body modification work done, though."

"What the hell does that mean?" she shouts. I glare at her to shut up but the bathroom door opens and a shell-shocked Ana looks back and forth between us. She takes one look at my hands and my guilty wide-eyed expression and bolts.

"Ana!" I shout and take off after her, nearly knocking Holly off her feet as I push through the bathroom door and into the motel room. She's already out the door and half way to the staircase when I catch her by the waist and drag her back to my room, kicking and screaming. I dump her down on the bed, remembering only at the last minute how carefully she was moving last night. In the daylight I can see he really fucking did a number on her, and I curse myself again for being such a fucking pussy and not gutting the bastard.

"You promised," Ana sobs and I make a move toward her, but suddenly Holly is beside her on the bed, holding her in her arms, and I feel like I've been shunted aside like old garbage. "You promised you wouldn't tell. You said you wouldn't go after him."

She's right. I did promise that. But I also made myself a promise the night the Angels attacked us, when she was almost raped right there in front of me. I promised myself I'd do everything within my power to keep her safe and if it's one thing I know about spoilt little rich kid fucks like Scott Turner it's that once they get away with something, they're cocky enough to try a second time. I'll be a rotting corpse before I ever let him near my Ana again.

Holly surprises us both by saying, "He did the right thing, Ana."

"What?" Ana and I ask at the same time.

"You need to go to the hospital. You need to let them carry out a rape kit and then you need to report this to the police."

Ana shakes her head. "My dad, he can't … this will destroy him."

"No. It won't." I peer out through the curtains at the car park below. "Learning that you covered it up and let that arsehole walk, that will destroy him."

She glances up at me. Her voice is just a whisper when she says, "What did you do?"

"I didn't kill him, Ana. I wanted to." I shake my head. "I *want* to, but then he's still not really paying for what he did. It'd be giving him an out. Report it, get the rape kit and he'll be locked away," I say, before adding, "It might not be as long as he deserves, but a pretty boy like him will spend every day in prison wishing he'd never laid a hand on you."

I glance at Holly. "Can you give us a minute?"

"Sure." She squeezes Ana's hand and then steps out onto the balcony, closing the door behind her.

"I'm sorry, baby girl. I know I betrayed your trust, but I hope you know I did it because I thought it was for the best."

"That wasn't your call to make," she snaps and looks up at me from behind a curtain of the prettiest hair I've ever seen.

I hear the wail of sirens in the distance and I know I don't have long. I pull her to her feet, wondering whether these precious few minutes with her will be the last I'll ever get. God, I hope not because I love this crazy, naïve, insanely beautiful woman more than I've ever loved anyone. The thought of never seeing her smile again or never hearing the way she moans when I bring her exquisite pussy to the brink with my mouth, forces something inside me to snap and my throat constricts around a lump I can't swallow. I know she's furious with me, and she has every right to be, but those sirens are getting closer and she and I are drifting further apart.

"Promise me you'll report this?"

"What, like you promised me?"

"Ana, please, I'm begging you." It's a low blow, but it might be the only thing that gets through to her, so I clear my throat and say, "If you care about me at all, you'll report it."

"What does that mean?" The sirens get louder. It finally falls into place inside her head because tears well in her eyes and she sucks in a deep breath and says, "They're coming for you?"

I nod.

"No." She closes her eyes, her quiet sobs filling the room. "What did you do?"

"It doesn't matter," I say and take her chin in my hands, because I'm afraid touching her cheeks will only cause her more pain. "I love you, baby girl."

I press her into me and kiss her hard on the mouth. It's not a lingering kiss, she doesn't open her lips and I don't force her, but for a moment I feel her soften and melt into me and that's good enough.

"I'm sorry you have to see this," I say, as I pull away and study her face one last time. The screeching of brakes outside sets my hair on end. I count three pairs of footsteps thundering up the stairs.

Holly swears. "Ah, guys?"

An officer kicks in the motel door and two more pull me away from Ana. She cups a hand over her mouth and shakes her head in disbelief.

I'm asked to put my hands behind my head, and I do. I also bend a little at the knees in order for the officers to reach my arms but some fuck-rag shoves his boot in the back of my knees and I drop like a tonne of bricks. Then I'm being shoved face down on the floor with some arsehole's knee between my shoulder blades as they slap a pair of cuffs on me and yank me up by my wrists.

"Elijah Cade, you're under arrest for the mutilation of Scott Turner. You have the right to remain silent …" The officer continues to read me my rights but I don't hear any of it. I'm too focused on Ana and the way she's mouthing "mutilation" at me like it's a question she thinks I can answer. I feel the officers restrain my hands and slip the cuffs into place and then I'm being hauled to my feet and carted out the door.

"Wait," I hear Ana say behind me and my walk of shame comes to a grinding halt. "I need to report a rape." She blurts out, and for a heartbeat no one says a thing.

The officer holding my arm yanks me around to face her. "This guy?"

"No." Ana's shaking like a leaf but her gaze slides over me and she steels herself, wipes her tears and says, "Scott Turner is the one who raped me, in the cane fields outside town, last night."

The officer nearest me sighs and pushes me toward the door, and I overhear the cop who read me my rights telling Ana to follow him down to the station.

I don't know what lies ahead of me now, but I'm bursting with pride over how fucking brave my girl is. The officer forces my head down as he guides me into the back of the paddy wagon and, for the first time in my life, I smile as I'm carted off to the station.

*T*he next six hours of my life are a living hell.

Holly drives and we follow the police to the station where I deliver my statement of last night's events to a man who has known me all my life, and is equally familiar with Scott Turner. I cry as I recount the drinking, the struggle and several times I have to stop to catch my breath as I tell Constable Miller about waking up alone in a cane field, about the pain lancing through my insides as I struggled to find my clothing and then walking the 2 kilometres into town to Elijah's motel room.

Afterward, I'm taken into a room where the Constable photographs my face, the bruises on my legs and the bite over my breast. Then I'm released and taken back to the hospital where the same nurse who had set my cast and taken care of me the night of the lantern parade carries out a rape kit, takes vials of my blood to be checked for STIs and HIV/AIDS, and hands me a tiny pill to swallow to prevent an unwanted pregnancy. I'm sent for x-rays to ensure my cheekbone is not broken and then I'm given a prescription for painkillers and the all clear to head home.

The police confiscated my clothing for evidence back at the motel. I only have the paper gown I'm wearing and the oversized t-shirt and tracksuit pants Elijah dressed me in last night. The thought of staying in his clothes, inhaling his scent the entire way home turns my stomach. I'm so confused right now as to how I feel, I'm almost numb. Thankfully Holly has a change of clothes in her car and she steps out to retrieve them. I lie back against the pillow and stare at the water stains on the ceiling. For the first time today my eyes are dry but when I hear a gruff, all-too-familiar voice out in the hallway they tear up again. My heart drops through my stomach.

Not here. Not like this.

"Sir, you can't just walk in there," a nurse calls from outside my door.

"Like hell I can't," he booms.

My door flies back on its hinges and across the room stands my dad. I watch him take me in and then his face crumples into a mask of anguish and my big, burly, rough-as-guts and tougher than a twenty-foot crocodile father sobs. Tears stream over his ruddy, sun-weathered cheeks and he cradles his face in his huge grease-stained palms.

For a moment I have no idea what to do. The nurse is watching me for some sign as to whether she should call security. I briefly shake my head and she leaves us alone.

"I'm so sorry, Daddy," I whisper and he crosses the room in two strides and wraps me up in his arms.

"Ah, Ana girl, this isn't your fault." He pulls me to his chest, cradling his thick arms around my head the way he used to when I was a kid, making me feel as safe and protected as I did back then. We cry together until Holly comes back with the change of clothes, and then Dad pulls her into his arms and holds us both as he sobs.

I don't need to ask how he knew we were here. News travels fast in small towns like ours. Which is part of the reason why I never wanted to tell—I can't stand the thought of people looking at me with pity in their eyes, and I can only imagine what this does to their "Ana Belle the town bike" theory, but I'm grateful to have my dad here with me all the same.

Once I'm finally dressed and on my feet again, I thank Holly and tell her how much I love her and how thankful I am to have her in my life, and then I ride home with my dad. I close my eyes as we drive past the cane fields and then again as we drive by Elijah's motel room.

I don't know how I'll continue living in this town with so many horrible memories around every corner. I don't know how I'll ever forgive myself for the decisions I made that night, or how I'll forgive Elijah for the ones he made, but I'm glad now that I reported it. I don't have room in my heart right now to think about how he's doing behind bars or how long he'll be there. The word "mutilation" keeps running through my mind unbidden and I can only guess what it means, but I'm hoping to god it's not what I think it is because it would mean that Elijah, my Elijah, was as sick as Scott and it hurts too much to think about that.

ELIJAH

I spend all day at the station knowing she's in a room nearby, wishing I could be there to hold her hand through what comes next but knowing that I deserve this, to be locked in a cell for a very long time for what I did.

The cops have already informed me that I won't be getting a trial. Instead, because I'm already a convicted felon with two priors, I'll stand before a judge in some bullshit courtroom hearing and have a sentence handed down to me. I don't give a shit about the details because, deep down, I know that though what I did was barbaric, it was also the right thing.

Thankfully, I'm in a cell alone, and I don't have to listen to some other fuck up fart and piss and complain about how he's innocent. Instead, I lie back on the cold metal bunk, close my eyes and pretend that I'm in that shitty motel room and Ana's wrapped in my arms where she belongs.

Much later in the day I'm taken before the judge. Despite what my legal aid lawyer says, I plead guilty to malicious intent to harm another individual. When he asks me why I committed such a heinous crime on an "innocent" young man I laugh so hard I almost die. Then I turn to him in all seriousness and say, "What would you do to the man who brutally raped your wife?" For a half-second he just blinks back at me and I think I see pity or even understanding in his eyes, but then he lifts his gavel, glares at me like this is the last place on earth he wants to be and sentences me to one year in prison with parole for good behaviour. He brings down the gavel with a hard knock. The finality of that all too familiar sound rings in my ears and makes my heart squeeze.

I'm handcuffed again and driven for two hours in the back of a paddy wagon to Grafton Prison where I'm stripped, hosed down and some big Maori guy buzzes off all my hair. Then I'm shoved out in the yard for playtime, where every badass motherfucker in a bad mood is eye-raping me like I'm fresh meat. This is nothing new; it's not my first time at the fucking rodeo, but it is the first time I've been inside without the weight of the club at my back. MCs have connections everywhere, from prison staff to inmates, and I may be a long way from home but that doesn't mean the Angels don't have contacts inside this prison. If they do, I'm as good as dead.

I pour two vodka shots and slide one over to Holly before leaning back in the faded lounge chair. Dad and the dragon are out on some weekend-long bike run to the mountains and Sammy has long since gone to bed. These kinds of nights have been almost a regular occurrence for us since Elijah went away and Cooper up and left town for the city lights and the stage. Holly and Coop drove me crazy with their kissy faces and their pet nicknames, at least for the first two months; after that things began falling apart, swiftly.

Coop missed the city, he missed his band and he missed being worshiped by his groupies in the mosh pit as he belted out songs from the stage and, despite wanting an out almost her entire life, Holly didn't want to leave Sugartown. I hope that wasn't on my account, but I suspect Elijah being behind bars and my impending trial might have had something to do with it.

Things got messy between Holly and Coop. They fought, they made up, and then they fought again. One day he showed up at the diner with a loaded car and an even more loaded ultimatum. Holly, being the stubborn woman she was, was determined to prove her point, so she sent him off without so much as a kiss goodbye.

"You know, I've been thinking," she begins.

"No."

"What do you mean, no? You haven't even heard my brilliant plan."

"And yet the answer is still no."

"Hey, I'll have you know I'm excellent with my hands, and I've never had any complaints in the sexy time department."

I laugh. "You're brilliant plan was that we should convert to lesbianism?"

She shrugs. "I'll try anything once."

"I think that's your problem."

Holly grabs the bottle and pours another round. "When did we get so pathetic, Ana?"

"When my boyfriend—no, when my *ex*-boyfriend—got carted off to prison and yours up and left you for fame and fortune."

"Right." Holly throws back her shot and beats her chest, coughing and wheezing like a decrepit old woman. Then she immediately pours another and raises her glass to me. "To men who fuck you over."

I clink my glass with hers. "To men who rip out your heart."

"To men and their stupid, beautiful, unforgettable cocks."

"Amen."

She opens her mouth, hesitates, and then asks anyway, "Have you heard from him?"

"No."

"Do you want to?"

I sigh. I don't know why she asks me this, but every week it's the same. I want to forget him so badly. If it were possible to cut him out of my heart completely, I'd do it. I'd do it and never look back, but I can't. So the ache and the longing just continue to build inside me until I'm drowning in it: drowning in how much I miss him, how much I still love him, and how I can never forget.

"No," I lie, but I know even Holly doesn't believe that.

"Yeah, me neither," she says and pours us both another drink.

*T*wo weeks later I'm enjoying a lazy Sunday lie-in before having to make my way over to the shop for more baking when the phone rings. Apparently no one else is capable of picking it up, because it rings out and then immediately begins ringing again. I throw back my covers and dash for the kitchen, yanking the receiver from the cradle before it cuts out.

"Hello?"

"Ana." It's Holly. Or at least I think it's Holly; it's hard to tell between all the sniffling and sobbing.

"Hols, what's wrong?"

"I'm pregnant."

"Uh … *ooooh*." I slump onto a stool at the breakfast bar and blink several times, hoping I'll wake up, because life couldn't possibly suck this much. *Could it*? "Um, are you sure?"

"I'm staring at twenty sticks with pee on them all screaming positive. My boobs hurt, I wanna simultaneously chuck my guts up and inhale a vat of ice cream, oh and that condom that Coop said was still good after he'd been carting it around in his car since the beginning of time was not even fucking close to being *still good* because I have his baby taking up space in my uterus. So yeah, I'm pretty damn sure."

"Holy crap."

"What am I going to do, Ana?"

"Hols, we'll figure this out. Just sit tight, I'm coming over."

"Okay," she says, but I can tell from her tone that everything is not okay. We're far from okay. "Ana?"

"Yeah?"

"Bring ice cream."

"Okay." I hang up the phone and stare at the countertop and the remnants of a big Sunday cook-up that Dad's left in the sink and I kind of want to throw up myself. Then I shake off the shock as best as I can and head back to my room. I throw on the first thing I see, yank my hair back into a ponytail and dash out the door.

It's not until I'm making a beeline for the frozen produce aisle that I remember why I've not set foot in this store in over two months. The surreptitious glances, the sombre silence as I leave a trail of gawking shoppers in my wake. It seems a couple of months aren't long enough for Sugartown residents to get used to the idea that the town "whore" was in actual fact as pure as virgin snow, and their beloved town sports star was a rapist scumbag. My bruises may have healed on the outside but these people remind me daily of the damage done on the inside with their stares and their weighty silence.

I steel my nerves, straighten my spine and avoid their gazes as I turn the corner into the frozen foods section. There are two shoppers at the end of the aisle but I don't pay them any mind; I don't even glance in their direction. I just scan the freezer for Holly's favourite brand and dive in when I see one tub left at the very back. Twenty seconds later I yank it free, and emerge from the cold covered in goose bumps and come face to face with Scott.

The ice cream falls to my feet and my heart leaps around inside my chest as I take in his face and the chicken scratch on his forehead.

RAPIST.

Elijah's handiwork.

I'd heard about it, of course. Between the town and my dad I'd known exactly what Elijah had carved into his face, but that knowledge couldn't compare to seeing it firsthand. The letters are etched into his skin with crude red scabs. It's so disgusting and barbaric and yet fitting, all the same. It's obvious he's growing out his hair in an effort to hide it. Seems a stain that dirty should be imprinted on his soul, not just his forehead. Still, I guess it does what Elijah intended it to do, though that doesn't make it any easier to see up close.

"Take one more step and I'll scream so loud I'll bring this place down on top of us."

"I'm not here to hurt you," he says holding up his hands in surrender. "Just shopping with my mum."

"And violating a restraining order, but then, the rules don't really apply to guys like you, do they?"

"Ana, I'm really sorry about what I did. I was drunk. I didn't know about you being ..." I suck in a sharp breath and he peters off.

I glance at his mother who doesn't even have the sense to pretend she's not watching this exchange like a hawk.

"Did your parents put you up to this?"

"No, I wanted—"

"You think you can smooth this over with an apology? Make it all go away?"

"That's not what I'm trying to do—"

"Bullshit. Let's call this what it is, a last ditch effort to get me to drop the case. Which, by the way, is never ever going to happen. You might be walking around like a free man now, but when this trial happens you're going away for a long time." I point my finger at his forehead. "The man who did that happens to be in the exact same prison you're about to call home, and I'll bet everything I have he's counting down the days until he sees you again."

"Ana—"

I turn on my heel to walk away but Scott reaches out and grabs my arm. I rip it out of his grasp and seethe. "Don't you dare touch me, you filthy pig."

I quickly walk away, holding my head high. I stalk past the gawping faces of shoppers and past the cashier who'd been working that register since I was five years-old and out into the midday sunshine of the parking lot where my heart drops through my stomach and I promptly fall apart.

"Where's the ice-cream?" Holly asks as I step into her bathroom and quickly shut the door behind me.

"Probably still on the supermarket floor," I mutter and then elaborate when she sends me a curious look, "I ran into Scott."

"Holy fuck, Ana! Are you okay?"

"Oddly, I think I am. Or at least I will be." I sit down beside her and she leans her head on my shoulder before handing me a pregnancy test. I glare at the little plus sign as if it personally offends me. "So you went and got yourself a Mini Coop, huh?"

She lets out a humourless laugh at my terrible joke and bursts into tears. I throw my arm around her shoulders. "Hey, we'll get through this. We'll get a house, sell pies by the side of the road and raise this kid together."

"I'm not keeping it," she whispers.

"You sure this is what you want?"

"Come on, Ana, you really think I'm Mummy material?"

"I think it doesn't matter what I think. If you want to do this, I'll be there with you. If not, I'll help you look into your options."

"I already made the appointment."

"When?" I slide my fingers through hers and clasp her hand tight, the way we used to do when we were little and our only worries in life were running away from boys in the playground trying to catch us in a game of catch-and-kiss.

"Monday week."

"I'm driving you."

"Okay." She rests her head on my shoulder again and we stay like that until the sky outside the window turns dark and her parents call us down for dinner.

ELIJAH

*M*y eyes dart around the visitors' room and I scan every face before finally coming to rest on a familiar pair of clear, blue eyes, so much like his daughter's. Bob sits at a round table, his chunky arms folded against his chest and a wistful smile on his face. I know he's thinking I wish he wasn't sitting there alone, but when they said I had a visitor today I wouldn't let myself believe it would be her. I'm not sure my heart could handle that hope being crushed once I found out she hadn't come. Still, it's good to see a familiar face.

I smile and the cut on my lip opens up again. It's probably a good thing she hasn't come. I'm already sporting a fat lip and a nasty cut over my left eyebrow from the shit storm of a fight in the yard yesterday. I don't need to land myself in any more trouble, and beating the other prisoners' faces in for looking at my woman the wrong way could see my parole offer for good behaviour revoked.

The guard plonks me down in the seat opposite Bob and moves to stand near the wall to watch over his band of criminals.

"How you doing, son?" Bob asks and his eyes zero in on my face.

"Can't complain, no one would fucking listen." I smile and hiss when my lip opens up again.

"They treating you alright?"

"What, this?" I point to my face. "Just a couple of playground bullies. They got theirs, and now they're both in isolation. I'm keeping my nose clean, though."

"Good, good." Bob nods. His eyes are unfocused, as if he's thinking long and hard about something, and then he snaps his attention back to me and says, "I brought you something."

"It's not a gorgeous blonde is it?"

"No. But it's a picture of one." He glances at the guard and indicates with his hands that he's going to pull something out of his pocket before reaching in and placing three photos on the table before us. The first is one of Sammy and Ana huddled on the couch, stuffing their faces full of popcorn. Their attention is focused away from the camera, it's a candid side-on shot. Ana's not wearing any make up, her hair is piled on top of her head in a messy bun and she has popcorn all down the front of her shirt, but there's a smile on her face that's the most beautiful fucking thing I've ever seen. Sammy's head is in her lap and her hand rests gently against his hair. There's so much love in that one tiny gesture that my heart practically splits open. I miss her so goddamn much.

The next photo looks like it was taken immediately after the first. Ana's attempting to hide under a blanket while Sammy pulls it off of her. Her face is contorted into a grimace, but it's still as beautiful as ever.

The third is Ana alone. The light around her is grainy and quite a bit darker. She's asleep on the couch with her hand curled under her cheek and her face slackened in sleep. There's the barest hint of cleavage on display, her t-shirt is rucked up around her chest exposing her flat stomach and the short shorts she's wearing show every perfect inch of her lean legs. She looks amazing and so completely fuckable that I feel my cock twitch in my pants. I shift uncomfortably, clear my throat, and shoot Bob a questioning look.

"Hey, I'm not handing that one over lightly. That's my daughter you're erecting a fucking tent for under this table, but I know how you feel about her and I know what you did for her, so I'm making an exception this once." He's blushing. Fuck, I wish I had a camera so I could immortalize this moment forever. It's funny how much has changed between the two of us. It's hard to believe this big, blushing mountain of a man is the same guy who bailed me up against a wall and warned me away from his daughter. Now he's visiting me in prison and handing over pictures like this.

"Thank you."

"You're welcome," he grunts.

"How's she doing?"

He sighs and folds his arms over his chest. "She won't admit to it, but I think she's hurting bad."

"I'd give my left nut to talk to her. Just to hear her voice, just once." In the months that I'd been inside I'd used my one phone call a week to talk to Bob. Seems kind of irrelevant when he visits every Sunday anyway, but I have no one else to call, and sometimes the need to speak to someone on the outside even about the most trivial of things was so great you'd sell your soul for the experience. I only ever called when I knew she wouldn't be there to answer. Once no one had picked up and I hung on, just to listen to the message she recorded.

"If she wants to talk to you she'll come visit. Until then, you gotta let her deal with this shit the best way she knows how."

"Yeah, I know. I just wish she'd deal a lot quicker."

"Court case is this week."

I nod because this isn't new information to me, and every time I think about her having to face that scumbag, knowing I won't be by her side, I wanna attack every guard in this place and smash down every wall that's keeping me locked away from her. "You're going, right?"

"Finally getting to see that animal locked away? You bet your arse I'm going." His eyes turn a darker shade of blue and he starts gritting his teeth. A muscle in his jaw pops.

I know how hard it must be for him to not dish out his own form of punishment when he sees that little turd-burger around town. If I were on the outside it would take a fucking miracle for me to let him walk away. I guess, in a way, it did. That night, if I hadn't been thinking of Ana and what she'd think of me if she saw me like that,

I'd have put a bullet right between his eyes and never looked back. Ana saved me from spending the rest of my days locked in a cell.

"You thought about what you're gonna do if he gets sentenced to serve time here?"

"When," I add.

"If. The evidence might be concrete but Turner's got a big old pile of money and they've hired the best defence attorney in the state. He might walk away from this unscathed."

"Then it's a good thing I'm up for parole in three months."

"Son," Bob begins.

"Yeah, I know. I just can't have him out walking around after what he did to her, you know?"

"I know, son, but you can't be saying shit like that in prison either."

I glance down at the pictures in my hands and sigh. "God, I miss her so fucking much."

"It may not seem like it, but she misses you, too." He follows the line of my gaze and gives me a consolatory clap on the shoulder. "She hasn't been the same since the two of you broke up."

I inhale hard through my nose to keep the tears at bay. After Mum and Lil died I went over half my life without ever tearing up, but since I met Ana it's like a fucking dam opened up and every couple of months I'm bawling my eyes out like a fucking pansy-arse girl.

"Ah, hell kid," Bob says when I finally lift my head and jam the heels of my hands into my eye sockets to keep them from leaking. "It breaks my heart to see you kids hurtin' the way you are. She'll come around, you'll see. You just work on keeping your nose clean and you tell that parole board whatever you have to in order for them to sleep better at night and you'll be home in time for Christmas."

"Yeah," I agreed, though the thought of spending another Christmas alone held little appeal. At least inside I'd be spending the day with others. Despite what Bob had said, I was pretty sure that if Ana hadn't come around by now, there was a good chance she wasn't going to. It was just another of life's losses that I'd have to get used to, but as I sat there, staring down at her picture and talking to her father—the kind of father I'd never had—I realise that getting over Ana Belle will be the hardest thing I've ever done, and the lure of the white line no longer calls to me the way it used to.

"Christmas," I say and shake my head in disbelief. "Can't wait."

Since I met Ana my whole life feels as though it's spiralling out of control. If I could hold on to her, even just for a minute, I feel like maybe it would slow down long enough for me to get my bearings, but the spinning never stops and neither does the hurt. I smile like I'm excited about coming home, but all I feel is numb and pain, like the two are trading blows in the ring. Truth is, without Ana, I have no home. And that hurts more than any of the losses I've encountered so far.

ANA

The day of the hearing was quite possibly the worst day of my life, next to the day my mum died—and the day Scott held me down and stole my virginity after pulverising my face, that is. Holly had stayed over the night before, but even her usually cheerful disposition was absent today. Instead, it was like a black cloud had settled over the Belle household and there wasn't a chance in hell it was going to lift.

I'd made the decision to allow my lawyer to speak on my behalf, and would be waiting out the verdict here at home. Despite my bravado in the supermarket, I couldn't stand the thought of facing Scott again and I didn't trust myself not to go postal if the judge let him walk free. Our evidence was concrete, the police had collected DNA and sperm samples from underneath my nails and from the rape kit, and they'd also taken photographic evidence of the bruises he'd left on my face and body. I needed to have faith in the system. I needed to know that the humiliation and horror of having strangers poke and prod at me wasn't all for nothing.

Holly and I walk into the kitchen and my entire family stare up at me with wide, pitying eyes. My dad is fully dressed for court. He and Kerry will be sitting in on the hearing. I wanted to be the girl strong enough to face her attacker and watch as they carted him off to jail, but I'm not. I'm just trying to deal with what happened the best way I can, and I hope there's no shame in that.

Dad walks over and pulls me into his arms, engulfing me in the smell of leather and his aftershave. He doesn't say a word, but after a beat his big body shakes with unshed tears, and the carefully constructed wall inside me holding everything together just crumbles.

Gut wrenching sobs tear from inside me and fill the room with their weak and horrible sound. I shake and sink to the floor and Dad sinks with me. He never once lets me go and he never says a single word, but I feel safe and loved inside his embrace so I cry out every tear I have for what Scott Turner had done to me, and I cry some more that the man I love is behind bars and that my best friend is pregnant with an unwanted baby and the fact that my mum isn't here to hold me today like she should be.

And then I dry my eyes and I rise and I pour myself a bowl of cereal that I don't eat, and I sit down on the couch with my best friend and try to pretend that today is just like any other.

*F*ive hours into our chick flick marathon, Holly runs screaming and tearing through the house to throw up the ten zillion calories she'd just consumed. I want to throw up too, but for different reasons. I should get up and make sure she's okay, but my whole body feels numb and I don't think standing would be the best thing for me right now. Just as she's coming back from the bathroom, my phone vibrates against the tabletop. We both freeze as we stare down at the screen displaying my dad's picture.

"You gotta answer that, Ana."

I tuck my hands beneath me and gently rock from side to side. I don't know if the swaying is helping or making me feel worse but right now I'm nervous and sick, and it's the only thing keeping me sane and not pitching my phone at the wall. "I can't."

Holly snatches up the phone and says, "Hey Bob. No, she's here. She's just having a hard time dealing. Uh-huh, okay, I'll let her know."

She hangs up the phone, sets it back down on the table and takes my hand in hers. She gives me a sad smile. Tears spill over her lashes and onto her cheeks and I feel bile rise up my throat. "Seven years. No parole."

The relief I think I should feel at hearing those words doesn't come. I'm glad he's being locked away, but no amount of time behind bars will ever bring back what he took from me and what he will continue to take every time I think about lying down with a man. There is no amount of years great enough to make up for what he's sentenced me to.

ANA

One month on

The phone rings for a fourth time and I contemplate not answering, but I know I have to. I've already spoken to Holly three times this morning, one more and I'm going to be late, but I can't not answer, especially not today. In just a few short hours, she'll be taken into a room to have her baby aborted. I can't even imagine what she might be going through, the fear and uncertainty she must feel. If I could switch places with her I would, in a heartbeat. I hate to think of my best friend going through this all by herself, and that's why I'll be gluing myself to her side for the entire day. I will not let her go through this alone.

I pull the receiver from the cradle and press my ear to my shoulder to hold it in place while I pour some Nutri-Grain into a bowl. "Hello?"

There's static over the line and then I hear a click and a smooth husky voice fills my ear. "Ana?"

I sit down hard in the kitchen chair, knocking over my bowl full of cereal. Milk runs all over the tabletop and down onto the floor, but I can't move to clean it up. My heart hammers so hard I feel like it might explode. I'm not ready for this. I don't know what to say.

"Ana? You there?"

"I'm here," I whisper, though I'm at a loss for what comes next.

A beat passes and I'm beginning to think he might have hung up. I'm wondering if maybe I should, and then he whispers, "I miss you so fucking much, baby girl." And all I can do is hold onto the phone and cry.

"I only get six minutes, darlin'." There's so much pain and vulnerability in his voice I want to reach through the phone and take him in my arms, but I can't. The reality that I might never do that again hits me and I cry harder. "Tell me you're okay?"

"I'm fine. I'm running late to pick someone up, though," I say and then regret it instantly. The sound of his voice stirs up so much pain and bitterness, my heart clamps in on itself because I still love him, and I wish it were enough. "Are ... are they treating you well?"

He chuckles, "It's a prison, Ana, not a day spa. But yeah, I keep my nose clean and I get by."

"Have you seen him?" I whisper. I don't need to elaborate. We both know there's only one person I'd be talking about when it came to inmates.

"Yeah, I saw him. My fist almost saw the inside of his brain, but I walked away. I'm up for parole soon."

"Wow, that's great," I mutter, but I'm only half-listening. I have too many thoughts spinning around in my head, and my heart feels like it's collapsing in on itself.

"Listen, I've been thinking about you, about us. I made so many goddamn mistakes, baby girl, if I could take them all back I would," he sighs. "Ah, shit. I'm going crazy without you, Ana. I need you to come see me. I have to see that you're okay. I have to be able to touch you again, just for a minute."

"I don't ... I don't think I'm ready for that."

"Ana—"

"I have to go. I'm running late." I can hardly breathe with the weight of the things he's saying. The guilt consumes me every night, as I lie safe in my bed while he's locked away in a cage. He's there because of me, and I don't know if I'll ever forgive him for what he did and the pain he caused and that terrifies me. I take a deep sobbing breath. "I'm so sorry, Elijah."

I hang up the phone and cry until there's nothing left. Then I drive my scooter to Holly's and pretend as if nothing happened. I know she can see my puffy, tearstained face for what it is, but I won't dump this on her today. She opens her mouth to ask but I just shake my head and walk over to her Peugeot.

"You wanna drive? Concentrating on the road that hard makes me want to blow chunks."

"Sure," I say, and bend over backwards to catch the keys she just lobbed in the air before they fall in a puddle.

"How are you feeling?" I ask as I climb in the driver's seat.

She lets out a short humourless laugh and glances at me across the centre console. "Like a horny teenager who went and got herself knocked up. You?"

"Like a rape victim who might die without ever once having had good sex."

"Wow. How did our lives get so sucktacular?"

"Just lucky I guess," I mutter, and take her hand in mine and squeeze hard. "This isn't your fault."

"Yes, it is."

"Coop is just as much to blame in this situation. He should be here with you too."

"Yeah, well, you know what they say about rock stars? A kid in every corner of the world, right?"

"Rock stars maybe, but Coop? Come on, Hols, he was crazy about you."

"Apparently not crazy enough. Now come on, this baby isn't going to abort itself."

'd give anything not to have to be here right now. The smells, the sad looking roses in the reception and the desperate looks on the women's faces as they contemplate what they're doing here and wonder if they're making the right decision.

Poor Holly is a shaking mess. Every two minutes she fusses with her hair and holds it in place so I won't see her cry. I know why she's so upset, and I also know she hasn't entered into this decision lightly. A baby at our age, in her current situation, just doesn't make sense. She's not financially stable, she could work for my dad until the baby comes screaming and tearing out of her right there on the shop floor, but it still wouldn't be enough. I'd help her as much as I could, but when it really comes down to it, she'd be alone.

I squeeze her hand to let her know I'm here and a nurse comes into the waiting room with a clipboard and calls her name. Holly stands. Her legs are shaking. She follows the nurse but then stops and looks back at me. "Can my friend come back with me?" she asks the nurse.

"She's welcome to stay throughout the consultation, however she won't be able to be present for the procedure." I stand and take her hand, and together we walk quietly behind the nurse.

We're led into a small room where the nurse closes the door behind us and checks all Holly's vitals before telling her to put on a paper gown and lay down on the bed. The smell of the antiseptic burns my nose. I let out a deep breath.

Holly goes behind the curtain and removes her skirt and t-shirt, but when she gets to her shoes she curses and has to sit down on the chair in the corner of the change room. She begins to cry and I tentatively take a step forward, not sure if I should say something or hold her or grab her hand and run, springing her from this joint. Then I remember that she's been the one to hold my hand through all the worst days of my life, and I ease past the curtain and drop to my knees to undo the laces on her Wonder Woman Converse.

She's sobbing so hard I'm afraid she's going to choke. Once her shoes are off I pull her into my arms, and we stand like that for a long time; Holly crying as if she were a wounded animal and me trying to hold myself together, to be strong for her. "You don't have to do this you know?"

"Yes, I do."

"I know I'm not Coop, but I'll help you any way I can. We'll move in together and raise this baby ourselves. To hell with men."

"I can't. Imagine what my parents would say, imagine the disappointment."

"Hols, you're a grown woman. You haven't been a teenager for years. Neither of us have. You have to make the decision you can live with. You can't make it for your mum and dad, and you can't make it for Coop. This is your decision alone. If you want to keep this baby, then don't you dare let anyone stop you."

"No, I have to go through with this."

"Okay." I exhale loudly, but it isn't just my lungs deflating, my heart does too. If this were the right decision, she wouldn't be so broken up about it. She wouldn't be shattered and defeated as she is now. Other women might still feel that loss all too keenly, but once Holly makes her mind up, that's that. This might not be the right choice, but it's her choice.

The woman comes back in. She doesn't make a face when she finds us wrapped up in one another's arms. Not that I'd really care if she did. "Do you need a little more time? We still have a few minutes." She's really very sweet, and I'm so thankful for that. I can't imagine the heartbreak she must see on a daily basis.

"No. I'm good," Holly says, though I know she's not.

"Alright then, let's get started." The nurse talks us through the procedure and most of it goes straight over the top of my head, but soon she's helping Holly up onto the bed and politely asking me to leave. I give my best friend a gentle squeeze before walking out the door.

I wait until I'm in the waiting room to completely fall apart. One of the women gives me an odd look, but the rest of the people ignore me.

I saw in Holly's eyes just how much her heart was breaking and mine breaks for her. I wish my mum were here. Holly's parents have never been overly affectionate with her. They pushed her to get good grades and, as far as providing for their child went, they ticked all the right boxes, but emotionally they're somewhat stoic people who forget that kids need the emotional support a parent provides too.

My dad is surprisingly astute at knowing when his kids need a cuddle and yes, he certainly can be a boar of a man but underneath the fleshy, frightening exterior, he's a big old teddy bear. Still, only a female would know how to really deal with this situation, and right now I wish to god Holly wasn't lumped with some inexperienced nineteen-year-old who has no idea what she's going through.

I feel, rather than see, someone sit down next to me. I'm so lost in my sorrow that it takes me a beat to realise they're sitting uncomfortably close. "Are you about done with the waterworks?" Holly says. "Because I could really go for some Baskin-Robins right now."

I stare at her, my mouth agape. "What are you doing—"

"I couldn't go through with it." She shrugs like she hasn't just made the biggest decision of her life.

"You're not alone in this, I'll be there. And if your parents won't help you, we'll move in together. Dad told me this morning that Jackson's coming to stay with us for a while. He can't stand being in that big old house in Tenterfield all alone after my aunt died, so he's selling and going to be crashing on our couch. Maybe we can get him to move in with us someplace and it will cheapen the rent."

"Oh joy, your hot cousin—with whom I had the best sex of my life—is coming to stay, and you want me to live with him while I'm pregnant with a fat arse? Geez, Ana, you couldn't have told me all this before I got myself knocked up? Jackson Rowe moving to Sugartown is fucking monumental!" she yells, and everyone in the room turns to look at us. "Oh, go back to reading your magazines and pretending like you aren't all here to kill your babies."

I blink up at the madwoman formally known as my best friend, and she waves her hands at me to hurry up and get out of my seat. She starts to move toward the door, but before she turns completely, I see her hands briefly rest on her stomach.

She turns around to glare at me for taking too long. "Come on, woman. I want ice cream before you drive me home, and I need a whole damn pint of chocolate-chip cookie dough."

ANA

The following day I sit at the kitchen table sulking over my cereal. I'm in one hell of a mood, thanks to sleeping on the lumpy couch all night. Holly's occupying my bed at present, and is the reason for me not getting a whole lot of sleep—her pregnant arse snores.

After we got home yesterday, she came clean to her folks and the bastards gave her a pretty hefty ultimatum: destroy the child inside her that was going to "ruin her life", or ship out and pretend she has no family left. I swear it took a freaking miracle to keep me from punching them both in their snobby, bitter faces.

I threw together a bag for her and dragged her out of that house before they could change her mind. This was her decision to make; how dare they not support her in this? That was their grandchild they were talking about offing.

Now, my dad runs around the kitchen, tearing the place apart in an attempt to find something he's lost. Probably just the number for Gary's Pizza Palace down the road.

"Dad, can I talk to you about something?" I hadn't told him yet that Holly was pregnant and would be crashing with us until the two of us could find our own place. Not that he'd care; Holly is like the daughter he never knew he wanted to have. I'd just rather he hear it from me first, than the rumour mill in town.

"Can it wait, sweetheart? I'm running kinda late."

"Yeah, okay," I mutter, and take a clean spoon and a bowl from the rack on the sink, and the cereal from the cupboard. I grab the milk from off of the bench and sit down at the breakfast bar. Then it dawns on me that it's Sunday morning and my dad never goes anywhere this early on a Sunday, unless it's to the shop to buy more bacon. Assuming that this is what he's looking for, I fish the keys to his Harley from under a wrinkled and well-read newspaper and hold them out to him. "Where are you going?"

He glances at me briefly and takes his keys from my outstretched hand, then averts his eyes like he's guilty of stealing the last slice of pie from the fridge. "I'm visiting a friend."

"Okay, cool," I mutter, but my dad's staring at me with an odd expression that makes me think over what he just said.

He's not visiting a friend at all.

I narrow my eyes on him. "You've been going to the prison? For how long?"

"Since he went in," he replies, and he at least has the good grace to look a tad bit sheepish.

I want to be sick. Knowing my dad has been visiting Elijah brings all the guilt rushing back to the surface. He's just Dad's employee, but he was everything to me. It hurts to know my father's had that kind of interaction with him, even though I'm still not sure I'm ready to.

"He never mentioned seeing you," I whisper.

Dad's brows shoot skyward. "You spoke to him? When?"

"He called me yesterday, while you were out." I replay our conversation in my head, the surprise in Elijah's voice when I answered the phone, and the way he hadn't wasted a single second in telling me that he missed me. I stare at my dad and the realisation hits that Elijah wasn't calling me at all—he was calling my father. "*You're* his weekly phone call?"

"He has no one else, Ana."

"That's why you asked me to take Sammy to rugby on Saturdays, isn't it? To get me out of the house?"

"I knew you weren't ready to talk to him, but the kid's all alone in the world, Ana. We're all he has left. I gotta get going. I've got a two hour drive, and if I don't haul arse I'm gonna miss visiting hours." Dad sees me wince and his whole face softens. He steps toward me and takes my hand in his. "You could come, too. He'd love to see you."

I catalogue my dad's strange behaviour over the last few weeks and yank my hand away from his. "That's why you took that picture of Sammy and I on your phone the other day, isn't it?"

"It was a nice picture."

"Are you giving it to him?" I accuse.

"I already have, baby girl."

"Don't call me that." I dump my bowl in the sink. The spoon makes a loud clatter against the stainless steel and I wince.

"Ana, we owe him a lot."

"We don't owe him anything. He carved up a guy's face, Dad!"

"Yeah, and if he hadn't, I would have. He told me the truth about the night you hurt your arm. He saved you then, maybe it's your turn to save him back?"

"I wouldn't have needed to be saved if it weren't for his ties to the Hell's Angels."

"Maybe not, but he loves you, kid. He's a good man and he'd do anything to protect you. That's good enough for me."

"You can't build a relationship on all the shit we have buried beneath us, Dad. One day, it's all going to come floating back to the surface, and what then? All we ever did was hurt one another, and everything and everyone around us. Sometimes you've got to cut your losses before you gamble away everything you have left."

"That's not living kid, that's barely surviving."

Tears prick my eyes and I swallow hard around the lump in my throat. "Yeah, but at least it's not dying."

"Look, I'm not saying you have to jump back into bed with him. I'm just saying, maybe think about what he's going through on the inside," Dad says, gruffly. "Alone."

"It's all I think about!" I yell, and the tears escape my lashes. Thick, fat drops of salt water splash against my cheeks. "Day and night, every minute for the last four months it's *all* I've thought about. So don't you dare accuse me of not giving this enough thought. I love him, but he betrayed me, more than once. He behaved like an animal, no better than Scott—"

"Ana!"

"It's the truth. I love him so much it's crushing me," I sob. "But I don't know if I can forgive him all the same."

"I'm sorry to hear that, kiddo," dad says solemnly. "But you know where to find him if you decide you can."

"Yeah, I do."

The weight of my words hangs suspended in the silence between us and Dad turns to leave. Before he walks away though, he stops and looks back at me; his eyes are gentle and full of sympathy when he says, "I've never pushed you to do anything you didn't want to, Ana, and whether or not you decide to forgive him is up to you, but he's up for parole in two months' time. Now, I don't know if he's going to stick around in this shithole town but he has a job with me for as long as he wants it.

"Despite what you think, that kid is the only reason I'm not serving time for murder. So I want you to think long and hard about this before you make any rash decisions. What he did may not have been civil, but I know him well enough to know he made a choice he could live with. Question is, can you live with yours?"

Could I? I didn't know.

ANA

My annoying cousin drove an even more annoying Holden Ute. He'd been here for two weeks and I was ready to shove the beast's muffler where the sun don't shine and strangle him with the fanbelt. His precious and shiny new toy managed to wake the entire street almost every morning when he'd pull in before dawn and whistle his way up the drive. I didn't know there were that many available women in Sugartown to sneak out on before dawn, but if anyone could find them it'd be Jackson Rowe.

Jackson is gorgeous in that typical Aussie kind of way: tanned skin, summer sky-blue eyes, blonde hair that curls into Simon Baker ringlets if he lets it get too long, a body like Chris Hemsworth and a face like Ryan Kwanten. Even *I* have trouble taking my eyes off of him and our mothers shared a womb—it's sick and twisted, I know, but I've made my peace with it.

Right now, though, I wasn't making peace with anything, I was on a warpath and my beloved cousin was about to feel the wrath of a sleep-deprived girl interrupted.

"God damn it," Holly yells as she pulls back the covers and shoves two dry crackers in her mouth to stave off the morning sickness. It's pretty rare for her not to have crackers or another form of baked goods in her mouth these days. "How is he still finding women to screw in this town?"

"I don't know." I say with a sigh. "Just be thankful you're pregnant and unlikely to fall prey, too."

"Yes, thankful," Holly mutters caustically. "That's exactly what I am. Ana, I don't know how much longer I can pull off this I'm-not-pregnant-I've-just-eaten-one-too-many-tubs-of-ice-cream ruse. If Jackson keeps looking at me like he wants to get all up in this, I'm afraid I'm going to cave and let him bang my brains out."

"You do, and I will personally shoot both of you. As much as I loathe the thought of having to see him dragging girls in by the hair at midnight and tossing them out before the sun comes up, we need him to move in with us. We won't make the rent otherwise."

Holly sighs and flops back down on the mattress. "How the hell am I going to live with that?" She gestures to the shared wall between my bedroom and the bathroom, where we can hear Jackson running the shower, and then she flings herself out of the bed and dashes for the door.

"Where are you going?"

"I have to peeeeeeeee." She switches her weight from foot to foot and crosses her legs, one in front of the other, her hand tucked between them like she's a little kid. "How is it possible that this kid is the size of a jellybean—he's not even a real jellybean yet, he's like one of those overpriced Jelly Belly things—and he's already pushing on my bladder?"

"You don't know it's a he," I reply.

"Oh, it's a he alright. Little punk arse bastard. Only a male would wake me up this early. He's banging around in my vagina, Ana. Then he's going to tear it up from the inside and stretch it all out of shape so no man will ever want to look at mummy's pink bits again. Of course it's a male." She stalks over and bangs on the shared wall. "Only a male would be that inconsiderate."

Jackson taps back in the same spot she had and then we hear his deep chuckle through the wall. Holly screams and lunges for the door.

"You can't go in there, Hols." I sit up in bed. "Jackson's in the shower. Naked."

"Thank you for pointing that out, Einstein. I'd wondered how people did this fancy pants showering thing. God, Ana, I so did not need that image in my head right now," she snarks and stalks out of the room.

"I meant what I said," I yell after her, "keep your horny pregnant vagina in your knickers!"

The bathroom door opens and then there's a long guttural groan, which I'm hoping is just Holly finding relief in the fact that she finally got to pee, and not something else. I climb out of bed and go in after her, just to be sure. She's standing up and rearranging her pyjamas into place when Jackson pushes the shower curtain back. "Nice as it was to see your pink bits again, Holly, I don't remember there being an open invitation on that door."

"Well, if some jack-arse man-whore didn't come striding in and waking up the whole goddamn town before sunrise and then hog the shower and steal all the hot water before anyone even has a chance to see some, I wouldn't have to barge in here to pee."

"That what's wrong here, Holly? You not seeing some?" Like a complete arsehole he waggles his eyebrows at her.

"Jackson, don't be a dick," I mutter, but neither of them are listening to me; they're both too absorbed in this sick little flirty power play they have going on, and I'm starting to think the three of us moving in together is going to be a colossally bad idea.

"Oh, I'm about to see some," she declares with a snide smile. Holly turns the hot water on in the bathroom sink, causing the pipes to groan and complain as Jackson leaps out of the shower in all his naked glory to escape the deluge of cold water. I avert my eyes from his very obvious arousal, and Holly nearly doubles over with laughter. "Why, Jackson, I think you're shrinking in your old age."

Jackson grabs a towel from the rack and hastily wraps it around his waist as he grins down at Holly, whose face is so smug it looks like she swallowed a whole aviary full of canaries.

"I don't recall you having any complaints sweet, sweet Holly," Jackson murmurs, and his smile grows wider. "In fact, I recall you begging me for more, on your knees, on the bed, in the back of my mum's car. And then there was that one time you let me stick it—"

"Shut up!" Holly snaps, and her smug smile is completely gone.

"Maybe the three of us moving in together isn't such a good idea," I say.

"Oh, we're moving in together," Holly says and strides defiantly from the room.

"Well, I, for one, can't wait." Jackson says, with a grin that always meant trouble. "Better make sure there's a sturdy lock for the bathroom door, though. I'd hate to have my roomies walk in on me while I'm bludgeoning the beefsteak."

"Gah! You're such a pig!" Holly calls out.

"Oink," he shouts back, and my bedroom door slams.

I frown at my cousin. "Why do you have to provoke her?"

"Because she's so much fun to poke," he laughs and then deadpans. "Oops, I mean provoke."

I quietly close the bathroom door and lower my voice, "She's in a vulnerable place right now, could you lay off for just five minutes? Please?"

"Why is she vulnerable?" His brow furrows, and just when I think I see a hint of genuine concern for her in his expression he ruins it all by saying, "Don't tell me some guy finally managed to locate her cold, black heart and break it in two?"

"Do you ever get tired of being such a complete tool, Jackson?"

He makes a show of thinking about that and then smirks. "Nope. Never."

"Lay off," I say and walk back to the door. "I mean it. She's not up for your stupid playboy power trip right now."

Jackson's brows knit together again and he frowns. "Wait. You're really serious, aren't you?"

"As a heart attack."

"What's wrong with her?" he whispers, and there it is, the concern I'd suspected was lurking somewhere behind his clear blue eyes. They can pretend to hate each other all they want, but Holly and Jackson don't have anyone fooled. In their own weird, twisted way they actually care for one another. Which makes them moving in together the most horrendous idea I've ever had. "She's not sick, is she?"

Both our mums died of cancer before they could see out their fiftieth birthday, so it's not unexpected that he'd jump to that conclusion before anything else. Losing more loved ones to the big C was my biggest fear in life, too.

"She's not sick, and it's not my place to tell you. Just please, go easy on her." I gesture to his half-naked body. "She doesn't need to be distracted by all this."

"Hey, I can't help it if she's gagging for—"

"Jackson Rowe, so help me god, if you finish that sentence I will tell every available woman in this town that you have the clap and you will never get laid again."

"Okay, okay." He holds his hands up in surrender. "Geez, when did you girls get so fucking uptight?"

"The moment we started trusting guys like you," I retort and perform a little slamming doors routine of my own.

ELIJAH

I press the plastic prison phone to my ear and wait for someone to pick up the other end. I know it won't be the person I want. She won't answer the phone and smile at the sound of my voice, and she won't whisper that she misses me into the receiver—probably ever again—but that doesn't stop me from praying to whatever god, entity, or chasm of void space yawning over us to let it be her.

The phone's been ringing too long. If no-one picks up then I've officially wasted my six minutes, though it's not like I have anyone else to call.

It's a miracle the club haven't found me on the inside, though most of our guys would have been sent to a Sydney lock up. The Bandidos chapter in Byron means there's a few blokes from our rival MC stationed here at Grafton prison, and I'm thanking fuck right now that no one but the cops know I'm the son of a Hell's Angels Sergeant-At-Arms. I have just one and a half months to make it through before parole. One and a half months and I'll be able to see her face again.

Just when I think the phone's about to ring out, Ana answers. She sounds annoyed, and out of breath, as if she just ran for the phone. I get lost in her laboured breaths, remembering how she used to look when my hands and tongue were the cause of her panting.

"Hello?"

"Hey," I say, and give myself a mental smack-down. *Fucking wake up, man!* "I didn't think you'd pick up."

"Expecting your boyfriend, huh?" she jokes.

I have no idea what to say. This is such a turnaround from the last time we spoke, I feel like I've just been bitch slapped. I laugh softly and smile bigger than I have in months.

"It's good to hear that sound," she whispers. And fuck me, if there isn't a whole fucking world of longing in her voice. "It's been a while."

"Been a while since I had something to laugh about, baby girl."

"Are you okay?"

Fucking hell! I feel like I've stepped into the twilight zone. Are we really having this conversation? Is she coming around? Has she already forgiven me for the things I did?

"Yeah, I'm alright. I got a parole hearing in a month's time."

"Dad told me."

"Is he there?" I ask cautiously. I don't want her to quit talking to me, but I hate to think she's only doing it because she feels she has to.

"You'd really rather talk to my dad than me?"

"Hell no!" I say, too quickly. *Fuck, I sound desperate.* I can't help it though, it's driving me crazy hearing her voice and not being able to see her, touch her. "How you been, baby?"

"I'm okay. Holly and Sammy are keeping me pretty busy. Jackson is driving me nuts, though. I'm kinda wishing he'd haul his arse back to Tenterfield. I don't think the women of Sugartown have been acting this crazy since you rode into town."

"Who's Jackson?" I say, and try not to sound like a possessive dick. I have no right to do that, she doesn't consider herself mine anymore, but no matter what she might think she'll always belong to me. Fucked up logic, I know, but it is what it is.

"Would you relax? He's my cousin. My aunt died last year, before you came, and he's been living in that big old farmhouse by himself. He finally sold it and moved his big oafish butt in here and he's been helping Dad at the shop ever since."

"He a mechanic?"

"No. When you get out you're going to have more cars to fix than you know what to do with. Assuming you want to come back to this hellhole of a town, that is?"

Christ! Is she fishing?

"Well that depends." I take a risk and flirt. You only live once, right? "Do I have a girl to come back to?"

"Elijah …"

Fuck! Not fishing. Not fucking fishing!

Even though I've more than likely just fucked everything up, I can't help sinking myself further in. "Yes or no, baby girl?"

"Honestly? I don't know. It sucks, but that's all I can give you right now. You'll have a job when you come back, and I'll always be here as a friend."

"You wanna be my goddamn friend, Ana?"

"Elijah—"

"Do you still love me?" There's a pause, and just when I think she isn't going to answer the beep that signals the last thirty seconds of our call sounds in my ears. "Do you still love me?"

"I—"

"Yes or no, Ana?"

Frustration seeps from every pore in my body as I wait for the answer that never comes. The phone cuts out and I slam the receiver down and fight against the urge to go postal on the useless piece of shit. If I destroy prison property it'll go on record. If the parole board see that shit in my file this close to my assessment they'll knock me back, for sure. The only way I'm getting an answer to that question is if I see it coming from her lips when she's standing right in front of me, and I'll be fucked if I'm going to wait another six months to see her and hear those words.

(Yep, Holly)

I heave up the last of the dry crackers I'd shoved down my throat this morning and curse men for all of eternity. When this kid finally claws his way out of me I'm going to celebrate my vagina by purchasing stocks in We-Vibe and drinking myself into a stupor. Then I'm going to find every battery-operated boyfriend I can get my mitts on and screw myself into an orgasm coma. I'll more than likely die alone, crushed by the mountain of falling dildos, but at least I'll never have to look at a real penis again.

Falling back against the cool tiles, I contemplate jumping off a bridge for the thousandth time since I found out I'm growing a person inside me—which is just wrong, on so many levels, if you really think about it—and then decide that my fat arse would probably never make it over the railing. I'd likely get stuck halfway and have to wait for emergency services to come and hoist me down from an embarrassing, half-arsed attempt at offing myself. Plus, once Ana found out she'd likely kill me, and then I would have wasted all the emergency service's time.

"This is bullshit! I'm taking her arse to the doctor," Jackson yells out in the hallway. He's talking to Ana, but the threat was as much for me as it was for her. He knew I would hear him. We always hear one another. The walls in this old farmhouse may as well be made of paper. I cast my gaze around the bathroom, spot the vomit splashed against white porcelain, breathe in the acrid stench of puke, and panic. He doesn't know I'm pregnant. I don't know how he hasn't figured it out yet. I don't know why I so badly want to keep this dirty little secret from spilling out. All I know is that I feel alone and confused on an almost hourly basis, but when Jackson's in the room? All that goes away and I can breathe easier and think clearer and forget I've got a person inside me, sucking all the joy from my bones.

Sharing a house with him these past three weeks without the buffer of Bob, Sammy and the evil bitch stepmum has been torture of the very best—and worst—kind. It turns out the man is terrible at fixing up cars, so he's been jobless since Bob locked him out of the garage, meaning he's been spending an awful lot of time here in this big house by himself. Most of the time, I'm torn between wanting to tear off his clothes and wanting to pulverise his face with our new magic bullet, but I have to admit that there's some sort of inner peace I find in watching *Friends* reruns on the couch with him. Until he opens his great big mouth, that is.

"You don't need to take her to the doctor," Ana says, "she's fine."

"She needs help, Ana."

I grab a handful of toilet paper from the roll and wipe away the mess I made of the bathroom, then I climb to my feet and brush my teeth. I spray a bit of perfume, which of course makes me dry retch again, and I stand over the sink fighting back the urge to vomit.

Jackson bangs on the bathroom door. I swallow back my fear. "Holly, get your arse out here. I'm taking you to see someone."

I pull back the door and a gust of fresh air swirls around me, carrying the pungent scent of vomit and toothpaste toward my nose. For a heartbeat I just stand there, trying not to throw up again, and then I step out of the bathroom and close the door behind me. I glare up at him like I'm more annoyed with his overall Jackson-ness than usual.

To look at me, you would never know I was pregnant. There's no baby bump to speak of, and though I should already be showing, I've actually lost weight from the morning sickness. My boobs are definitely bigger, but do guys ever really notice anything past "Oh look, boobs"?

My moods have been kinda crazy, in fact I've probably seen days where I've looked like less of an escaped mental patient, but outwardly, I guess I seem kind of normal. Or as normal as I get, anyway, so I guess it makes sense he'd jump to the conclusion that I choose to chuck up my guts for kicks.

I stare up into his sky blue eyes and realise this is the moment that I have to come clean. It's also the moment I stop being the sexy little minx that rocked his world once or twice in our not too distant past, who he might like to bend over the kitchen counter and screw senseless, and instead become a walking womb.

"I don't need to see a doctor, Jack. I'm pregnant, not bulimic," I blurt out, and try to edge past him while his face is frozen in shock. He grabs my wrist and pulls me toward him.

"What?" he whispers, and I'm surprised by the hurt I see in his gaze.

"Jackson, meet Mini Coop." I wave my arm back and forth between him and my stomach.

He glances at my flat stomach, my face and then at Ana, as if he's hoping that this is all some fucked up joke. "Tell me you're shitting me, Hols?"

I don't know what to say. I wish someone would tell me that this is all a mistake, and then I'd grab his hand and run off to the nearest available horizontal surface to bang his brains out. *Yeah, that ain't happening, and this shit's still real.*

"It's true," Ana confirms, and Jackson swipes his hand over his face. His other hand is balled into a tight fist and I can tell he's dying to hit something, or someone. I guess it's a good thing Coop's nowhere to be found, after all.

"Fuck!"

"No thanks, that's kinda what landed me in this position in the first place," I deadpan, but that just makes him angrier. Jackson's really not taking this news well. I know we flirt and fight and carry on like an old married couple, but I didn't know he'd be this affected by finding out I was pregnant with someone else's baby. When he narrows his gaze and pens me in against the wall, my breathing becomes heavier. Wetness pools between my legs and my nipples harden into stiff peaks beneath my singlet top. Holy crap, I have a total lady boner for Jackson Rowe right now.

"How could you be so fucking stupid, Hols?" he's seething as he says it, but there's not just anger and disappointment in his tone—there's hurt, too.

Aaaand the happy feeling's gone.

"Jackson!" Ana chides.

"You know what, Jack?" I say quietly. I'm a nanosecond away from crying, but I swallow back the tears and the hurt, and I meet his steely gaze head on. "I ask myself that on a daily basis."

"But you're always careful?"

"Yeah, except for that one time where I wasn't, and I trusted my boyfriend enough to believe that the condom we were using wasn't centuries old, but then: surprise! Turns out you can't trust any man these days, even the ones that claim they love you. Who knew, right? Now, if you're done with your caveman bullshit, I have to get ready for work."

"Who is he? *Where* the fuck is he?"

"Don't know, don't care."

"What do you mean you don't know? He's gonna take care of this shit, isn't he?"

Why the hell does he care so much? I know there's this out of control chemical pull between the two of us, but I have no idea why he'd be acting like some jealous tool. This is Jackson Rowe we're talking about. Jack doesn't form emotional ties to anyone, that's what makes him so freaking fantastic in bed. There are no inhibitions when it comes to sex with Jackson, only intense animal heat and multiple orgasms.

"I really hope you didn't just refer to my baby as *this shit*. Because pregnant or not, I will take your arse down. And no, Coop won't be taking care of this baby. He won't even know about it."

Jack's eyes narrow. "What do you mean he won't know? You're not telling him he has a kid?"

"No," I shake my head. "I'm not telling him shit."

"What the fuck, Hols?"

"Jackson, lay off," Ana butts in.

"Don't tell me you're alright with this shit?" Jackson shoots Ana an incredulous look before turning back to me. "The man has a right to know about his kid."

"As far as I'm concerned, he gave up any rights he had when he left me here with his demon seed to go become a rock star."

"Did you just call your baby demon seed?" Jackson says.

"Hey, I'm allowed to call him whatever the hell I like, he's *my* baby. Just like the decision to tell his father is mine and no one else's."

"Oh yeah? Well, when the hell were you going to tell me about this? When I'm giving up my room for a nursery, and kissing my sex life goodbye because there's a baby screaming into all hours of the night?"

"As if that would ever stop you." I place my hand on his strong forearm and attempt to push past, but he doesn't budge, he just cages me in against the wall. "The entire house could be on fire, and you wouldn't notice a thing until you'd blown your load."

"Are you fucking serious right now?"

"Oh, I'm deadly serious," I snap, inching away from the wall and getting up in his face. "What I'd like to know is why you think you're so fucking important that you deserve to be informed on every little detail of *my* life? You're my roommate, Jackson, nothing more."

Jack flinches as if he's just been slapped. I didn't mean for that to come out the way it did, and his wounded expression tells me I've hurt him badly. *Crap.* I didn't mean any of the things I just said to him and—oh, how wonderful, now I'm acting like a complete and utter girl because tears are springing into my eyes again and this time I know they won't be swallowed down. God, I'm so damn mad I could choke him and yet all I want to do is wrap my arms around his middle and beg him to forgive me.

These pregnancy hormones suck arse!

"Both of you shut up!" Ana points at Jackson. "You need to back the fuck off," she says and then turns on me, "and you need to chill the fuck out. This kind of stress is not good for the baby."

Just as she says that I feel a sharp pang in my abdomen. I cry out and bend over, breathing rapidly through my nose. Ana's by my side in a heartbeat, taking my arm in hers and leading me to the bedroom. "Holly, are you okay?"

"Yeah I …" I begin, and then pivot on my heels and run for the bathroom. I barely manage to get the lid on the toilet seat up before the vomit comes gushing out of me. My stomach cramps down on itself over and over again as I empty it into the bowl. Ana's beside me holding back my hair, which is just about the sweetest thing she could ever do because she's one of those people that loses her shit just seeing someone dry-retching. Jackson stays over by the door, which is typical Jackson, but when I ease back from the toilet and finally rise to my feet my eyes meet his, and he's clearly stricken. Either that, or he's just fighting the urge to throw up now, too.

"Do you want me to call your doctor?" Ana asks, as she steers me over to the sink and preps my toothbrush for me.

"No. I'll be fine. I may have to call my boss though," I kid.

Ana smiles and heads over to the door as I freshen up. "Well, good luck. I heard she was a raving bitch."

"Nah, she's okay. I think she mostly just needs a good lay," I mutter. She rolls her eyes and heads out of the bathroom.

In the hall a moment later, she grabs her handbag and keys with a promise to call me at lunch to make sure I'm okay. Then she turns on Jackson. "You. Take care of her today. If she wants something, go get it for her. Do not let her get out of bed unless it's to pee."

"Yes ma'am," he says, but the second the words are out of his mouth he goes back to clamping his jaw so tightly that a muscle pops in his cheek.

She points at me. "And you, keep your bloody temper on a leash."

"Okay, Mum," I reply, and then she's gone, leaving Jackson and I to stare at one another, our earlier argument abandoned. Though I know the world hasn't changed within these last few minutes of fighting, everything in our world has. Silence fills up the space between us until I finally turn away and trek back to my bedroom to hide beneath the covers and wish like hell that the zombocalypse was upon us. At least that way I'd have a legitimate excuse to punch his lights out.

 ELIJAH

*T*here's nothing like the rush of endorphins you feel when the gate slams closed behind you and your feet touch the bitumen of the world 'outside'. I close my eyes and inhale the country air. It's no different than the stuff we breathe in the yard every day, but somehow it always feels better, more, free.

I open my eyes and look around. The prison sits pretty much in the town's centre, so it's only a short walk from here to the bus station. I don't know how I'll get to Sugartown from there—maybe get off on the highway and hitch, maybe walk the whole damn way, it doesn't matter. What matters is that I can walk anywhere at any time for the rest of my life, 'cause I ain't ever planning on going back inside.

A prison supply van pulls out of the parking space in front of me and my heart just about leaps outta my fucking chest when I see the hot blonde leaning up against my bike. Fuck me, is that a sight for sore eyes! I have this overwhelming urge to bend her over that bike and take her sweet pussy with my mouth, to force her to open to me and cry my name as her thighs squeeze the sides of my head and her heels dig into my back. My cock twitches and I gotta take a deep breath and think about nuns again in order to calm myself down.

"Easy tiger," I mutter as I run my hand over my freshly buzzed hair, and then cross the parking lot towards her.

"Whatcha doing here, Ana?" I ask as I come to a stop in front of her. I'm careful not to touch her, though it takes a fuck-load of restraint. "Not that I'm not happy to see you, or my bike, for that matter."

"I thought you could use a ride."

"How she handling?" I say, pointing to my baby, though to be honest, the thought of Ana riding my bike is causing blood to pump and flow to places it shouldn't be right now.

"Good. Dad and I have been starting her up every few days. I know how precious you are about her, so I'm the only one taking her out."

"And how are you holding up?"

She gives me a wistful smile. "I'm okay. I don't get a lot of sleep on account of the nightmares, but I'm dealing with it."

Fuck! I'd give my left nut to touch her right now, to hold her, to kiss her. I'd squeeze her tight enough that another bad dream would never enter her mind again. I'd keep all the bad thoughts away, forever, or for as long as she'd let me. *Christ, I sound like a fucking pussy.*

"What about you?" she asks.

"Today's a good day." I wink at her and the sweetest blush of colour floods her cheeks. "A very good day."

She glances down at the bike, and then at the near empty carpark and the prison gates, anything to avoid my gaze. "Listen, I don't want you to get the wrong idea here, but Holly and I have our own place now. It's a big four-bedroom farmhouse outside of Sugartown. It's not much, but we've already talked it over and you're welcome to stay as long as you want."

I'd just assumed that after making my way back to Sugartown I'd stay in the motel again but this, this is so much better. It's a chance to try and win her back. A chance to prove we can't live without one another. Every cell within me is pushing me to reach out and touch her, but I fight it.

"You sure? Last time I checked, Holly wasn't a big fan of mine." I cock my head to the side, an attempt to get her to look at me. She does, briefly, then she bites her lip and shrugs.

"She's changed." She gives a small humourless laugh. "A lot, actually. But she's okay with it, if you are?"

"Yeah, that'd be great." I jam my hands in my pockets to keep from touching her. I step closer. The bike is still between us, a buffer, a barricade I could easily hurtle over in order to get to her, but I don't dare. Few things frighten me. I've seen and done shit no man my age should have, but the idea of losing Ana for good scares the crap outta me, so if she needs me to take it slow. I'll wait for her move, but I won't wait long. "I've got some money saved up. I'll pay my way."

Ana shakes her head. "You don't have to—"

"I said I'll pay my way, baby girl." I give her a stern look and she swallows hard.

"Okay." She nods and tosses my helmet toward me. I catch it and run my hands over the beat up surface. "Then let's take you home."

She doesn't realise that I'm already home, because wherever she is, is home to me.

I always thought there was nothing better than the freedom you feel when you step outside prison. Clearly I'd forgotten the way it felt to have Ana's legs wrapped around mine, the press of her beautiful tits against my back and her head tucked into my shoulder as we fly down the highway toward home.

Fuck, I've missed that.

Now, as I pull up the long gravel drive leading to the farmhouse, I kinda wish I'd taken the drive a little slower. I shut off the engine. Ana jumps off the back of the bike and I instantly miss her heat pressing against me. She pulls off her helmet and I stare as she walks her fine arse up the path to the front steps.

"You just going to sit there all day?" she asks when she opens the front porch gate and realises I'm not behind her.

"No, I'm coming." I flip the kickstand down and slide off the bike, following after her like a stray puppy needing an owner, which I guess isn't that far from the truth.

Ana leads me into a big Victorian-style farmhouse with huge stained-glass windows and wooden floors. I've never been into all that interior design shit, but if I had a house to call my own, this is exactly the kind of thing I'd want. Quiet and homey with a big-arse kitchen for my knocked up wife to bake pies and biscuits all day, and there'd still be enough room to plant her sexy arse on the bench and lick her out before dinner. Yeah, yeah, that makes me sound like a sexist, chauvinistic dick, but I'm okay with that.

We walk through the lounge room. All the furniture is mismatched and second-hand, but it only makes the house more endearing. Ana comes to a stop in the kitchen. I'm busy looking at the beautiful red, gold and green stained-glass windows with the sunlight filtering onto the wood floor in a swirl of distorted colours, so it takes me a while to notice the half-naked man standing in front of the fridge.

"God, you're such a pig," Ana mutters.

"Love you too, sweetheart." The dude's wearing only a towel around his hips. One tiny scrap of terry towelling between his Johnson and the world. My blood runs cold, then hot, then to boiling as I realise this guy might be my replacement. There's certainly enough tension between them.

The dude closes up the carton of milk he was drinking from and burps in our direction. He's pretty cut and he's above average height, though not as tall as me. He looks like he's never been in a fight a day in his life, so I'm as sure as fuck I can take him.

"Hey man," he utters as his eyes roam over me. "Cool tatts."

"Ana, you wanna tell me why there's a half-naked man in your kitchen?" I say in her ear, though it's loud enough for Captain No Pants to hear the threat, too.

Ana shivers, and is it my imagination or did she just lean back into me?

The dude holds up his hands in surrender, "Whoa, mate, you've got the wrong idea completely. It's not like that."

"Then why don't you tell me what it's like?" I say and take a step forward.

"Elijah, meet Jackson," she says—and damn if that name doesn't sound familiar—before clarifying, "my cousin."

"Cousin, huh?"

"Unfortunately." They both say at the same time, and now that I'm not thinking of pulverising the dude's face, I can see a family resemblance. Actually, Jackson looks more like her brother than Sammy does.

"Good to meet ya, mate," Jackson says, and steps forward to shake my hand. While my hand is grasped in his, he pulls me toward him to whisper-yell in my ear. "Just so you know, she's been through hell. You break her heart again and I'll kick your arse."

"Jackson!" Ana's making a slicing hand gesture at her throat in my peripheral vision.

This whole exchange makes me smile, not because I'm being an arrogant, cocky arsehole—for once—and laughing at the threat, but because it feels good to know someone else has her back. He clearly loves Ana, and he's going to keep an eye on me because of it. I nod and say, "I wouldn't dream of hurting her again."

He studies my face for a beat and then gives my hand one last shake before nodding his approval and moving across the kitchen.

Ana sighs. "If you two are done with the pissing contest, can I show Elijah to his room?"

"Knock yourself out," he says. "Just don't do anything I wouldn't do."

"*Is* there anything you wouldn't do?"

"Yeah, you're right." Jackson nods. "Okay, don't do anything Holly wouldn't do."

"You do realise that's even worse?" Ana asks.

"What's worse?" Holly asks, as she stumbles into the kitchen. Her hair is sticking up all around her head like a copper bird's nest, and her clothes are swamping her. She's clearly just woken from a nap, though she looks as though she hasn't slept in days. She hasn't seen me yet on account of me standing up against the wall beside the fridge, and she's rummaging through the cupboard like her life depends on it. "Where's the jailbird? I could use me some eye candy right about now."

"Hey, I take offense to that," Jackson says, and winks at her.

"You can sit on the fence, for all I care." Holly shoves his shoulder and Jack grins. "Preferably one of those über pointy pickets."

"Hey Holly," I say. She spins around with her mouth gaping open. We've always rubbed each other the wrong way when it came to Ana. I know I don't deserve Ana, I could work on redemption my entire life over and the next one, too, and I'd still never be enough for her. But I love her. I need her in my life, in any way she chooses to be in it, and I'm worried Holly is going to have something to say about that.

"You're back?" Her eyes widen a little and glitter with unshed tears, and the next thing I know, she's throwing herself at me. After a moment of blind panic where I assume she's going to start using me as a punching bag and I realise that there's no way in hell I can hit a woman so I'll have to just stand there and take whatever fucked up punishment she thinks I deserve, I nearly keel over. Her arms wrap around my waist and she cries into my chest. I have no choice but to wrap my arms around her.

"It's good to see you too, Holly." My eyes are saucer-wide as they dart between Ana and Jackson for answers.

Jackson sniggers, "Feeling a little clingy today, Hols?"

Holly uncurls her arms from around my waist and glares at Jackson. "Shut up, fuck-face! Did you eat the rest of my crackers?"

"Holly's pregnant and tends to get a little … er … emotional lately," Ana explains.

Jackson hides his next dig behind a fake cough, "Psychotic!"

"Fuck you, Jack!" She stalks from the room, and a door somewhere in the house slams behind her.

"You just name the place, sweetheart," he calls after her. "You know where to find me."

"Would you stop provoking her, please?"

"She's really pregnant?" I feel like I've stepped into the twilight zone.

"Yeah, she's fourteen weeks along." Ana gives me an uneasy smile. "Come on, let's get you settled in." She grabs my hand and leads me from the kitchen down a narrow hall, pointing out Holly and Jackson's rooms at one end. In the middle is a decent-sized bathroom, and further along two more rooms sit opposite one another. The one on the right is covered in clothes, and there's a yellow doona sitting bunched up on top of the bed. No guesses as to who occupies that room.

I follow Ana into the room opposite. There's a black and grey doona sitting on top of a double bed that barely looks like I'd fit in it, two bedside tables and a chest of drawers leaning against the side wall with chipped and peeling black paint. On the top sits a framed picture of my bike and another of Ana and her family, Jackson and Holly included. I pick up the frame and stare down into the posed shot.

"Do you like it? You can take it out if you like. I just thought you should have at least one picture of … family. I know you don't have any of your mum and sister and no one should have a room without pictures." She's rambling again, and it's so fucking sweet it's giving me a damn toothache.

"I love it, I love all of it." I make a gesture that includes the room around me. "Thank you."

She smiles. "The police confiscated your clothes; more like they confiscated everything in that motel room, even your bike. Dad had to buy it back at a police auction."

He hadn't told me that. When he'd visited me that first week in jail, Bob had just said that he'd kept it for me, that it was safe. He didn't say he had to buy it back from the cops. It would have cost him a shitload of money too, considering how rare they are here in Australia. Money I'll be paying back, down to the last cent.

"Anyway, Holly and I went shopping last week for some basics. There isn't much, but I'm sure we can take some things back if they don't fit. And sorry about the bed, it was the only one we could find within our price range. I have a queen-sized one, and we can swap them over if you like? I really should have thought of that before. I guess I just forgot how big you were and now that you're here—"

"Ana?"

"Yeah?"

"Shut up. Everything's perfect," I say and then realise that doesn't even begin to cut it. I take a step toward her. "You're perfect."

She backs out of reach. "Well, I should see about dinner. You probably felt like a quiet night alone, but my family doesn't really do quiet. Ever, actually. So everyone is coming around for a BBQ a bit later. Surprise." She throws her hands up and turns to leave.

"We gonna talk about this?"

"Talk about what?"

I raise my brow at that, and she steps back into the room and sits down on the bed, my bed. "You know, I haven't had one of these since I was sixteen."

"A bed?" she asks, as I sit down beside her.

"A bed, a room, a home." I flop back onto the mattress and rest my hands on my chest. "My dad had a room at the clubhouse. After I went to juvie he sold the house. I wasn't there anymore, and he hardly ever stayed there as it was. I think it just held too many memories of Mum and Lil, so he sold it. Sold all my shit, too. When I got out of lock-up the first time, the club came calling. I became a prospect, and prospects don't amount to shit until they're patched in, so I stayed on a clubhouse couch for the next year. Then I spent three years on the inside and after I got out, I roamed from one shitty motel to another, until now. Until you."

"Well I'm glad you have a room—a home, now," she says, and her voice cracks a little on the last word. Ana sat there, stiff as a board, throughout that story. She's so different now. We're different now. I grab her elbow and yank her back so she's lying beside me, her arm flush with mine. She lets out a frustrated yelp that quickly turns into tears. For a moment I just let her cry, because though I hate the idea of her hurting, I know she has to work through everything she's feeling with me being back.

When I can't handle the silence any more, I link my hand with hers and say, "Talk to me, baby girl."

"I can't."

"'Course you can." I nudge. "If there's one person in the world you *can* talk to about this it's me."

"I can't fall back into things with you," she blurts, and I'm glad we're not facing one another because that hurt like a motherfucker and I'm sure it's written all over my face.

"Can't now? Or can't ever?"

"I don't know," she whispers, like saying those words quietly is going to hurt me any fucking less.

"You still love me?"

"I don't know that either." She gets up and walks over to the door. The tears are openly streaming down her face now. She makes no move to wipe them away, she just stares at me from the doorway. "I'm sorry."

"Yeah, me too," I say.

Ana walks the few steps into her bedroom and closes the door. Her gut-wrenching sobs are all I can hear. It tears and claws at something inside me, but I make no move to go to her. Right now I'm not what she needs, and that hurts more than hearing her say the words that ripped my heart into shreds.

As good as it'd been to see Ana's family again I breathed a sigh of relief when the door closed behind them and the last dish had been wiped and put away. Bob was giving me a week off before he wanted me back at work. I should have been grateful, but all I felt was frustration that I'd be sitting around playing with my cock until I could get under the hood of a car.

Now, Ana and I sit side by side on the couch, watching some shitty reality show about bogan Brits who should all be banned from fucking one another to spare the human race from having to deal with their fuck-knuckle spawn. The temptation to pull her into me is so great I curl my hands into fists and allow the bite of my nails to sting my calloused palm and chase that thought away. I can't be thinking shit like that or I'm gonna fuck this up and wind up not having her be a part of my life, even if it's not the part I want.

In prison, it's not just pussy a man craves, it's the peace, the connection that touching another person brings. It grounds and centres, makes us whole where we might've been incomplete. Right now, I'm so fucking incomplete I feel like a man on death row.

Ana yawns, bringing my attention back to her. She lays her head back against the couch. Her feet are tucked away under her body and she looks so damn fuckable with her hair all dishevelled and her make-up smeared.

"You wanna go to bed?" I ask her, and I swear I meant that to be an innocent question. Maybe it's the way I'm watching her, maybe it's the two Stolis she had with dinner, or maybe it's the fact that I want more than anything to know that keeping our distance from one another is as hard for her as it is for me, but a small frown turns down the corner of her lip and I think I see the crease form in between her brows, the way it does when she's about to cry.

She rises and heads towards the hall. "Good night, Elijah."

"Night," I mutter, hating myself for constantly making her cry.

"Welcome home," she says, and then she's gone.

Home. I'm beginning to think that word isn't worth shit.

I sit bolt upright in bed. For a half second I forget where I am, and think the screaming across the hall is just another inmate seeking attention. But I know that shriek, and it's a sound I hoped to never hear again. I jump out of bed and push open the door to the room opposite mine.

Ana thrashes on the mattress. Her blankets are pulled tight around her, restraining her, and she's whimpering in her sleep.

"No!" she cries. "Get off me!"

I race over to the bed and untangle her limbs, which may have been a piss-poor decision on my behalf because she lashes out and punches me square in the jaw. She's sobbing and screaming, and I'm wondering how the hell she hasn't woken the whole house.

I don't bother trying to restrain her. I think that may only make things worse, so instead I sit on the edge of the bed and gently shake her shoulder while calling her name. She lunges upright with a gasp and lashes out at me again. I don't fight her, I just sit there and let her beat on me until she comes to enough to realise that I'm not him. When it does finally dawn on her, she lets out a wounded, sobbing cry that tears me all to pieces.

"You're okay, baby girl. You're safe." I fold her up in my arms and she clings tightly to me, tucking herself in against my chest. I'm buck-naked and she's wearing only a pair of cotton knickers and a singlet top, but none of that matters. The only thing I feel right now is love and hurt and helplessness that I wasn't there to save her that night. But I'd willingly spend all of my nights awake in bed with her body wrapped around me until she fell asleep if it meant she felt safe in my arms.

Safe with me

ANA

I woke this morning feeling lighter than I have in months. For the first time since the rape I've slept the whole night through, which makes me ecstatic and gives me the hope that maybe I'm slowly coming to terms with it. I'll never be able to erase it, or wash it out like I would a stain, but I might finally be able to look in the mirror and not blame myself.

Of course, the downside to being nightmare free is that, for the first time since Elijah moved in two weeks ago, I woke up this morning alone. And I actually kind of missed him—though waking up to a naked man who's tenting the sheets with his morning wood has been increasingly awkward and impossible to ignore. I'll never admit it, but I'll miss the way he held me in the middle of the night, and not just because he was the only one who could chase the nightmares away.

Holly has been bugging me to make my special macadamia pancakes for weeks now and, thanks to the public holiday on Monday, I don't have to spend my entire day slaving over a hot stove so I've decided to give her what she wants. She's always been a tad bit demanding, but pregnancy seems to have pushed her over the edge and into homicidal maniac territory. If I didn't know that was Coop's baby turning her into a crazy person, I'd think it was the second coming of Satan.

After having Holly buzz around me like an over-excited kid as I pulled together ingredients and a mixing bowl and turned my skillet on to preheat, I headed down the hall to see if Elijah's awake and ready to eat. I knock but don't really wait for a reply before opening the door, partly because I'm not thinking clearly this early in the morning, and partly because I'm sure he's still dead to the world. But when I walk into the room I see it's not sleep that Elijah is immersed in, it's something entirely different.

His overly large body is buck-naked and stretched out on top of the doona, and the muscles in his chest and arms are straining as he pumps his fist up and down his shaft. I know I should look away, I should walk out and quietly close the door behind me, but I can't. Has there ever been a more magnificent sight then a man pleasuring himself? If so, then I haven't seen it. This is not the first time I've witnessed Elijah touching himself, but it is the first time I shouldn't be allowed to watch. He's not aware he has an audience—not that I think he'd mind if he was made aware of it, but it's the principle that counts here. I shouldn't be watching because he's not mine anymore and this sight, as glorious as it is, is not mine to see because I gave up that privilege when I told him we couldn't be together.

It's at the exact moment, when I decide to leave quietly, that he opens his eyes, rolls his head toward me and says, "You just gonna stand there, baby girl, or are you gonna join in?"

"I didn't know you were … I am so sorry," I blurt and grab for the doorknob behind me.

He slows his stroking and looks me dead in the eyes. "I'm not."

I swallow hard. "I'm just going to go now. So, have fun. I mean, enjoy your … bye."

I'm just about to slink from the room like a dog with its tail between its legs when he whispers, "Stay."

"I shouldn't."

"You shouldn't be entering my room without knocking either, but you still did and here we are."

"I did knock," I mutter. "I just didn't wait for a response … I really should go."

"You should, but you won't," he says with certainty, and begins stroking himself again, faster this time.

He's right. A hurricane couldn't tear me from that room. I lean my weight back into the door and ignore the humming sensation between my legs that quickly turns electric. His hand glides up and down over his length, and he makes no effort to pretend he's not staring at me. And why should he, when I'm clearly eye-raping him?

"Take off your clothes."

The hint of a smile pushes at my lips, despite the fact that I know we're walking on dangerous ground. "No."

"Please?" he grunts.

"Come on, Cade, you and me, naked in a room together? That spells disaster."

"No, baby, that spells fucking incredible sex." He moans and his eyes glaze over. I don't know how he hasn't come yet. I'm ready to explode from watching him alone. "Please, Ana, don't make me beg. Just this once, let me come while I'm looking at that fuckable little body. I won't touch, I swear. Please, just let me see you and then we'll pretend this never happened."

Maybe it's the pleading in his voice or maybe I've just lost my ever-loving mind, but whatever the case, I find myself slowly peeling off my singlet top. I let it fall away to expose my breasts. My nipples harden into peaks and I can practically feel his tongue gliding over them as he wets his lips, though I'm still standing several feet away.

"Pants too, baby, don't cheat me outta seeing that beautiful fucking pussy," he commands, and I hesitate with my hands on the elastic waist of my PJs. I'm not sure I'm entirely ready for something like this.

"No," I whisper.

"Ana," he warns.

"No. This is as far as this goes," I whisper, afraid I'll break the spell. Afraid to walk away and more afraid to stay. "I don't trust either of us with any more than that."

"You drive me fucking crazy, you know that?"

"The feeling's mutual, Cade."

He lets out a long sigh and begins stroking again. One hand cups his balls and his eyes never leave my body as he drives himself closer to orgasm. My heart kicks into overdrive, my head is spins and my body screams out for his touch, but I don't do anything more than lean against the door with my breasts exposed as I watch the single most erotic scene I've ever witnessed. I don't know what I'm doing here and yet I can't turn away. My heart feels as though it's cracking open.

"Touch yourself," he commands.

"No."

"Come closer."

I shake my head. "No."

"Fuck! Why is it always no with you?"

"Because I don't trust myself with you." There. I said it. It's a dangerous admission, especially in a situation like this, but I said it all the same, and oddly enough the sense of relief I feel is overwhelming.

As if in retaliation, Elijah quickens his pace. His hands on his body are no longer languid but almost punishing. He's brutalising himself as penance, and I don't know if it's meant solely for him, or me, or for the both of us.

His eyes lock with mine as the first wave of pleasure rocks through him and that's exactly where they stay until his creamy semen spurts from his cock all over the bed. As Elijah rides out the euphoria I swiftly throw on my shirt and then I quietly creep out the door, the way I should have before I let it get this far.

Have I just ruined everything by allowing that to happen? And what exactly did just happen? God, I really have to learn to knock.

I lean against the door for a beat until I hear Holly calling out about wanting her pancakes, so I quietly tread up the hallway and head into the kitchen like nothing has happened.

"Oh my god, what took you so long? Mini Coop just about shrivelled up and died of hunger waiting for you to get back."

"Sorry, I had to go to the bathroom."

"Well, is he joining us? Because if not I am so eating his share," Holly asks and then narrows her eyes on me as she glances between my clothing and face. Her mouth gapes open as her eyes zero in on something. I follow her gaze and realise that, in my haste to leave

Elijah's room, I've put my singlet on inside out. "Oh my god! Did you? Did he? Did the two of you finally bump uglies?"

"Will you keep your voice down, please?" I slip it off and turn it the right way out before Jack comes running to find out what all the fuss is about and draws the same conclusions as Holly. In fact, why stop at just my housemates? Why not have a giant neon sign made up that says I'm a dirty slut who takes her clothes off so her ex-boyfriend can get a glimpse at the goodies as he jerks off, so the whole town can see it? Oh, right, the town already thinks I'm a slut, so I guess I can probably save my money and forgo the sign.

"No. I did not have sex with him." I go about throwing my ingredients into the bowl and mixing up the batter.

Holly folds her arms over and chest and arches a brow. "Then why does your sweet little face look so goddamn guilty, Ana?"

"Because I might have done something I shouldn't have." I glance down at the mixture and sigh. "Now can we please stop talking about this?"

As usual, Holly ignores me. "Hell no! I want details, what did you do?"

"I walked in on him."

"You walked in on him?" She frowns. "Walked in on him what?"

"You know," I say and give her the wide-eyed head nod that comes with letting someone fill in the blanks.

Holly's mouth forms an "O" and she slaps me hard on the arm. I flinch and take a step away from her. "Holy shit, did you walk in on him jerking his chain?"

Someone clears their throat behind us and I spin around to find Elijah leaning against the refrigerator in only a pair of faded old jeans. His buzzed hair is still damp from his shower and with all that ink and muscle on display he's every bit as enticing as he was in his room just moments ago.

"Mornin'." His eyes meet mine, and heat claws at my cheeks because for the second time today I just got sprung ogling him from head to toe.

Holly chuckles and I tear my gaze away from Elijah to look at my best friend. She smirks as she gives him a once over. "And what a glorious morning it is."

I turn back to my pancake batter and whisper in an aside, "Would you please stop referring to his morning glory?"

"That it is," Elijah says, and I know without even having to look at him that the smug smile is back on his face. "A perfect morning, in fact."

Twenty minutes later, we're all sitting around our kitchen table eating pancakes. I look at my flatmates and think that we may be an unconventional family and we might fight and scream and yes, admittedly some of us might want to tear one another's clothes off from time to time, but we are just that—a family. And I wouldn't change that for the world.

Elijah's eyes lock with mine across the table, and instead of seeing the intense heat he's been spearing me with all morning, I see them soften in a silent question; are we okay? I smile back at him. It's not seductive, coy or even playful; it's the kind of smile I've been giving Holly since the day we met. It's the same smile I give Jack when he says something so unbelievably stupid that I burst out laughing. The same smile I give Sammy when he gets the green light to leave the bench and join the game in rugby. And the same smile I give to my dad when he's being a pigheaded, bull of a man who suddenly quits yelling and guffaws out loud mid-sentence because he can see what a shit he's being.

It's love in its purest and unsullied form, without desire and sex and greed and complication. It's just love.

Are we okay?

We're better than okay.

We're home.

ELIJAH

Christmas morning I'd been woken just after six by two girls bouncing around half naked on my bed. No, it's not as naughty as it sounds, and yes, do I ever wish it had been. Ana and Holly had been like little kids, giggling, jumping up and down and screaming that Santa had come while we'd slept.

I'd mumbled some half-arse reply about him coming again if they kept jumping around in their underwear and they'd laid into me with their tiny fists of fury. Which, surprisingly, had hurt more than it should have. Then they'd dragged me and Jackson out to the living room to exchange gifts under the tree with bleary eyes and hangovers from hell.

We'd all gone a little nuts this year, pooling our money together to buy one another gifts. Ana had been harping on for ages about buying herself some overpriced fancy electric beater, and I'd gone with Holly earlier in the week to pick one out. She'd been over the freaking moon when she unwrapped that sucker and Holly had already requested a long list of baked goods to come from it.

I had something else small for her, but I wanted to wait until we were alone before I gave it to her. It wasn't much, but it meant the world to me, and I hoped it would mean the same for her, too.

Holly had been given a new car stereo, which we'd fitted last night, but the excitement she'd felt over that little piece of machinery was swallowed completely when Jackson hurried off to his room to get "something" and came back pushing a baby cot he'd made and painted himself.

Jackson got a new toolkit and I was the proud new owner of a bottle of Blue Label Johnnie Walker. Best fucking Christmas I ever had, and the sun hadn't even risen properly yet.

Now, I groan and sit back in my seat, waiting for the food coma to take me under. While the rest of us had gone back to bed, Ana had been dashing around the kitchen like a blue-arsed fly. She'd made Christmas lunch for the whole family and still managed to look like a fucking goddess in her little white cherry dress.

Sammy's sitting beside me shoving asparagus spears up his nose and pretending to be a walrus. Fuck, I love that kid. He's like six-year-old me with ADHD. He shoots one of the veggies out of his nose and giggles hysterically, and then from out of nowhere he turns to me and asks, "Hey Lijhie, do you and Ana Cabana thleep in the thame bed?"

I choke on my beer. How to answer this one without having Bob cave my head in with his meaty fist? "Er …"

"Sammy!" Ana chastises.

Holly's laughing her pregnant arse off. Jackson's shaking his head and Bob's turned white as a sheet. He's been eyeing me suspiciously from the head of the table throughout the entire meal, probably because I've been staring at Ana like I want to put her over my knee and spank her for making my naughty list this year. I feel my mouth tip up in a crooked smile as Ana's apologetic gaze meets mine.

"What? I wath just athking if you guyth ever have thleepoverth. When I'm growd up I'm gonna have thleepoverth wif girlth all the time."

I bump my fist with his tiny one and say, "I don't doubt that at all, little man."

"Please do not encourage him. The women of Sugartown are still recovering from you two—" Ana points to me and Jack "—they're definitely not ready for Sam Belle."

I laugh. "You just stick with me, mate. When you're old enough, I'll teach you everything I know."

"And the women will run away screaming," Holly deadpans.

"Ah," I grin. "But it's what they're screaming that counts."

Ana shoots up out of her chair. "Who wants dessert?"

Everyone mutters their approval and Ana hurries off to the kitchen. I follow after her. Despite the fact that it's thirty-four degrees outside, she pulls a couple of pies out of the oven and places them on the bench.

"Holy shit, that smells amazing," I say, breathing in the sweet, homey smell of caramel, pecans and pie crust. "Need some help?"

She just glares at me, so I get to work pulling out bowls and cutlery and the ice-cream from the freezer. As she serves, she sings along to some folky, sweet-sounding song playing from the stereo— thank fuck it's not Christmassy—and she sounds terrible. Kinda like a cat in heat, but when I look over she's swaying her hips in a way that makes me want to dance with her. I don't. Because I'm an Aussie bloke and we don't fucking dance. Ever. But that doesn't stop me from fantasising about sliding my hands from her waist to her sexy-as-fuck full hips and down to her completely fuckable arse and back up again.

I move closer and she glances up at me. I half expect her to rim me out for not helping but there's a hint of curiosity in her gaze. "I have something for you."

"For me?"

I nod. "It's my real gift to you."

She arches her brow and twists her lips into a disapproving frown, like she expects me to whip out my cock and dangle it before her. "Okay, I so do not have time for this."

"Get your mind out of the gutter, dirty girl," I tease and then I make out like I'm going to kiss her as I lean over and hook my hands behind her neck. It takes some effort to get the tiny clasp to open and then close on account of my giant hands, but eventually the necklace complies and I let its weight fall and rest against her chest. I step back and allow her to take in her new gift.

A tiny golden swallow rests on a gold chain, just above the line of her cleavage. It's just as perfect on her as it was on its previous owner—maybe more perfect, and seeing it again on someone so beautiful makes me smile like the cat that didn't just get the cream, he got the whole fucking carton.

Ana runs her fingers over the swallow and tests its weight in her hand. "It's beautiful."

"It was Lil's. It's been taped under the seat of my bike since she died. I had a jeweller clean it up and fit it with a new chain a couple weeks back."

She shakes her head. "I can't accept this."

"Yeah, you can."

"No, Elijah, it was your sister's. It's all you have left of her. I can't take that away from you."

I ignore all this. It suits her, and I'd rather see someone as perfect as her wearing it than know it was collecting dirt and dust under my bike. Lil would want that, too. Lil would have loved Ana. She would have idolised her, the same way Sammy idolises me. Hell, one look at Ana and Lil would have asked if she could swap siblings. "You know what they mean?"

She shakes her head, no.

"Love, freedom." I stick my hand out in front of her and turn my palm up, then I trace my finger around a tiny shape beside the reaper, hidden amongst the rest of my tattoo sleeve. It's Lil's swallow. Ana's swallow, now, I guess. Maybe that tattoo was always intended for her and I just didn't know it. "Loyalty. A swallow represents the loyalty of a person always returning to them. I'll always return to you, Ana. There's never been anyone else for me."

Ana stares up at me, all doe eyes and sad smiles, but there's something else in her expression, too, and it's as clear as the day is fucking hot. She wants me. Right here, in this moment, Ana Belle wants to fuck my brains out. It doesn't change anything, though. She still won't allow herself to give into it and I won't push it upon her because she's not ready yet, and when I do finally get that woman beneath me I won't ever be giving her up. Not even if she begs me to.

I pull her in and place a soft kiss to her lips. I hadn't meant to linger there, but her mouth is so god damned inviting and she doesn't push me off, so I take the opportunity to draw out the moment I've stolen. I don't force my tongue down her throat, it never even leaves my mouth, but there's heat all the same because our eyes are open and neither one of us is walking away.

"Ewww, dude," I hear Sammy whine behind us. He runs back to the dining room complaining, "Dad! Anath's thucking on Elijath's face again!"

I place once last kiss against her lips and then I saunter away, feeling satisfied. I'm probably about to be murdered by Ana's father in the next few minutes, but I don't care. Every second was worth it.

I'm halfway to the dining room when Ana says, "Elijah?"

"Yeah, babe?"

"I love it," she whispers and gives me a megawatt smile.

Best fucking Christmas ever.

ANA

"**H**urry up, bitches, or we're starting this lame-o movie without you," Holly yells from the lounge room. Elijah and I are in the kitchen; apparently we're the designated snack providers for our impromptu cinema night. I swear, sometimes being the only person that can cook in a household of constantly hungry boys and cranky pregnant women kinda sucks arse.

"Yeah, and don't forget the beer," Jack shouts.

"Popcorn and beer? That's disgusting!" I hear her say, and Jackson rattles off a list of reasons as to why 'that shit is the fucking bomb'. "My baby is crying right now inside of me, you know that, don't you? You're making him cry with your disgusting eating habits and then he's going to throw a tanty and start kicking my vagina and then I'll want to throw up all over you, so could you please, just for once, shut up? And where the heck is my chocolate milk? I had like, half a glass left."

I finish dusting the popcorn with icing sugar while Elijah fishes out two beers for himself and Jack. "You want one?"

"No thanks, could you grab me a Stoli though?"

"Uh-oh. You better tell me now if you're planning on getting so shitfaced you have to be carried to your room." He waggles his brows at me. "I'll go easy on the beer so I don't drop you."

"Very funny."

I grab the bowl of popcorn and head for the lounge. I'm halfway there when Holly yells, "Can you bring the chocolate milk, pretty please?"

I swing back and run smack bang into Elijah, who clearly wasn't watching where he was going because I'm pretty sure his eyes were firmly fixed on my bum.

"Shit. Sorry." He rights the bowl of popcorn before it falls from my hands, but not before several pieces fall and find a new home in my cleavage, which of course turns him into a drooling boob of a man—pun intended. "You've got popcorn … uh."

I fish the pieces from my bra and pop them in my mouth, then I push him back a step before heading over to the refrigerator. "Geez, Elijah, it's like you've never seen boobs before."

"I never seen boobs as perfect as that." He points to my chest with his stubbie and then takes a long pull while openly ogling my breasts.

I shake my head and retrieve Holly's milk from the fridge. I almost make it out of the kitchen before she yells, "Bring a glass too, Jackson drank from mine and I think he has cooties."

"You ever feel like we're running a hotel here?"

I let out a sigh. "With those two? Ha! More like we're running a daycare."

"You know that's actually a pretty apt description."

"Oh, like you can talk, Mr I-Go-Gaga-for-Boobies."

He shrugs. "They're nice boobies."

I roll my eyes and follow him into the lounge room. Holly and Jack are hunkering down on the couch. Despite sitting at opposite sides from one another, their legs stretch out in the middle of the sofa, leaving no room for anyone else. Elijah plonks himself down on the recliner and I shoot all three of them dirty looks.

"Where the heck do I sit?"

"Jackson, get up," Holly commands.

"I'm not getting up, you get up," Jack says, and shoves her foot with his.

"I'm pregnant! Besides, Ana's a woman. You're supposed to give up your seat to women and the elderly; it's the gentlemanly thing to do."

"Gentlemanly?" Jack smirks. "Since when do you care about gentlemen?"

"It's fine," I say impatiently. "I'll just sit on the floor."

"Sit with me," Elijah ventures.

"I'm not sitting with you."

He frowns. "Why not?"

"Because you're ... big, you hardly fit on that thing as it is."

"Fuck," my cousin groans. "You two are worse than a couple of tweeniebopper virgins trying to figure out where the condom goes. Just sit on him already and be done with it."

"Jackson!" I chide.

At the same time Holly pouts at him and says, "Hey, that's my line."

I'm thinking I might just forget this whole movie night thing and go to bed, but Elijah's looking all too sure of his ability to ruffle my feathers so I smile snidely and say in my most seductive voice, "Where do you want me?"

The cunning in his gaze is immediately replaced by desire, and I bite down hard on my lip. I shouldn't be flirting with him. It's cruel and wretched, and yet I can't seem to make myself stop. I don't *want* to stop. From the looks of it, Elijah doesn't want me to stop either, because the challenge is back in his eyes, the one that says he doesn't think I'll do it.

"Right here," he says and—surprise, surprise—he pats his lap.

It's just sitting on his lap for goodness sake, it's not like I haven't done it before, I think, and then that evil voice in my head helpfully supplies, *Only the last time we were completely without clothes and trying to get as close to one another as possible.*

Ignoring that judgemental bitch in my head, I casually stroll over and lower myself onto his lap. I'm only resting half my weight on him and the rest is on my knees and feet as I push them against the floorboards in an effort to ground me. Elijah's not happy with this arrangement, though. He wraps his arm around my waist and pulls me into the hollow created by his open legs. Before I can get my wits about me enough to move away, he pulls the lever for the footrest and I'm flung back against him in a reclining position.

The first thing I notice is his hard body pressing against my back. The heat and delicious all-male scent of him blurs my senses, forcing me to momentarily lose my mind and fall prey to how good it feels to be in his arms again.

The second thing I notice is that he's rock hard … everywhere. I try shifting away but he presses his large hand to my abdomen to secure me against him. I squirm in my seat, my breath labours and my knickers are soaking wet.

Elijah tilts his head so that his lips are pressed against my lobe. "Unless you want me to blow my load, baby girl, stop squirming and watch the movie," his words are low and hushed, but the authority in his tone causes goose bumps to break out all over my skin. They also cause a streaking bolt of alarm to shoot through me. Until now, I wasn't aware the movie *had* started, but Paris Hilton's plastic-fantastic face is plastered all over the screen and her friends have just made a gruesome discovery in the woods.

I glance around. The lights are off, Holly's eyes are growing heavy just a few minutes in, the popcorn's been demolished and Jackson's madly typing away on his phone.

I'm hyper aware of Elijah behind me, around me. It's intoxicating and frightening, all at once. I also don't think I've ever been this turned on—which, given that all my past sexual experiences, bar one, had included this man, is really saying something. Elijah knows exactly how to seduce me and he's certainly not pulling any punches. One hand is grasping the back of my neck with only the barest hint of pressure, just the way I like it. The other is splayed against my lower abdomen, his pinkie and ring fingers resting against my pubic bone and causing pleasure to arc between the gentle press of his hand and my core.

I hear him inhale and then whisper, "You smell so fucking edible, baby girl. I'm gonna die if I don't get to taste that sweet pussy of yours soon."

My breath leaves me in a rush that sounds an awful lot like a whimper. I hate that I can't control myself around him, that even as I sit here I've been turned into a whimpering ball of need and longing and he knows it. He knows just how to slink past all my defences and twist the knife deeper into my heart. It's the night outside the Sugartown Hotel all over again, only this time I'm the only one he's screwing over. And he's enjoying every second of it.

"Would you like that? My mouth on your beautiful cunt? Licking and sucking until you come screaming my name?"

Before I can think about the ramifications of what I'm doing I rock back into him and nod my head. *I shouldn't have done that,* I think. *I shouldn't be leading him on when this can go nowhere.* This man ripped my heart out a few short months ago. He broke me completely, he pissed on everything we had by keeping his dirty little secrets and tore whatever we had left apart by fucking another woman in front of me.

"Do you still love me?"

"I don't know."

Lies, lies, lies.

All of it.

If anything, our time apart has made me love him more, but I can't give myself over to him again. I let him take my heart once, but I won't let him take what's left of me.

"Jesus, babe, you're wound so tight," he murmurs against my neck and slides his hand inside my skirt. "Fuck me! And so wet, too. I'm gonna take care of this, baby girl, and then you and I are going to talk about this shit between us. Cause I'm not going another day without possessing you completely."

A quiet moan escapes my mouth as he teasingly strokes his fingers around my clit, careful not to actually touch it. I want to scream my frustration at him to stop playing games and make me come already but I don't, because the anticipation of being touched is just as good as the sensations produced when his hands actually connect with my flesh.

When they finally do make contact it's the sweetest kind of torture. It's been months since I've been touched like this, touched by him. His fingers feel like they're burning me as one slides inside, knuckle deep, while his thumb grazes back and forth across my clit. The pressure of his erection digs into my arse and I rock back into it until Elijah's hips are moving with mine. His fingers maintain their steady assault as we rock into one another, both chasing the release that the other is so willing to provide.

Elijah shifts his hand so that his palm is cupping my clit and his fingers are now touching the front wall of my vagina. He wiggles them back and forth and I practically come apart in his hands. I can feel my orgasm building, but all my previous experiences with the big "O" have never felt like this. His fingers aren't gentle as they push back and forth, but I couldn't care less. I'm not thinking about the room around me or the fact that I shouldn't be using him like this. All I care about is that he never stops.

I rock my hips back and forth in time with his fingers. He groans. "So fucking sweet, baby. I want you coming all over my hand."

And I do. I come hard and fast, and it's more intense than any orgasm I've ever felt before. It's wetter, too. So wet that my knickers and Elijah's hand are drenched. He doesn't seem to notice though, because he's busy losing himself in his own release. His free hand slides up my side and squeezes my breast, as his own orgasm rocks through him.

I lay back against him, exhaling loudly, breathing the same air, sticky and luxuriating in the feel of his arms and the saccharine sent of sex in the room. And then he eases his fingers out of me and I get a sense of just how wet we are.

I am beyond mortified. He just gave me the best orgasm of my life and I returned the favour by peeing on him. The embarrassment amps up a notch when I turn and see him licking his fingers clean of me.

"I'm so sorry," I blurt.

"I'm not. That was the hottest fucking thing I've ever experienced."

"I just peed on you." Elijah guffaws and I glance around, wondering where our roommates got to, though I don't really blame them for leaving. "Why is that funny? Where did Holly and Jack go?"

He gives me the smug smile, like he's over the freaking moon hearing me admit I was so distracted with him that I didn't notice our flatmates leaving. "They left about the time you started moaning. And that wasn't piss." He laughs again. "Fuck, baby, that was some of the hottest shit I've ever seen. I don't think I've ever been this hot for a woman after watching her come."

I'm completely confused and I'm probably staring at him like he's some fetishist freak who enjoys golden showers because he smiles like I'm a goddamn piglet that's so bloody endearing you can't help but want to pinch and coo to it. "That was your G spot, Ana. Oh, the things you have to learn about your body. Lucky for you, I'm a very hands-on teacher."

I haven't the foggiest idea of how to respond to that, so I push the lever on the side of the couch and the chair comes lurching upright. My heart is racing, and now that the afterglow is wearing off I realise what a colossal mistake I've just made. This could obliterate all the progress we've made toward being regular flatmates. To my peace of mind. To the fact that we've both tried our hardest to be civil and adult about living together and pretending like we're fine when our hearts are breaking. With ten minutes of touching, we've managed to destroy any hope we had at a normal friendship.

After the rape I stopped thinking about my wants and desires. I forgot that I was a young woman who needed to be loved, to be touched, just as I had been before. I focused on my family and my friends and began lovingly taping band-aids over their problems because they seemed so much bigger than mine when the reality was that my bandages had come undone, ripping and tearing off my skin, and I hadn't even noticed.

And now? Now, I noticed. I just had no idea how to put them in place again.

I unseat myself from his lap and head for the bathroom.

"Hey, where are you going?"

"I have to take a shower."

"I thought we were going to talk about this?"

"No. You said we were going to talk, I don't remember agreeing to anything."

"Like you didn't agree to coming just now?"

"Fuck you."

"What the fuck, Ana? Why are you fighting this so god damned hard?" he shouts and I spin around, stung by the harshness in his voice. "I can see how much you want me. I can feel it. Fuck me! I can't stand in the same room as you without feeling the longing seeping out of your pores, and yet you refuse to acknowledge that you're still in love with me." The surprise I feel at that last confession must be written all over my face because Elijah comes closer, until he's staring right down into my eyes and says, "Yeah, you can drop the fucking act, baby girl. I know how you feel about me, the question is, why don't you?"

"You need to stop pushing this. Stop pushing me!" I shout. "Yes, I still love you, but you tore my heart out, Elijah! You left me broken in a million fucking pieces! You don't get to be the one to put me back together."

I storm into the bathroom. Slamming the door behind me, I quickly undress and slip underneath the hot spray. I'm too numb to cry and, despite seeing myself shake like a leaf, I don't feel a thing, not the sting and burn of the water against my flesh and not the fresh wound gaping in my chest.

I let it go too far. I let him in again, I think, as I lean my head against the tile. My chest hurts, my head hurts. I'm made up of millions of tiny exposed nerves, all trembling and clamouring at once with the aftershock of being prodded by sharp implements. I'm raw. There's no other way to describe it. How many times can we do this to each other before we realise we're completely broken with no chance of ever being put back together?

I don't know how long I stand there, letting the water soak me to the bone, but sometime before it turns cold the shower door opens and Elijah steps in behind me. Slowly, I turn to face him. The spray soaks his clothes, his hair and face.

"Get out!"

"No," he says quietly. His eyes narrow with anger.

"Fine then, I'll get out."

"No. You won't," he says as he pushes me back against the tile. "You're not making this decision for us."

"Jesus Christ, Elijah, how many times do I have to push you away before you get a fucking clue? How many more times can you stomach hearing that I don't want you, that there is no more us?"

"Bullshit! The only reason we aren't together right now is because you're too fucking stubborn to admit how you feel, because it might mean being hurt again. Well guess what, baby girl, life is all about hurt. From the day we're born to the day we die, we fucking hurt and we cry and we pick ourselves up and, if we're really lucky, we have people to help us pick up the fucking pieces."

"You think I don't know this shit? You're not the only one who knows hurt, Elijah, so quit with your fucking world weary patronising."

"You know hurt, huh?" Elijah snaps. "Then why the hell are you putting us through more of the shit?"

I shove him up against the glass and clench my hands into fists to keep from scratching and clawing at him until there's nothing left. "You did this to us! Not me. I'm just trying to deal the best way I can. I'm trying to save myself from you, because if I give you what's left I'll have nothing leftover to pick up when you leave again." A sob tears free from my throat, and my hands thump at his chest while he holds me to him. "I hate you!"

"Don't hate me, Ana," he coos in my ear, and his voice is so soft and so full of hurt that it only makes me cry harder. "I love you. I'd go to fuckin' ground for you. I can't deal with this shit any more. For six months I waited in that hellhole and you never once came to visit, and then the day I'm released you show up like some fucking miracle, an angel who wants to give me a home and care for me like a stray puppy. But the funny thing about angels is you can't touch them, just like I'm not allowed to touch you, though I know you want me too as badly as I do. I need you, Ana. I'm fucking dying without you, baby."

"I don't have anything left!" I shout. "I gave you everything I had and you tore it all up. I can't allow you to do that again. I wouldn't be the girl you love if I let you destroy me again."

I try to push him away but he won't let up, and so he ends up clutching me to him in a vice grip while I cry and scream until all the hurt and tears and heartbreak just dissolve around us. We stay that way until the water runs cold, with him fully clothed and me stripped bare before him, and then I slide his arms from around my waist and pull him down to kiss his lips before I push open the shower door.

"You need to find somewhere else to live." My throat hurts from crying, my heart hurts from squeezing out those words, but it had to be said. We can't live like this anymore. Some things are just too broken to fix. "I'm sorry, but this is just too hard."

I wrap the towel around my chest and walk out, wishing it hadn't just felt like I left a piece of myself in that bathroom.

 ELIJAH

I've decided I'm going to have to kill Jackson in his sleep. After spending all day on the couch versing one another on Xbox he's killed me thirty-seven times in some random fighting game and nine times in *Race Pro.* There's only so much of a beating a man can take before his masculinity feels threatened. And therefore, Jackson Rowe must die.

I hear Ana pull up in the drive. She's been at work by herself all day on account of Holly being sick again. Jackson drove her to an appointment earlier in the morning and we haven't heard a peep out of her since. Bob hadn't opened the garage today because we've been having a dead week and he had some tax audit shit going on, so Jackson and I have put our time to good use by wasting an entire day playing video games.

I glance at the food wrappers lying on the coffee table and then over my shoulder into the kitchen where I can see dishes piled all along the bench. Shit, I should have taken care of that already. I should have made dinner or pulled out a fucking vacuum or something. God, I'm such a cunt. No wonder she wants me out.

Ana comes storming in the door. She's pissed, but that only gets worse when she sees the mess we've made. She closes her eyes, takes a deep breath and then turns without a word and stalks down the hall to her room, slamming the door firmly behind her.

"Mate, your woman is fucking pissed," Jackson grunts.

"She's not my woman," I grunt back.

"Come on, you really believe that shit?"

"There's nothing to believe. She wants me out of here."

Jackson laughs. "Jesus, you really are fucking clueless. She wants you alright, but it's got nothing to do with wanting you to move out. She's just scared."

I toss the controller on the couch beside me and give him a look like he doesn't know shit. "I don't know, man. You didn't see her when she told me to go. I think I broke her."

"Christ, do you not know anything about women? If she says she's broken, you get out your fucking araldite and glue that shit back together."

I shake my head and run a hand over my hair, wishing I had the length back so I could rake my hands through it properly when I'm frustrated as all shit. "I tried."

"Bullshit! If you'd tried, you be in there right now fucking your woman, not sitting out here bitching and moaning to me like a fucking pussy."

"Alright, I'm going. Keep your fucking knickers on."

Holly comes stumbling out of her room, looking all puffy and pregnant and like she could murder someone for a steak. I cock my head to the side as I watch her and then whisper to Jackson, "You gonna heed your own advice, Don Juan?"

He glances at Holly and a goofball smile breaks out across his face. He can pretend all he wants, but he's just as pussy whipped as I am. "That train wreck? Nah, I'm not into homicidal bitches."

"Right," I agree with a healthy dose of sarcasm. "'Cause that's what that face means."

"What face?" he protests as I walk away. "Dude, what face?"

I walk down the hall, a little afraid of what I might find. The woman I love is as mad as a cut snake, and I can't stand to see her angry or hurt unless I know I can fix it in some way.

I knock lightly on the door and hear her sniff before telling me to come in. She sighs when she sees me and says, "I'm not in the mood to fight right now, Elijah."

I hold up my hands in surrender. "Not here to fight. I come in peace." I pat down my pockets and find a fun-sized bag of M&M's

I'd stashed there earlier so Jackson didn't scoff them all down. They're probably a little warm, but chocolate's chocolate, and that's exactly what she craves when she's upset. I set the bag down on the end of the bed and she snatches it up and tears into it while she leans back against the headboard.

I climb onto the mattress beside her and lean my back against the bedhead, stretching out my legs. I'm so close that the heat from her side threatens to scorch me, but I don't touch her and she doesn't touch me. It hurts. It's awkward as fuck, but that's the way it has to be. "Now, you gonna tell me what's bringing you home in tears, or do I have to threaten to take away the chocolate?"

"I ran into Mrs Turner today."

My whole body stiffens and I have to clear my throat to get the words out. "Why didn't you call me?"

"Because you can't fight all my battles for me."

"Doesn't mean I don't want to," I whisper.

"I know," she says softly. "I had to deal with this on my own though. Can you believe that bitch actually blamed me for her son being in prison?"

"What did you say to that?" I ask, and even I can hear the quiet tremor of rage in my voice.

"I told her to go fuck herself." She laughs half-heartedly and then adds, "Then I asked her how it felt to raise a rapist, and whether she was proud of his fondness for virgins."

"Shit, baby girl, you got some lady balls, that's for sure. Remind me never to take you on again," I say and we both chuckle at that until the realisation of our last argument punches us in the face again and leaves us both speechless.

Ana tips out the last of the M&M's. She eats the remaining chocolate with the exception of one, which she places on her outstretched palm and offers it to me. When we were together she always did that. She'd eat the majority and offer me one tiny morsel, like it was the most important gift she could consider parting with, but I never minded because the taste of it on her lips was always sweeter than the lolly itself. I take it from her palm and pop it in my mouth.

We settle into the silence, both of us side by side and resting against her headboard until I can't take the weight of the hurt between us. "You should know I've been looking for somewhere to live. I'd go to the motel, but the smoke damage from their fire means they have to gut the entire place and start again and, funny enough, no one wants to rent to an ex-con. I'll find someplace and I'll make things right between us, it might just take a little longer than we wanted."

Ana's quiet as she chews that over and then she places her hand in my upturned palm and whispers, "Don't move out."

"I should," I mutter like I'm on autopilot. I don't want to go anywhere. I can't think of anything worse than not seeing her face every day, of not being able to touch her in passing and pretend like I was just reaching for the milk. I miss her like fucking crazy and I haven't even left yet.

"You should," she agrees and then adds, "but you won't."

I won't let myself believe she means that until I hear it directly from her lips. "You sure?"

"Yeah. If there's one thing you've taught me, Cade, it's that running solves nothing. It just hurts your feet in the long run."

I laugh. "Amen."

She rests her head on my shoulder and I tuck my arm around her waist. It's a force of habit but she's not making a big deal about it so I decide neither will I.

"Hey," I say, "I got that bottle of blue in my room, whaddya say we crack that sucker, order a pizza and drink away all the shit behind us? All our mistakes, all the hurt, all the shit we've waded through to get to this point, everything?"

"That actually sounds like a nice idea," she replies, and so we do. We hole up in her room with our old friend Johnnie and we eat and laugh and forget about all the hurt we've caused one another. We wipe the slate completely clean. I'd be lying if I said I didn't think about fucking her. I think about it at least a hundred times a day, and I could tell she was thinking about it too, but the point was that, for maybe the first time ever, we didn't give in to that physical shit that always seems to screw us over.

Sometime around two am she fell asleep in my arms and I tucked her under the covers and held her until I passed out.

That night I slept more soundly than I have in years.

 ANA

I rest my head against the edge of the tub and try to think about something else. I always knew this day was coming. I said I was fine with it, but I'm not fine at all. I'm furious. I want to ride around town until I find his bike and go and give his new fuck buddy a brand new face. Preferably one with my fist-print in it.

This is not the first time he's been out on a Friday night. The shop closed its doors hours ago, so I know he's not working late. The same time I pulled the diner door shut and flipped the sign around, Elijah had been jumping on his bike. He gave me a wave through the window and took off in the direction of home, but just like the last few times, he wasn't here when I pulled in the drive.

Jackson and Holly were getting ready to head to a movie when I walked in. They offered for me to come along, but I declined. No one wants to be a third wheel to a relationship as dysfunctional as theirs. I thought Elijah and I had it bad, but there just aren't words for how messed up those two are. So, instead of sitting through two hours of awkwardness, I decided to drown my sorrows in vanilla-scented bubble bath, only with Elijah out screwing around I wasn't feeling so damn relaxed. I was about ready to annihilate someone.

I hear the front door slam and begin thinking that maybe Jackson's said something to piss off Holly before they've even made it out of town. The lights are on and the bathroom door is closed, but I haven't bothered to lock it because I knew no one would be home before I'd begun pruning. I'm halfway considering standing up and scooting out of the bath to flip the lock in case an axe murder's just walked through my front door when the bathroom door flings back on its hinges and Elijah comes striding in, angrier than a red-bellied black snake. He immediately begins toeing off his boots and socks. His back is to me as he lifts his shirt over his head and he hasn't even noticed that the room is otherwise occupied.

I'm torn between watching the show and stopping him from shedding his remaining clothing when a cough sneaks out my throat, spoiling all my fun.

Elijah whirls around. "Shit, I'm sorry. I thought you were out."

"Is that why you're in such a bad mood, or did your Girl Friday call and cancel your date?"

"Girl Friday?" he asks, and both his dimples pop out as if he finds this hilarious. He holds his hand against his chest—which I guess isn't all that odd, considering I did just scare him half to death—but there's a clear plastic film peeking out from behind his large palm.

"Did you hurt yourself?" I nod towards his chest.

"Yeah," he mutters, and I'm not sure if it's to himself or if he's speaking the words to me because he drinks in my body with a pained expression. I know he can't see much on account of the half bottle of bubble bath I poured into the water but that clearly doesn't stop his mind from wandering. I know because I can see it in the way his eyes glaze with desire.

"What did you do?"

He frowns. "What?"

"The bandage?" I ask. "What did you do?"

Elijah shakes his head, "Nah, it's … nothing—a scratch."

"You want me to take a look at it?"

"No," he says quickly, pressing his hand tighter to the plastic covering. "Where's Jack and Holly?

"He took her cranky, pregnant arse out to a movie."

"Like a date?" Elijah's brows knit together.

"Honestly? I don't know." I shrug and the bubbles swirl around me. Elijah's gaze follows their movement. He wets his lips. "I don't ask any more. Holly and Jack are complicated."

"Well, if anyone knows complicated, it's you and me." He laughs and runs his free hand over the back of his neck and up to his hair, which I think he's growing out again after I'd consumed half a bottle of Johnnie Walker and told him women like something to hold onto when they come.

"True." I smile up at him.

"I'll, ah … I'll leave you to it," Elijah says and turns to leave.

"You can take a shower if you want to. It's nothing either of us hasn't seen before."

His Adam's apple bobs. "Maybe so, but that doesn't mean I'll have the restraint to keep my eyes from wandering and my hands to myself."

I roll my eyes. "Elijah, take a goddamn shower."

"Alright, if you insist," he says, and makes a move to undo his jeans but catches me staring and straightens up. "You keep looking at me like you want a taste, baby girl, and I'm not gonna lie, I'm gonna let you have it."

My gaze shoots up to his smouldering one and I quickly avert my eyes. "Sorry. Old habits die hard, I guess."

"Yeah, no shit," he replies as his eyes trail over my pink flesh. He breathes deeply and turns around to remove his jeans and the plastic bandage and slips into the spray of the shower, which is situated directly in my line of sight. The clear glass does nothing to hinder my view of the hot water cascading down over Elijah's perfect bum. He keeps his body turned away from me as he lathers and rinses and then he stands beneath the spray with his hands against the tile and his head bowed.

I could live a thousand lives and never forget the way he looks, the way it feels when his large, powerful body engulfs mine, the way I feel about him. All of him. Not just the good, but the bad too. I miss his hands on my body, I miss his mouth claiming mine with his own. I miss touching him and being touched and for once, my need to be claimed by him, completely, overrides the caution I have in my heart.

The desire to touch him is so great I don't give myself a chance to second guess it as I quietly rise from the water and pad over to the shower. Opening the door, I step into the steam filled cubicle covered neck to toes in bubbles.

Elijah's shoulders stiffen, his head rises and he slowly turns to face me.

"Ana?"

Shock quickly turns to desire as his eyes slide over me and he wets his lips like he wants a taste too. I place my hands on his chest and push him back against the tiles. He rests his too-large hand over mine and holds it to his chest. The skin beneath my palm feels hot and slightly raised. I begin to pull my hand away but he pushes it harder against his flesh, as if he doesn't want me to see.

"Let me look," I say and when he shakes his head no, I plead.

Elijah closes his eyes and removes his hand. On his left pectoral is a new tattoo. Where there used to be a gothic graveyard scene with his sister's name now sits an intricate antique-looking compass emblazoned right over his heart, but instead of sporting the traditional North, East, South, West icons a simple cursive A is written at each of the compass points. Beneath it are the words: "Conscience is a Man's Compass".

Holy shit! Was he saying that I was his moral compass?

I tear my eyes off the beautiful tattoo—and it is beautiful, not just the sentiment behind it but the artwork, too. "When did you get this?"

"I had the last of it retouched tonight. I shouldn't be showering right now, but I needed it after work." He looks down at me, as if he's expecting me to freak out. Instead I trace my fingers over the lettering with a wistful smile. "You didn't wonder where I was going every couple of weeks?"

"I wondered. I just didn't think it was my place to ask."

"Ana, there isn't a single thing you could ask of me that I would refuse." He smiles and my heart just about leaps out of my chest. "But you already knew that, didn't you?"

I didn't actually, but I don't doubt his sincerity now as he says it.

"I love you," I blurt out, and for the first time, I feel vulnerable telling him that. Since he got out all I've done is try to shove him into a box he never fit in to begin with. Elijah was never my friend. Someone that you love and desire that much could never be just a friend. It was stupid of me to believe we could be anything less than this.

"I know," he says, and his face lights up with the admission. He brings his lips down on mine and lifts me so that I have no choice but to wrap my legs around his waist. I can feel the length of him pressed against my belly and it starts a heat unfurling again in my core, seeking him out, calling out to the fire within him.

"I want inside you so fucking bad, baby."

"I want that, too. I'm just … scared," I whisper.

Elijah cocks his head back to look at me. "Of me?"

I shake my head. "Of the pain. I'm terrified, actually."

"I promise you, baby girl, it's not going to hurt. I'm gonna kiss you all over and then I'm going to eat you out until you're screaming my name, and then I'm going to do what I should have done the day we met and make that beautiful pussy mine." He grasps the nape of my neck, and kisses the spot below my ear that drives me crazy. "Okay?"

His lips keep up their wonderful assault on me and I can only nod my acquiescence, as he shuts the water off and carries me into my bedroom without bothering to dry us off.

He lays me down on the bed and envelops my body with his. Elijah's lips cover mine, his tongue gently coaxing. There's none of the brutality that usually comes with the two of us clawing at one another in an effort to get closer, and I think I understand why now. Because now there's nothing between us, there's nothing holding us back, all our cards have been laid on the table and there are no more secrets. There's also no more fear. Just love and desire and an aching need to fill one another up.

Elijah intensifies the kiss and I fall willingly into him, into moulding my body to his. His heartbeat echoes my own, a steady pounding rhythm that reverberates throughout my entire body and centres itself in my core.

I moan into his mouth. He pulls away to study my face, his big hands smooth the hair back from my head and he places a gentle kiss to my nose before trailing his lips and tongue from my throat to my breasts. He sucks a nipple into his mouth. Pleasure arcs through me. I moan. Elijah's breath is hot against my wet flesh. "You like that baby girl?"

I nod. "I love anything that involves your mouth."

"Well, isn't that a nice coincidence? I fucking love using my mouth," he chuckles, and glides his tongue down my ribs and across my stomach. His mouth rests over my pubic bone where he places a series of gentle kisses before darting his tongue out to tease my hot flesh. He settles himself between my legs and gently licks and sucks all around my lips, avoiding the one spot where I need to have him.

"Please, Elijah?" I beg, "I need to feel you on me."

He groans and lowers his head to my mound, gently prying apart my lips. His eyes meet mine up the length of my body. "I'm gonna take real good care of you, baby girl."

He laps at my clit and I feel my insides quicken. Gently, he eases one finger inside and then another, and begins working them the way he did that night in the lounge room and my brain goes into meltdown, though the desperate need to come is suddenly replaced with the urgency of having more of him inside me, around me, driving us both toward release.

"Elijah please?" I beg, unable to stand the wait any longer. I've been waiting for this moment since the day we met, and now that he finally gets a green light he wants to dick around? "I can't wait any longer. I need to feel you inside me."

"Fuck me, Ana," he groans. Climbing up my body, he rests between my legs. His cock butts up against my slick flesh. I ache with need, from the tips of my toes to the roots of my hair. "Do you have any idea what you do to me when you beg?"

I smile because I know exactly what it does to him, and he smiles back because he knows that I know.

"You drive me fucking crazy, you know that, right?" he asks, but it's said with such reverence that tears sting my eyes.

"I love you, too," I whisper.

Elijah smiles down at me with this huge goofy grin that quickly turns into a pained expression as I push myself closer and gently rock my hips against his. "Don't suppose you have a condom in here?"

"No." I stop moving and frown. "You don't have any in your room?"

"Well, no, considering the one woman I want to bury myself deep inside rejected me. I haven't needed to use one since ..." he peters off, and I know we're both thinking the same thing—the night he fucked Nicole. I wait for the anger, the burning hurt that usually overcomes me when I think of that night, but it doesn't boil over the way it used to. We both made mistakes, terrible, stupid mistakes, and they led us here.

"I'm on the pill," I say breathlessly.

He narrows his eyes. "Since when?"

"Since Holly got pregnant, and no I'm not sleeping with anyone either. I just thought it would be a good idea in case what happened with Scott happens again. It's one less thing to worry about."

"It's never gonna happen again, you hear me? I'm never gonna let you outta my sight," he says with such vehemence that I swear my heart swells ten times its regular size. "I should have been with you that night. I—" I place my hand over his mouth and he frowns down at me.

"I don't want to talk about that." I wait for him to nod before I take my hand away. "I don't want to talk, I just want to feel you."

"Yes ma'am." He smiles and lowers himself over me again. Taking his cock in his hand, he glides it through my wetness from front to back. I'm almost giddy with anticipation, but a small part of me is scared shitless, too. I know that Elijah would rather die than hurt me and I trust him implicitly, I just have to learn to trust that I'm safe in his hands.

I feel him press against my opening and gently edge his way in. He can't have gotten very far when I feel my muscles clench around him, tightening to prevent him from entering me. I'm catapulted back to that night in the cane field when Scott shoved his way inside me, when he brutalised me. I close my eyes, willing it away, wishing I could concentrate on the here and now, wishing there was some way to forget.

"Hey, you okay?" Elijah asks in a gentle voice that just about shatters me from the inside out. Tears roll down my cheeks and he kisses them away. "You need me to stop?"

I shake my head, even as my mind and body are both screaming for me to run. *God, I'm such a fuck up.* I'm much too psychologically damaged for someone like Elijah. He's a man who clearly likes to fuck women and I'm a broken little girl who can't even crawl outside of my own head long enough to allow myself this one shot at happiness.

"Ana, look at me," he commands. "I love you, baby girl. So fucking much. It's just you and me here, we got this, baby. If you tell me to stop, I stop. Anything you want, it's yours. Just let me do this, let me take care of you and we'll erase him together. We'll erase every bad memory, every nightmare, every second you've thought about it since. We'll do it together, okay?"

I swallow hard and nod my head. There's no point searching for words because all my senses are jumbled up and I feel hurt and raw and I'm afraid if I open my mouth I'll start bawling and I won't stop, so instead I take a deep breath and relax my body enough to allow Elijah to push in a little further. He shifts his weight and snakes his hand between us, teasing my clit with his fingertips, coaxing me to open further for him. He slips the rest of the way inside, until I feel him hitting the end of me.

I'm not met with blinding pain like I expected to be. Instead, I'm met with hardness and heat and the delicious ache of him stretching me. His fingers keep up their ministrations and heat unfurls inside me, burning me up from the insides until all the world is a flame. I moan with the intense pleasure, the newness of it all, and then, when he starts to gently thrust inside me, I lose my ever-loving mind.

"You're so fucking perfect, Ana," Elijah whispers in my ear as he moves into a steady rhythm inside me. "So tight and so fucking beautiful it hurts."

My orgasm builds within me to a point where it hurts to stave it off, but I don't want to come without him, so I try my best to bring myself back down into our own stratosphere. Elijah thrusts, harder, faster and I bite down hard on my lip; it stings but it's all I can do to keep me grounded.

"Don't hold back, baby girl," Elijah grunts. "Come for me, I wanna hear you scream my name as you squeeze my cock."

I do. I let go of everything. Every hurt I ever caused him, of every time he made me cry, of everything that Scott did to me and everything that's happened since. I let it go as I'm catapulted into sensation and I cry his name over and over as he pumps into me and my orgasm rocks through my body.

"Fucking incredible," he whispers in my ear. I don't have a response, I'm too raw, too strung out on sensation, too overwhelmed. I'm feather-light, weightless, limbless, and boneless. I ache all over, but still I want more. Elijah shifts and places, his hands under my arse, lifting me so that we're both sitting upright, my legs wrapped around his waist. I grind my hips against his as he rocks into me.

"My turn," he whispers as he tightens his arms around my waist, pulling me as close as he can. I wrap my arms around his shoulders and we rock into one another slowly, delighting in sensation and the unhurried heat of pleasure building inside. When I think he's close I slip my hand between us and circle my fingers around my clit the way he does.

"Fuck that's hot," he pants.

I smile down at him, my body begging once more for release. Elijah pistons his hips, his cock jerks and we both cry out as he comes in hot spurts and I clench around him, following him over the edge, lost in the pleasure and the sweetness of it all.

When we're satiated and spent, he falls back on the bed and takes me with him. We lie still for a moment, breathing the same air, luxuriating in the warmth of each other and the stickiness where his hard places meet my soft ones. He traces a finger up my spine and I shiver and then he grasps the nape of my neck and forces my mouth down to his. That one kiss contains more heat and desire than any we've ever had because for once, it doesn't symbolise the end.

It's a beginning.

And a damn good one, too.

Follow Ana, Elijah, Jack, Holly and Sammy
in the remaining Sugartown books Enjoy Your Stay,
Greetings from Sugartown and Now Leaving Sugartown.
But first, continue reading with a Valentine's Day short story
from Sugartown's favourite couple.

A WELCOME TO SUGARTOWN VALENTINE'S

ELIJAH

I bring the bike to a stop in our drive and kill the engine. Before my feet have even moved to set the kickstand down, Ana jumps off the back and heads for the house.

She is pissed.

I get it, chicks dig Valentine's Day. They love all that shit; flowers, chocolate, and an excuse to drag their men to the movies to watch those shitty Rom-Coms. I know what women want. *Or at least I thought I did.* Apparently, what they don't want is to be taken to a pole dancing class. They also don't let men into those things just to watch their smoking hot girlfriend gyrate on a pole in order to fill their spank bank fantasies for a lifetime. Learned that the hard way. I don't think the offer to take her to McDonalds afterward really helped my cause either.

"Baby girl, wait up," I say, as I slide off the bike and unclasp my helmet.

"I really would rather you didn't talk to me right now, Cade." She spins around on the gravel drive and nearly loses her footing. I put a hand out to stop her, but she pulls out of my grasp, doubles over and yanks off her heels, hurling them off toward the fence surrounding the house. "Stupid fucking heels."

I stare longingly at the offending red satin shoe hanging suspended from our barbed wire fence. *Damn, I was kinda hoping she'd leave those on while I fucked her senseless.* She glares at me a little longer, and then turns and stalks up the stairs.

"Baby, I'm sorry." I follow her closer than her shadow.

Holly and Jack are mauling one another on the loveseat, or maybe she's beating the crap outta him again—it's kinda hard to tell with those two. Despite the fact that my bike roared up the drive a few seconds ago, they look surprised to see us and they break apart like kids caught screwing around on formal night. Ana swipes the wine from the table in front of them and swigs it straight from the bottle.

Fuck, she even manages to make winos look hot.

"Hey, you guys are home early, how was your night?" Holly says, but her grin falters when she sees the pointed look Ana gives me. She too levels me with the wrath of a thousand bitter harpies baying for my blood. "What did you do, Cade?"

"I don't really see how this—"

"He took me to a pole dancing lesson," Ana snaps.

"Dude, sweet." Jackson throws his hand up for a high-five, but Holly elbows him hard in the chest. He lets out a disgruntled noise, shakes his head and adds, "You are never getting laid again."

I shrug. "I thought she'd be into it."

Ana pulls the bottle from her mouth and slays me with another dirty look. "Because nothing says Valentine's like strippers and McDonalds."

"You took her to McDonalds?" Holly accuses. "You are never *ever* getting laid again."

I roll my eyes and fold my arms over my chest. "I offered to take her to McDonalds, but the glare she gave me made me drive on past. I didn't make a reservation somewhere because I thought we'd be otherwise occupied."

Ana scowls. "Elijah's idea of a special Valentine's Day date is watching me and ten other scantily clad women gyrate on a pole."

"They have clubs for that, man," Jackson says. *Way to throw me under the bus, fucker.*

Ana thrusts the wine at me, forcing me to take it. "Hold this. I'm going to change out of this ridiculous dress."

Earlier tonight when she came out of our room in the little red number, I almost lost my shit right there. I muttered all the appropriate half-witted replies a man is supposed to when his girlfriend walks out in a dress that accentuates all his favourite parts of her bangin' body, but now I know she's taking it off, I feel like I've barely had time to appreciate it.

"I'll help you," I say, and shove the bottle at Jackson.

"Haven't you done enough, Cade?" Holly asks with a sly smile. *Hopefully. Otherwise, I am never living this down.*

Ana stalks up the hall and I follow behind like a naughty puppy who knows he's in the doghouse. She pushes back the door to our room and gasps. A fragile smile tugs at her lips. Her brow crinkles and her eyes turn glassy as though she's about to cry.

"Happy Valentine's Day, baby girl." I slide my arms around her waist, pulling her back against my front as I usher her into the room and close the door with my foot.

Pink and red candles in little glass jars line the outside of picnic rug and in the centre sits a chocolate fondue set with a platter of fresh fruit, cheeses and a bottle of expensive red. I lead her over to the rug and press a kiss to her shoulders.

"How did you do all this?" Her voice is thick with emotion and wonder.

"You know how right before we left I said I had to change because I had grease on my shirt? I laid most of it out then, but I messaged Holly for help with lighting the candles and putting the food out while you were in the bathroom at the dance studio." I turn her in my arms so I can see that incredible face. Her eyes are watery but bright. Her smile widens as she stares up at me. "You didn't really think I'd take you to McDonalds for Valentine's, did you?"

"Elijah, you'd just taken me to a pole dancing class," she says dryly. "Nothing would have come as a surprise to me."

"Except this." I wink and gesture for her to sit. I hit the opposite side of the rug, attempting to fold my big body into the small space like a pretzel, but I have to shift half of the candles to make room for my legs. I pour us both a glass of wine and dip a strawberry into the melted chocolate. I bring it to her lips, but instead of letting her take it in her mouth, I slide it over her chin and down into her cleavage, then I toss the strawberry away and lick her skin clean of the sugary sweetness. Ana moans and I shove my hands into her hair as I follow the trail back up her neck.

"I fucking love this dress, babe," I groan against the milky flesh of her throat. "But right now I want you out of it."

"Really?" she asks, her voice soft and breathy, and fuck me I'm so hard right now I could probably club a seal with my cock. "You don't wanna eat first?"

"Oh, I'm gonna be eatin' alright." I slide my tongue across her chest to her other shoulder and hit that sweet spot beneath her ear. Her eyes fall closed, her ruby red painted mouth opens and her fingers move from my arms to her zip. She eases it down, and we both help her out of it. I toss it off toward the bed, avoiding the millions of candles around us. I'm already burning hotter than a fucking inferno, and we don't need another fire breaking out in this town.

I dip my fingertips into the chocolate, it burns a little, but it's cool enough by the time I place my hands on her body, so I paint her chest with it. I sully her creamy skin across her nipples, between her tits, over her stomach, and all the way down to the barely there underwear she has on. I hook my fingers into the lace and tear them off.

She gasps. I chuckle at her stunned expression. I love that after all this time I can still surprise her. *I am the luckiest son of a bitch alive.* The woman of my fucking dreams is kneeling before me completely naked—minus the chocolate, of course—what man wouldn't consider himself lucky in this scenario.

I sweep my arm out, the fondue set and plate of fruit clatter together as I shove them out of our way. The chocolate spills all over the rug and probably the hardwood floors too, but I just grin like the devil and lay her down in it.

"Who's going to clean that up?" she complains, as she squirms in the warm liquid.

"I am." I must look like a fucking maniac because my smile widens at the prospect. *This is a mess I'll gladly clean up.* I plunge my hands into the pool of smooth, warm chocolate and smear her skin with it from nipple to navel, and then I begin the satisfying and very fuckin' time-consuming task of licking her body clean.

Best goddamn Valentine's Day ever.

Acknowledgements

There are so many people to thank when it comes to bringing a book baby to life, but at the risk of sounding like an Oscar winner blubbering their way through their acceptance speech, I'd like to take a minute to thank the incredible people in my life that helped make this book a reality.

To my darling Ben, who supports and loves unconditionally. Who puts up with a partner who spends more time inside her own head than she does in real life—without compliant—I love you more than you could ever comprehend! Thanks for being an amazing partner, an even more incredible father, a freaking awesome cover/web/swag/blog designer, a sounding board, a saviour, a warrior and my best friend. The ideas man reigns supreme! Read my book!

To my babies Ava and Ari, I love you like crazy! Thanks for sharing mummy with the voices in her head. I hope when you grow up you're lucky enough to have a job you love as much as I do mine, and above all I hope you never stop dreaming.

To my niece, Zöe Jean—my Ana. Thank you for agreeing to let me plaster your beautiful face all over the original cover of Sugartown. You went above and beyond for our photo shoot and I'm so incredibly grateful. You're not only beautiful, but your grace, humility and humour make you an incredible young woman, and I couldn't be more proud.

To my mum for being the most amazing woman I know … Thank you!

My family and friends, thank you for understanding that writing a book isn't just about stringing together a few pretty sentences, it's spilling your blood and guts all over the page and rolling around in it for months, sometimes years, on end! Now you know why I'm so bloody crazy.

To Lauren K McKellar—the greatest editor in all the land—thank you! I gave you a very messy manuscript and you made it sparkle like a diamond! Yes, exclamation points and all!!

Heartfelt thanks to my amazing beta readers: Ali Hymer and Debbie Besabella from Black Heart Reviews, and author Emma Silver. I adore each and every one of you! Thank you for loving these crazy kids as much as I do, for championing and swooning—Ali, you're messed up, but I wouldn't have you any other way—right alongside me, for creating teasers, leaving AMAZING early reviews and helping to spread the word of Sugartown.

Ali, thank you for cyber bitch-slapping me when I'm freaking out—which, let's face it, happens a lot—for encouraging, and for just plain getting me. I don't know what cruel fate, soulless entity or cataclysmic events decided/led to us living on opposite sides of the world, but I am a better author, person and friend for knowing you!

To my motorcycle expert Steve Streater for going above and beyond for a little Aussie author who previously knew NOTHING about motorcycles. Thank you for finding a bike big enough to carry Elijah that still managed to be sexy, mysterious and a little bit run down—just like its owner. You were so kind and extremely generous with your time, and all for a complete stranger! Any mistakes in this area are my fault alone.

Special thanks to Lauren Perry of Perrywinkle Photography for the amazing cover image.

A massive THANK YOU to my wonderful blogging buddies, you know who you are, and to everyone who has shared, blogged about, squeeeeed, added, and requested ARCs of Welcome to Sugartown. I'm indebted to all of you!

And finally to the readers, the world is full of incredible books, thank you for choosing this one to grace your shelf/e-reader.

Welcome to Sugartown.

I hope you Enjoy Your Stay.

BOOKS BY CARMEN JENNER

Welcome to Sugartown (Sugartown Series #1)
Enjoy Your Stay (Sugartown Series #2)
Greetings from Sugartown (Sugartown Series #3)
Now Leaving Sugartown (Sugartown Series #4)
KICK (Savage Saints MC #1)
TANK (Savage Saints MC #2)
REVELRY (Taint #1)
Finding North
Toward the Sound of Chaos
Harley & Rose

COMING SOON

The Way Back Home
The Trouble With Us
CLOSER (Taint #2)
HURT (Taint #3)
JETT (Savage Saints MC #3)
GRIM (Savage Saints MC #4)
KILLER (Savage Saints MC #5)

ABOUT THE AUTHOR

Carmen Jenner is a thirty-something, USA Today and international bestselling author. Her dark romance, KICK (Savage Saints MC #1), won Best Dark Romance Read in the Reader's choice Awards at RWDU, 2015.

A tattoo enthusiast, hardcore lipstick addict and zombie fangirl, Carmen lives on the sunny North Coast of New South Wales, Australia, where she spends her time indoors wrangling her two wildling children, a dog named Pikelet, and her very own man-child.

A romantic at heart, Carmen strives to give her characters the HEA they deserve, but not before ruining their lives completely first … because what's a happily ever after without a little torture?

www.carmenjenner.com

Need more Sugar in your life?
Join Carmen Jenner's Street Team, The Sugar Junkies — a kick arse group of chicks dedicated to spreading the word of Sugartown … and man candy.

Follow Carmen Jenner:
Twitter www.twitter.com/CarmenJAuthor
Facebook www.facebook.com/CarmenJennerAuthor

Made in the USA
Columbia, SC
10 October 2017